CONFESSIONS OF A CONTRACTOR

CONFESSIONS

of a

CONTRACTOR

Richard Murphy

G. P. Putnam's Sons

New York

G. P. PUTNAM'S SONS

Publishers Since 1838

Published by the Penguin Group

Penguin Group (USA) Inc., 375 Hudson Street, New York, New York 10014, USA • Penguin Group (Canada), 90 Eglinton Avenue East, Suite 700, Toronto, Ontario M4P 2Y3, Canada (a division of Pearson Canada Inc.) • Penguin Books Ltd, 80 Strand, London WC2R 0RL, England • Penguin Ireland, 25 St Stephen's Green, Dublin 2, Ireland (a division of Penguin Books Ltd) • Penguin Group (Australia), 250 Camberwell Road, Camberwell, Victoria 3124, Australia (a division of Pearson Australia Group Pty Ltd) • Penguin Books India Pvt Ltd, 11 Community Centre, Panchsheel Park, New Delhi–110 017, India • Penguin Group (NZ), 67 Apollo Drive, Rosedale, North Shore 0632, New Zealand (a division of Pearson New Zealand Ltd) • Penguin Books (South Africa) (Pty) Ltd, 24 Sturdee Avenue, Rosebank, Johannesburg 2196, South Africa

Penguin Books Ltd, Registered Offices:
80 Strand, London WC2R 0RL, England

Library of Congress Cataloging-in-Publication Data

Murphy, Richard, date.
Confessions of a contractor / Richard Murphy.
p.   cm.
ISBN-13: 978-0-399-15507-9
1. Contractors—Fiction.   2. Los Angeles (Calif.)—Fiction.   I. Title.
PS3613.U7535C66   2008   2008016793
813'.6—dc22

Printed in the United States of America
1   3   5   7   9   10   8   6   4   2

BOOK DESIGN BY AMANDA DEWEY

For Cheryl

A Note to the Reader

I renovated houses and apartments in Los Angeles and elsewhere for nearly twelve years. I worked for lawyers, journalists, casting directors, real estate developers, actors, musicians, agents, producers, divorcées, and drug addicts, among others. While I was inspired by my experiences with these people, *Confessions of a Contractor* is a work of fiction. Any resemblance to actual events or persons, living or dead, is coincidental.

CONFESSIONS OF A CONTRACTOR

The first thing a woman needs to know about renovating a house or apartment is simple: do not, under any circumstance, sleep with your contractor, no matter what your husband or boyfriend is doing to you, or not doing to you. Some people in the building trade will consider this statement a direct violation of the Man Code, and you won't find additional information on this subject at Home Depot—even though it should be there, in its own department, right between electrical and plumbing, managed by a woman who has made this very mistake.

"Can I help you?"

"Yes, I'm renovating my house, and I'm using these imported tiles from Italy and I'm thinking about sleeping with my contractor."

"Don't do it."

"But he's an incredible listener. And he goes shopping with me."

"Because you're paying him. Thousands and thousands of dollars."

"Is there someone else I might be able to talk to?"

"Listen to me. He may be erecting the house of your dreams, but once you cross that line, your life will never be the same. Not to mention his craftsmanship."

That woman is right. It's trouble for everyone involved, especially the contractor, which is why many companies educate their employees with codes-of-conduct seminars and grounds-for-dismissal manuals designed to encourage abstinence. But it still happens. And when it does, as the pages of this story will testify, things get incredibly complicated, incredibly fast.

Now that you've been properly warned, how do you find this man you should not sleep with under any circumstance; a man who will spend weeks in your bedroom, bathroom, and closet doing pretty much everything you ask him to do; a man who will receive keys to your home at the end of your first or second date without ever buying you a meal, pouring you a glass of a wine, or making you laugh? You ask every single person you know, including the compulsive talker who lives on your street, the one who told you on three different occasions how her bamboo floors are more environmentally friendly than your hardwood floors because bamboo is a grass and it's the fastest-growing plant on earth.

Call her. Go for coffee. Listen to the bamboo.

If for some reason your inner circle can't produce the name of a contractor, you need to increase the square footage of your inner circle before people start thinking you're a renter, or worse yet, a *contenter:* someone who thinks their house or condo looks fine just the way it is.

Referrals are everything in this business, and for good reason. In time, this contractor you're seeking will develop more power than your nanny, your gardener, your computer technician, your colorist, your mechanic, and your Pilates instructor combined. Not because he has the ability to make you look beautiful on the outside, even when you're unraveling within, but because he has your house, your sanctuary, your sanity in the palm of his calloused hand, where it will remain until the job is finished. Not intentionally of course. This brief orientation is not intended to scare you into reconsidering your objective, or make you think people in the trade have ulterior motives. It's simply a reminder that cohabitation with a contractor (and his crew) is not for the weak. To find out if you have the stomach for it, consider these five basic questions:

Is your marriage or relationship in good shape?
Are you in excellent physical condition?
Are you mentally sound?
Are you financially secure?
Are you fully prepared for everything to go wrong and drastically affect your answers to the first four questions?

If you said "yes" to all of the above, you are ready to begin remodeling.

If you found yourself lingering a bit too long on a particular question, justifying certain answers in an effort to convince yourself that everything is okay in your world, you might want to consider a chemically induced coma with a medical directive that specifically states you are not to be awakened until the dust is gone, the noise has subsided, and everything in your newly remodeled home has been replaced with items that an overpaid feng shui expert has deemed feng shui. It's a long, hard road, but at least you're honest. No one is ever fully prepared for the things that go wrong once their walls have been stripped, and the secrets they shelter have been revealed.

Those who think they are, usually move or get divorced.

ONE

The dream went like this: Sally Stein was sitting across from me, completely naked, going through a list of tweaks and polishes in the breakfast nook of her Hollywood Hills home. She wanted everything to be perfect before I gathered up my tools and returned her keys. Her body was exactly how I had imagined it: taut, confident, beautifully hers. I found it odd that the dream was always set in the breakfast nook, and not some exotic place like Thailand, but not odd enough to wake up and demand my money back. Sally Stein was nice to look at, no matter where she sat.

Then something weird always happened, ending the dream before it had a chance to evolve. One time the roof collapsed on us, another time Willard Scott knocked on the kitchen window and wished me happy birthday. On the morning of April 1, the day that set everything in motion, the dream ended with a phone call.

The call entered in a hurry, like a compulsive shopper who spent Thanksgiving camped in front of an electronics store. I hadn't received a call on the landline since Gia moved out with my answering machine months earlier, and I had forgotten it was even hooked up. It sounded like it was coming from a different corner of the apartment every time it rang, which may have had something to do with the whiskey I drank after backing out of Sally Stein's house on my hands and knees, manipulating grout into the new sandstone floor in her kitchen. Whoever was trying to get ahold of me had either dropped dead while the line was still ringing, or they needed something very badly.

"Yeah," I said, picking up the phone just to make it stop.

"I'm looking for Henry Sullivan. I got this number from Allison."

The caller had one of those voices that belonged on the phone, the kind that made you want to stay on the line even when you had nothing to say. Out of habit, I started a personal profile in the one area of my mind that was still working: the caller was married, late-thirties, smoked Parliaments in the mid-nineties before she got serious about having kids. The nineties were over but the smoke lingered, wrapping even the simplest words in a thin coat of velvet.

"It's six o'clock in the morning."

"Allison said you get up early. Did I wake you?"

"I've done work for three different Allisons. Can you be more specific?"

"Sorry. My coworker, Allison Reed. She lives in Beverly Hills on Maple."

"Married to the gay guy?"

"Well, yeah, I guess. But she didn't know it at the time. They got divorced."

Saw that coming. "Allison, right."

"She said I should call you. I'm throwing a party at the end of August and my contractor just quit. The house is a mess. I have no idea what to do." I knew this tone well. The woman was a House Virgin, a first-time renovator trapped in the middle of a job gone bad without a single Google solution to set her free.

"Sorry, I'm not looking for new clients."

"I'll double your rate." Less than a minute in and her cards were already on the table. She waited for me to do the same. I swore I'd never take on another House Virgin after the last one hovered over my shoulder for the better part of a month, comparing my work to those carpenters on TV who transform entire houses in thirty-minute segments. But there I was, still on the phone, walking toward the kitchen.

"Do you have anything to eat?" I asked, looking into an empty refrigerator.

"Are you talking to me?"

"I haven't been to the grocery store in weeks, and I was out drinking last night. I need to eat something."

"You want me to cook for you?" replied The Voice, a little confused.

"I'm not interested in your money, or the job. But if you make some eggs, I'll at least come by and assess the situation. Tell you what you're looking at." The silence that followed provided more information. The woman's problems went beyond the condition of her house, and I could tell she was growing tired of pretending that they didn't.

"Allison said you were unconventional." She let this hang there for a moment, seeing if I would respond. When I didn't, she breathed in deep through her nose and exhaled while saying, "How do you take your eggs?"

*   *   *

I grew up in the Midwest helping my father work on houses. It was the seventies, and men always handled the remodeling of a home. These days, I usually work for women. Complex women. Women in their early thirties to late fifties, all looking to change something, no longer willing to wait. Most are college educated, residentially ambitious, and wealthy—some through their own hard work, others through marriage. If my clients are married, the husbands are rarely around. They're usually out hunting and gathering at a pace that seems to indicate they're planning an escape of some kind. These men had parachuted into The Land of Opportunity for one reason or another, and were in a race against the clock to acquire as much as they could before the other Ferragamo loafer dropped in the form of an earthquake, an actress, or death.

As my truck rolled west on Sunset, leaving the hills of Silver Lake for the central grid that separated me from my destination on the Westside, I wondered what The Voice's husband was out hunting, and if it had anything to do with her urgency to pull off the party in August instead of postponing it or moving it to a new location. What else did she have riding on the completion of this house? Was it a chance to rectify a mistake she had made? Or was *he* the problem, and this was just her way of trying to prove she still had an identity of her own? I tried to remind myself that I was simply stopping by to offer some friendly advice in exchange for a home-cooked meal, but that wasn't entirely true. If she had given me her name I could have filed her away in the phone book, among the anonymous and the easy to forget, but she hung up after giving me the address, leaving me to visualize a set of blueprints that gave shape to the sound of her voice, a voice that had me driving through rush-hour traffic on the first day of my vacation.

Renovating a home is a rite of passage, much like getting married or having kids. It's been this way ever since human beings lived in caves. At some point, a certain cavewoman grew tired of her space and began pressuring her caveman to find a better cave. Upon receiving this complaint, one of two things happened: either the caveman had no idea what she was grunting about and therefore died off, alone and childless as a result of his inability to understand the other sex, or he went out and looked for a bigger, better cave that afforded more light and was closer to the food source. If the caveman was unable to find a cave that fit these specifications, the couple was then forced to stay put and renovate their walls with rudimentary drawings that depicted their struggle. These drawings evolved through time into the paintings, photographs, and Nagel prints people hang in their homes today, which is how Nagel-lovers have been able to stave off extinction when they should have been the first to go. It's not a testament to the human spirit; it's in the genes.

This rite of passage that started with one cavewoman's desire to up-grade her cave is now a trillion-dollar industry. Even when the industry is hit by a recession, or a natural disaster, or a collapse of the subprime market, it always bounces back. Construction usually accounts for ten percent of the U.S. economy; Home Depot is nearly four times the size of Coca-Cola; and home-improvement shows, with all of their tips and promises that are sure to make us the envy of all our friends, rule cable TV. Yet for all of these advances in the never-ending quest for the perfect home, the question raised by that first boldly aggressive Homo sapien remains: can that home bring true happiness, and if so, how long will it last before it needs to be renovated again in a different color scheme?

The answer I was leaning toward reminded me of my own predicament. The lease on my apartment was up in September, and my landlord was selling the building to a developer who was planning to tear it down and replace it with one of those sixteen-unit, stucco monstrosities that desecrate perfectly innocent streets the way a goiter desecrates a perfectly lovely neckline. This left me about four and a half months to decide if I was going to finally take the plunge and buy a house myself, or find a new apartment that I could continue dating for as long as I wanted without the pressure to settle down. I'd been with a lot of houses over the years, but none that I wanted to spend the rest of my life with.

That's right, I was a renter. And proud of it.

Renting made absolutely no sense on a number of levels. While I was basically flushing cash down the landlord-drain, my clients were padding their pockets in a luxury home market that seemed to be recession proof. And I was approaching thirty-seven, an age when most people start to think you're an anarchist if you're not, at the very least, dozing off to sleep thinking about your future. The physical wear and tear of my occupation was making it harder and harder to ignore this timeline, but something was still holding me back. There was a certain comfort in the imperfections that came with renting. It provided balance, freedom, the ability to leave at any time without sentiment. I'd seen too many people stay in a house beyond their welcome, shackled by the amenities they had grown accustomed to, and I was determined not to make the same mistake.

Gia called this a fear of commitment. I called it seventeen years in the trade.

The Voice's house was located on a quiet, affluent street near Brentwood Country Club, close enough to make a last-minute tee-time, far enough away to avoid errant shots slicing toward the windshield of your import. The house itself was originally simple in design: an elegant, single-story ranch with high ceilings, built in the early fifties. Since then, someone with a bachelor's degree in bad taste had tried to turn it into something it was never intended to be.

At first sight, I'd say it went down like this: while returning home from the set of a Richard Marx video in 1987, one of the previous owners, a coked-out record executive who said things like *"Stop the presses"* and *"How the fuck should I know?"* found himself driving past Frank Gehry's iconic, postmodern beach house in Venice. After stopping for a full ten seconds to study the design (he was a very busy man), the executive returned home, scratched out a few haphazard drawings that looked nothing like Mr. Gehry's work, and hired the first contractor who would cash his check.

Not the type of house you want to renovate if you're a House Virgin.

For those of you playing along at home, if you're about to embark on this journey with a spouse or significant other, take a moment to ask yourself how you feel about that person's taste. It doesn't matter that you're in love, or that you've helped each other through the death of your parents. If you don't see eye to eye on aesthetics, you could be headed for a courtroom. And don't say he doesn't care about that kind of stuff. He'll care the moment he sees it inside your home. You may not see the man for a week, but don't underestimate his ability to step off a plane, enter the master bathroom, and say, in a near-perfect, passive-aggressive pitch, *"That's not going to be the color of the floor, is it?"* Do not give him this opportunity. Talk now, or get an attorney, before he becomes active-aggressive in front of a house designed by a famous architect, and decides that undulating scrap metal might look good on the outside of your home.

Sally Stein called as I was getting out of the truck in front of The Voice's house. Sally was forty-one, single by choice, and blessed with the type of energy that made her fully capable of starting a fashion trend, freeing hostages, or doing both simultaneously at any given moment. She wore glasses despite having 20/20 vision because she liked the way she looked in them, and her thick brown hair was usually bound tightly in a ponytail that she liberated in front of me at the end of each day, releasing the sweet smell of some exotic shampoo that had been marinating for hours, a scent that practically rendered me and my crew powerless.

While building a credenza in her master bathroom, I thought about investigating the scent to find out if Sally Stein seasoned her hair with additional fragrances before sending it off to cure in the secret weapon on the back of her head, but I ultimately decided that certain mysteries were better left unsolved.

"What's going on?" I asked, flipping open my phone.

"The sandstone floor looks A-mazing. I totally love it."

"You're not supposed to walk on it yet."

"I haven't gone near it."

"You're standing on it right now. I can tell by the acoustics."

"All right, all right, you caught me," she replied playfully, leaving the kitchen for what sounded like the dining room. "You don't have to be such a know-it-all."

"Hector or Miguel will be by this afternoon to seal it."

"You're not coming?"

"I'm on vacation, remember?"

Sally let out a soft sigh. She didn't like the idea of people like me taking vacations. "It's really quiet around here without you guys. I'm not sure I like it."

"You'll get used to it."

"I think I might have you do something to my garage."

"Can we talk about this later? I gotta run. I have somebody waiting."

"Run, run, run. I'll see you Saturday night. Everyone is dying to meet you."

Saturday night was the dinner party clients often threw after I completed a job. It was their chance to show off the house to their friends while I knocked back some good wine and answered everyone's questions, a ritual that usually filled my wallet with enough business cards to pick and choose what I wanted to do next.

"Saturday. Right. See ya then."

"Will you be bringing a date?" she asked in a way that made it clear there was only one correct answer. I took a moment to weigh my response, fully aware that this wasn't just a question, it was an invitation to something else entirely, something that had been building ever since I'd walked into her house. Sally Stein was no longer my client. The list of tweaks and polishes had been completed. There was nothing left to interrupt the dream.

"Nope. Just me."

"Excellent. You won't be disappointed." And with that, she ended the call.

The only sign of the contractor who defected was a mound of debris in the middle of The Voice's driveway. Demolished drywall, splintered molding, insulation, carpet, tackboards—all piled in a way that blocked access to the garage. I stopped briefly to right a fallen starter bike at the edge of the grass, and when I turned back toward the front door, I was met by not one woman but two, standing side by side in the door frame. "You must be Henry," said The Voice, stepping outside to greet me. "Rebecca Paulson. Thank you so much for coming."

Rebecca Paulson looked nothing like her voice.

She was attractive, but not in the traditional Southern California way. She wasn't the lead actress who stopped a room the moment she entered, she was the voice of that actress in the straight-to-DVD animated feature of that scenario. Everything about her was off. Her eyes were too close together, her ears and nose were too big for her face, and her long, curly black hair was streaked with a shade of gray that had nothing to do with age. Separately, imperfections like these made Los Angeles the capital of cosmetic surgery. Together, they made Rebecca Paulson one of the most beautiful women I had ever seen.

"The house is kind of all over the place," she said matter-of-factly, referencing the Frank Gehry situation. "We were supposed to remodel it when we moved in a year ago, but we kept putting it off."

"There's never a good time," I assured her, shaking her hand.

"This is my friend Tess." Rebecca turned to Tess, who was tall and thin with fair skin that brought out the suspicion in her eyes. "She's here to protect me in case you try to dine and dash. She ran track in high school."

Rebecca smiled. I smiled back. "Good to know."

It wasn't unusual for a potential client to invite someone to our initial greeting, except most people tried to make it seem like it was a coincidence, as if I would somehow think less of them for taking the sensible precaution of avoiding being alone in the house with someone they had never met.

Examples of these encounters:

"My mom just stopped by to borrow some cumin."
(Nobody stops anywhere to borrow cumin.)

"My gay friend Todd just stopped by to drop off some muffins."
(Your gay friend Todd should stop being your gay friend Todd because you just referred to him as your gay friend Todd.)

"These are the members of my contemporary nonfiction book club. I forgot we were meeting today."
(As if people in contemporary nonfiction book clubs forget when they're meeting.)

I stepped forward and shook hands with Tess, who looked me up and down as she formulated her thoughts on the topic that brought us all together. "Breakfast, huh?"

"Sounds good," I replied, pretending to misunderstand her. "Let's eat."

. . .

Every house has a story, and every story begins in the kitchen.

People usually straighten up their bedrooms before I arrive, but the kitchen remains closest to its natural state, providing the best insight into those who either use it or avoid it. Even if the kitchen isn't included in the renovation plans, I always find a reason to start the interview there.

In many parts of the country, contractors have to be willing to cut costs and rearrange their schedules to win a potential job. In places like Los Angeles, New York, San Francisco, Dallas, and Miami—where a good contractor rivals the importance of a good doctor—it's the client who has to be competitive. Many of the people who live in these cities look at their homes as extensions of themselves, canvases that should say exactly who they are even if they're still trying to figure it out. A surgeon cannot perform this operation, and psychologists rarely make house calls. Only a capable contractor can execute this procedure, and to land that contractor, a homeowner must have a good reason for him to accept the job.

Throughout the years, I have been offered all sorts of perks from people who tried to persuade me to choose their problems over the problems of others, perks that included courtside Lakers tickets, a weekend at a Malibu beach house, even a small part in a movie. Earlier in my career, I made the mistake of accepting a few of these gifts. Earlier in my career, I thought those gifts were free.

Having learned from those experiences, my criteria for accepting a job are simple: First and foremost, I need to like the people I'll be working for, knowing this might not be the case at the end of the job. Second, I need to have a good feeling about the environment I'll be working in. I need to believe the client can handle the assault of having their home turned upside down. Even when people choose to move out for a few months, their desire to return home often transforms them into very different people, people I no longer recognize. Finally, I need the client to provide an opportunity to create something inspiring in the space they are occupying. I don't build things just to build them.

I liked Rebecca Paulson.

The kitchen was clean, not spotless, and it smelled of food, not cleaning supplies. Everything else about the job told me to give her some advice and a referral, then leave and never look back. The departure of Rebecca's former contractor, and her reluctance to discuss the matter—all she would say was he walked off the job after an argument with her husband—was just one in a long list of warning signs that all pointed to the face of her refrigerator.

Refrigerators represent a small percentage of pictures taken by a couple or family, pictures designed to illustrate a certain universal happiness, so I always review them carefully. The Paulson refrigerator had only four pictures on it. Two of them were crayon drawings created by twins, both girls, enrolled in kindergarten at the prestigious Franklin School. Another was a photograph of Rebecca, her husband, and the twins on the Santa Monica Pier, a picture that featured Rebecca trying to manage unmanageable wands of cotton candy while her husband stood in profile, gazing out at the ocean as if all the answers to his problems swam just beyond the horizon. The fourth and final installment was a picture of the husband within an advertisement that ran in the *Daily Breeze,* promoting his upcoming real estate seminar in San Pedro.

Why bail bondsmen and people in real estate think the rest of the world has an interest in what they look like (you don't see pictures of accountants and chimney sweeps on the backs of bus stops around the country) is without a doubt one of the great mysteries of the twenty-first century. And Rebecca Paulson's husband, behind an acquired smile of synthetic white, was doing his part to make sure it stayed that way.

"Let's walk," I said to no one in particular. Both women had been busying themselves with breakfast, yet I could feel their eyes upon me, monitoring my interest in the pictures on the refrigerator.

"I thought you wanted to eat first," replied Rebecca.

"I changed my mind. I need to see the rest of the house."

Rebecca and Tess dried their hands and took me on a tour. I needed time to think, and movement usually improved the outcome. It wasn't just that Rebecca's husband seemed familiar to me, like I had made fun of him while passing by a bus stop. It was more personal than that. I was pretty damn sure I had met him before.

The various residents of any house over the years are all connected in a way. Some houses lure in certain types of people with their architectural style; others do it with their seclusion, their size, or their proximity to a particular school. I reasoned that Rebecca Paulson's decision was based on the last entry in that category. Anything short of a mother's desire to give her children the best-available education made no sense. Why else would she move into a house that appeared to strip each and every occupant of their ability to think clearly the moment they enter it?

As Rebecca guided me through her general state of disarray, Tess, an aspiring designer who was assisting Rebecca with the renovation, provided suggestions on how to improve the environment, an environment that would have looked considerably better if the previous owner had remodeled it with a handful of grenades. The house was that confused; the rooms were that disjointed. And grenades, despite their tendency to blow things into oblivion, would have at least given the space a sense of symmetry, something positive for me to comment on before leaving as quickly as possible.

"That's kind of interesting. That huge black hole in the hallway looks just like the huge black hole in the living room."

Forget the coked-out record executive's attempt to give the ranch exterior a postmodern "feel." That was an admirable effort compared to the occupant who went to great lengths inside the house to cross what can only be described as that anorexic line between Shabby Chic and Shitty Shack. If this was the line the record executive had snorted before running amok with the undulating scrap metal, his actions were more justified.

The occupant who flew over the suburbs of shabby and into the city of shitty was obviously distressed out of her mind. Nearly everything within her vision of the house had been altered to make it look old and weathered. When done right, and with great restraint, this process can make a home feel like a cottage on the shores of Cape Cod. When done wrong, it can make that same home feel like a bed-and-breakfast on the outskirts of Hell, a place you could find only on April Fools' Day.

The doors, the cabinets, and the stairway were all victims of faux-finishes. The walls around them, all washed with colors that should not be seen mingling together at an ice cream social, let alone layered over one another in a house in Brentwood. The lavender dining room speckled with green patina took away my hunger altogether. The violent yellow guest bathroom stenciled with daisies made me want to light a match just looking at it. And these were two of the better-looking rooms.

The biggest problem in the house was revealed in the master bedroom. The previous contractor had already started the demolition process without redistributing the weight supported by a load-bearing wall, and as a result of this oversight, the back corner of the roof was starting to sag. Blue tarps had been stapled onto the remaining studs, many of which suffered from old termite damage.

Normally, I am compelled to improve these conditions. It's what I like most about my job, taking a structure in need and giving it a second chance. However, on that day, in that house, my mind kept drifting back to the husband. My theory about Rebecca had survived the walk-through. The Los Angeles public school system was a mess, and a lot of parents were purchasing less-than-ideal homes closer to private schools just to avoid it. But what kind of man would move his wife and young children into a place like this, then wait an entire year before renovating it, or at least having it painted? Even if his reason was legitimate, it left me with a bad feeling, a list of questions I had no time to answer. This was not the type of environment that had any chance of getting me to postpone my vacation. Realizing that, I turned my attention to a framed wedding picture sticking out of a box near my feet.

Rebecca cleared her throat. "It's worse than you thought, isn't it?"

I glanced up and saw Rebecca Paulson looking more vulnerable than anyone ever should in the security of her own home. It was at that moment I remembered where I had met her husband. I looked back at the picture sticking out of the box.

"How long have you been married?"

"Six years."

I heard myself sigh, something I did whenever I was knowingly about to make a mistake. "And how old are the twins?"

"Five. Why? What does that have to do with my house?"

I felt myself nodding, a second and more troubling sign that I had passed the last exit on the freeway of no return. "I'll take the job," I said, reaching for the tape measure on my belt. "You'll have an estimate by the end of next week."

TWO

Bad decisions often come in threes in the Sullivan family.

I think it's an Irish thing. We inadvertently make a second bad decision to distract us from the first bad decision, and a third one to distract us from the second, artfully paving the way for a new trilogy of mistakes that we then begin at the most inopportune time. My great-grandfather turned down passage on an ocean liner because he wanted to migrate west in a boat he built with his own two hands. He didn't bring a compass with him because he wanted to navigate that journey using the sun and the stars. He ended up working in a cannery in southern Greenland for two years gutting fish because he couldn't admit it wasn't the country he was aiming for.

Attending Sally Stein's dinner party was my second mistake in a trilogy that began with me ignoring my assessment of Rebecca Paulson's personal problems. One more down, and I would be ready to start another. If Rebecca was the foundation of my demise, Sally Stein was the substructure—an equally important component in any house of cards.

Sally had first entered my life on the front lawn of a middle-aged oncologist who'd gotten involved in his wife's renovation. I was trying to convince the man that the entrance of his massive home would look better if I installed double doors as opposed to the single door he was demanding. I lobbied that a single door, while perfectly suitable for a smaller home, in a smaller archway, would look odd in the large space I designed for it, and therefore make the overall scale of his residence appear imbalanced. Sally was driving by on her way to Beverly Hills in search of an alternative cleaning product that might combat the strange, unidentifiable odor that was permeating the walls of her living room.

Sally's maid had tried every cleaning product in the grocery store, and all of them wafted away in defeat, a crisis that was undoubtedly polluting the powers of that secret weapon on the back of Sally Stein's head. Sally brought in a plumber to rooter the drains, a specialist to steam clean her Berber rugs, and a shaman to bless the entire house with sage. The odor only got worse. These details would come later, of course, but the urgency was right there in Sally's body language as she marched across the lawn to try and lure me away from the oncologist, in hopes that I would stop by and give her a second opinion.

Let's go back to you and your significant other for a moment.

You seem to agree on the aesthetic direction of the house you are about to renovate, and you are now in the market to find the right contractor, except you don't have any referrals for reasons we all understand. If you've purchased one of those self-help books to guide you through the remodeling process, chances are you won't hire someone like me. The book has warned you about disheveled contractors who drive rusty old trucks, because it might be a reflection of their skills. You've been instructed to look for someone who exudes success, a contractor or general contractor who—you'll have to read between the lines for this part—you may never see again once the job starts and he hands you over to a project manager.

The unbridled determination that fueled the steps of Sally Stein told me she hadn't read one of these books, or if she had, she didn't care about appearances. Dr. Rolland used the threat of Sally's impending interruption to remind me that he was in charge, not his wife, and if I didn't like his idea of a single door, he would find someone else to install it. I considered calling his bluff, tired of haggling with a man who had no real interest in his home beyond undermining his wife's creative decisions, thereby making my job more difficult.

Ever since I'd sided with his wife on an antique faucet for one of their seven guest bathrooms, the cancer specialist began questioning me and my crew at every turn. And while his resentment of me eventually morphed into the belief that I was sleeping with his wife, which I wasn't, his insecurities were much harder to manage than those based in infidelity. The doctor's fears were complicated. They entered unexpectedly through a faucet above a sink I was quite sure he would never use, and flowed freely each day thereafter. His internal dam had broken. There wasn't a shut-off valve to make him stop.

The doctor began leaving for work later and later each morning and returning home earlier and earlier each afternoon to patrol the renovation. He went out of his way to distract me. He would wait until I reached the top of a ladder, then ask me to come and look at something trivial in a room on the other side of the house. He'd approach me from behind when I was making cuts with the miter saw and try to compete with the sound of the blade despite my warnings that conversations and saws don't mix. Remember that shop teacher at your high school? The one who was a couple digits short of a full hand? Talking to freshmen at the time, ten to one.

If it wasn't for the doctor's wife, and the affliction that had metastasized in her eyes—an affliction that comes from arriving at a certain point in time and realizing you no longer recognize anyone around you—I would have pulled my crew and walked off that job without ever thinking twice. But every time I got close, every time I was ready to pack up my tools and move out, I thought about the repercussions his wife would face. Knowing the doctor would find a way to silently punish her every time he walked through the double doors she desired, I once again swallowed my pride and signed off on his preference for a single door, then broke for an early lunch in the Hollywood Hills.

I never made it to the refrigerator or the sandwich I requested in Sally Stein's kitchen. The odor she was battling in her living room was not to be taken lightly, making it hard to enjoy the view beyond the floor-to-ceiling windows. It smelled like broccoli that had been placed in a Ziploc bag and left in the refrigerator for nine days. I don't know what it is about chilled broccoli sealed in plastic, but it produces a musty, powerful odor worse than any vegetable, running shoe, or kitchen sponge gone bad. Multiply the radius of that odor by 3.14, and that's what Sally Stein was dealing with.

Sally put on a mask scented with Febreze and offered me one as well. My attention, however, was already on a set of planter boxes near the central air vent at the top of the atrium that crested the room. The architect who conceived the house was too smart to include such an impractical detail, which meant a previous owner had added the boxes, unable to tolerate the emptiness of a space where light was designed to be the only occupant.

"How do you change the halogens?" I asked, motioning toward the ceiling.

"The maid does it. I have a ladder in the garage."

"How long have you had this maid?"

"Marianna? I don't know, a year maybe."

"Is she eager to please?"

"Oh my God. She's amazing. I got her from The Four Seasons in New York. I've turned all my friends on to her."

Sally Stein wasn't the first person I'd met who used the five-star-hotel system to find someone to clean up the messes she left behind.

The messes were often large and intensely private. One had to be creative to find the very best. Unlike professional sports, there is no draft system. You can't select Albinka Guerro in the fourth round, then trade her for Rosario Delgado if she doesn't have a good eye for cobwebs. Recruiting maids in hotels with a proven clientele was a reasonable alternative.

These specialists were also my allies. We shared a common ground in the homes of others, and that produced a bond of mutual respect. This bond made my diagnosis feel like a betrayal.

"Why do you ask?" inquired Sally, looking concerned behind her surgical mask. "Did she do something wrong?"

I took a few steps back, adjusting my perspective on two small marks about sixteen inches apart on the wall below the planter boxes, marks left by the top of a ladder if the bumpers have worn thin. "No. Not intentionally. But someone has been watering the fake ivy. You've got yourself a mold problem."

Before you go judging Marianna, you should know something about these plants. This wasn't your mother's fake ivy. These greens were customized. They had been tested and retested to make sure they felt as real as they looked. With more and more people around the country switching from authentic to fabricated plants, both indoors and out (no, that's not a typo), the folks in Research & Development have been working overtime to stay competitive and meet the growing demand. If buyers *don't* feel the need to water their fakes, R&D hasn't done its job.

Although the mold in the basin of the planter boxes turned out to be harmless, it didn't keep Sally Stein from deciding the house needed a makeover just to be on the safe side. Sally had heard the horror stories playing on the dinner-party circuit about a toxic, potentially fatal mold called *Stachybotrys chartarum*, a mold that grows in areas that are constantly wet. The mold has been discovered in all fifty states, and even found its way into the home of activist Erin Brockovich, who promptly and rightfully brought it to the public's attention when she and her family got sick. Not exactly the home you want to start growing in if you're a toxic mold hiding from exposure.

I tried to assure Sally that she wasn't at risk, that her house was otherwise in good condition. Sally saw it differently. The mold problem, whether small or large, had driven her to an intersection in her life where she stopped her car in the middle of a street and shared her crisis with someone else's contractor. The result of that encounter was a sign from the universe that she had entered a season of change.

"It'll be fun," she informed me after describing her spiritual motivations. "You have good taste. I can tell that just by looking at you."

My attraction to this magnetic creature was not the reason I accepted the job. It was the manner in which she dealt with Marianna. A lot of people would have reprimanded my ally, humiliating her in a way that exercised their personal inches of power. They would have fired her on the spot and encouraged their friends to do the same. Sally Stein did neither. She took full responsibility for the blunder, then made me promise—even though at the time I hadn't agreed to anything—that if any of her friends ever asked why she was remodeling the house, I would never tell them the truth.

"Our little secret," she said with a twinkle. "No need to spread the fear."

.   .   .

I arrived at Sally Stein's dinner party half an hour late because someone slashed the tires of my truck, forcing me to take a cab, which in L.A. is a sure sign of trouble. Los Angeles is the City of Houses (ignore the brochure, the Angels all left years ago), and with those houses come

26

garages, and with those garages come millions and millions of cars that always appear to be on the road when I am. If you find yourself in a cab it usually means something bad has happened—not as bad as the circumstances that land you in a city bus, but still something bad enough to make you sit back and wonder how you got there.

My cab ride to Sally Stein's house had all the markings of a jealous oncologist.

In other cities, the back of a cab feels like you are exactly where you are supposed to be at the moment you should be there. In L.A., it feels like the back of a squad car. I hadn't committed a crime in the home of Dr. Rolland, I merely supported the aesthetic opinions of his wife and withstood his petty wrath for doing so. But in the months after my departure, something had spurred Mrs. Rolland to validate her husband's insecurities with a false confession that she was sleeping with me the entire time I worked there. Having witnessed the depth of this woman's loneliness, I figured she did this for one of two reasons. Either she was trying to drive the doctor away once and for all, or lure him closer by painting a different image of herself, reminding him that she was still a sexual being fully capable of attracting another man.

Armed with this new information, the doctor followed me home from Anawalt Lumber one evening and confronted me in front of my neighbors. I tried to tell him he was mistaken, and that he should discuss the accusation with the woman he was neglecting. Rolland, however, was incapable of recognizing the possibility that she had made it up, a defect that he conveyed to me through a series of insults as his pager beeped frantically, trying to notify him that someone other than himself was in need.

As hard as it was to imagine this same, middle-aged man sneaking around, slashing truck tires in the twilight of a Saturday evening, I could easily imagine him hiring someone else to carry out the deed. Random acts of vandalism involve graffiti, knocking over mailboxes, and choosing not to flush a public toilet, the latter being the most inexplicable of the three. Slashing a person's tires is what people do when they want to send someone a message. As for the exact text of this message? It was too early to tell. Doctors have notoriously bad handwriting.

The dinner party was just getting started.

Sally Stein poured me a Jameson and introduced me to fourteen of her closest friends. I had met a few of them during the remodel and acquainted myself with the others while Sally organized a tour of the house. I am never outwardly social at these functions. I make my living listening to people and speaking just enough to put them at ease. If the situation requires a story to make them feel more comfortable, I will offer them one. Otherwise, I usually just sit back and keep my mouth shut.

Sally's friends were all interesting in their own way. They were attractive, successful, and overly educated. A few worked in the entertainment industry, while others worked in law, finance, and manufacturing. One owned her own restaurant, and one was a trust-fund baby hell-bent on changing the world one drink at a time. Some were married, most were divorced, and all of them viewed Sally Stein as their unspoken leader.

Sally had made her money developing a line of expensive purses that became instantly popular when a well-known actress brought one to the Academy Awards. Shortly after that fateful walk down the red carpet, Sally sold her company and her product line to a major conglomerate for nearly seventy million dollars, allowing her to focus on some of the more important things in life, such as philanthropy and orchestrating the ultimate dinner party.

Unlike some of the women I worked for, Sally's desire to help others was genuine and deeply personal. She didn't donate money just to mingle at fund-raisers. She wasn't the type of person who wanted her name on a medical wing or a shelter for abused women. She was an everyday missionary, a tornado of kindness that could touch down anywhere, at any time. If she saw someone else's maid walking up the hill from the bus stop below, she stopped and gave her a ride. She didn't read the newspapers to validate her own pessimism about the state of the world, she did it to locate those who had been dealt a bad hand: people who had been sent to prison without a fair trial, kids who couldn't afford to go to college, families who lost their homes in natural disasters. After Hurricane Katrina, Sally flew out a family of five and let them live with her for three months while she found and purchased them a home in Baton Rouge.

"All right everyone, I will now hand the house over to Henry."

Sally turned and gave me a smile loaded with mischief, topped off with the understanding that I had very little interest in the walk-through she was requesting. She knew I wasn't looking for work. My participation was viewed as a sign of affection. This was Sally Stein's way of asking me to dance.

The real guest of honor should have been the man who originally designed and built the house back in the sixties. Other than a couple of poorly conceived flower boxes added to the upper atrium, the stone, steel, and glass structure had stood the test of time. And collaborating with Sally on the design was easy. The woman had style. She made everyone and everything around her look better.

That being said, I accepted the dance and ventured forward down the hallway that served as the main artery through the house, walking and talking my way across the Pebblestone floor we laid over the existing concrete.

I pointed out the new steam shower in the master bath and the credenza I built across from it. The reclaimed ironwood walls in the den were well received, as was the new cantilevered deck off the side of the house, which expanded Sally's view to the ocean. After brief stops at each of the three bedrooms, all soundproofed at Sally's request, I concluded the tour in the living room at the S-shaped bar we'd built using sandblasted steel and salvaged teak from a fishing boat. When the business cards came out and people asked about my availability, the conversation turned to my new client. The guests wanted details about the type of work I would be doing for her. They wanted to know where she lived, and when I would be finished.

"You're doing Rebecca Paulson's house?" asked Sally Stein, oddly intrigued. "I know Rebecca. We used to be friends."

"Used to be" was the key phrase in this declaration.

I'm not sure why this came as such a surprise to me. Los Angeles may be the second-biggest city in the country, but in the circles I work in, it's just another small town. Perhaps it was because Sally and Rebecca were so markedly different, making it difficult to imagine them as friends.

"I thought you said you were taking a vacation."

"I am. I was. It just happened a few days ago."

"Rebecca Paulson. Is that the woman you went to UCLA with?" inquired the guy with the trust fund. "The one who used to play tennis?"

Sally smiled and shrugged off the question. "Rebecca used to do a lot of things before she got married and had kids. Finish up your cocktails. It's time to eat."

"Rebecca Paulson, wow. I haven't heard that name in a long time," said the restaurateur in the group, turning to me to continue her thought. "Is she still married to that guy who does those real estate seminars?"

I confirmed this with a nod and downed the rest of my drink.

The caterers walked into the living room all wearing dark sun-glasses, moving like an iconic British band that had been up all night. But they weren't British, and they weren't in a band; they were literally blind. Sally Stein used their entrance, and what an entrance it was, to inform us that tonight would be no ordinary dinner party. The meal we were about to eat would be consumed in total darkness.

For those of you unfamiliar with "dark" dining, you are not alone. At the time, I had no idea what she was talking about. The concept is this: when sight is removed from the equation, your remaining senses become heightened and you discover a new appreciation for the sub-tleties and complexities of whatever you're experiencing. The craze was started by a blind clergyman who opened the first dark restaurant in Switzerland, where he employed blind waiters and waitresses to serve his customers. Soon, people were paying top dollar to eat in pitch-black settings in Paris, Tokyo, Berlin, Montreal, Hong Kong, London, New York, and, yes, the newly remodeled home of Sally Stein.

Before I could fully grasp the absurdity of what she was suggesting (leave it to Sally to assemble the only blind catering staff in the coun-try), she handed us each a blindfold, then shut off all the lights in case any of us felt the urge to peek. When everyone had been properly handicapped, the caterers guided us into the dining room and sat us down at the table, where my first obstacle was to determine who was sitting next to me without the use of speech.

Sally Stein freed her ponytail, letting me know that she was the per-son seated on my left. Once I made this silent deduction, she slid her hand between my legs and began gently caressing the center of my gravity as if her signature scent had been developed for this very mo-ment, when the two of us would be seated side by side, hidden in front of her closest friends.

It was a bold move even for the hostess with the most-est, which caught me by surprise, an impressive feat following the introduction of her caterers. As Sally's caressing became more sensual, more purposeful, more harmonious with the Jameson she poured me earlier, I began to realize that she wasn't just teasing my palate in preparation for the long night ahead, she was serving me an appetizer to tide me over. And she wanted me to consume it, all of it, right to the very end.

The hand that entered from my right became another story altogether.

It belonged to a woman who smelled of nothing, or at least nothing that would compete with the food. It arrived on my lap just prior to the tomato bisque, and left during the arugula salad with caramelized pears.

I wish I could tell you I stood up and removed my blindfold and said a few things about caramelized pears, and professional responsibilities, and how tag-team hand-jobs at dinner parties in the dark, while inventive and intensely stimulating, are also a recipe for disaster. But I didn't. I just sat there, mesmerized by their fingers moving in perfect synchronicity with one another on the outside of my jeans. This wasn't some random tryst that happened in the absence of light. It was premeditated.

I knew I was stepping up to the plate that night (bad pun #1), but Sally's lead-off triple and the discovery of a third-base coach waiting for her at the bag (bad pun #2) revealed a very different side of her. Sally had already amassed enough altruism to bring Ayn Rand back from the grave in protest, and when I compared my own small contributions to the world, it was hard not to feel selfish in her presence. Knowing she was capable of such a calculated act suddenly made her seem more human, less benevolent, even more desirable.

What else lingered beyond this window she opened for me?

Because no one was allowed to speak during the meal, I could not use a process of elimination to ascertain who, of the eight women at the table, was the other participant. The woman wasn't wearing a wedding ring, but she could have taken it off before sitting down. My own hand told me she was wearing a dress, but so were many of the other guests. When I began to realize that my quest to unveil this woman was in fact inhibiting the very experience her anonymity was designed to enhance, I called off the search and tried to succumb to the moment. Sally Stein had given me a gift in return for my services. There would be plenty of time to unwrap it later.

But I couldn't let go.

Don't get me wrong, I enjoyed what they were doing, quite a bit actually. I even reached out beneath the table to sell that enjoyment with my own hands, letting them both know I was getting close, I was almost there. Only I wasn't almost there. I was driving around in circles, lost, refusing to speak up and ask for directions on how this arrangement came about, a detail that was preventing me from the release Sally Stein was seeking.

Was this the feeling some women experienced when their husbands or boyfriends treated them like inanimate objects there for the taking? And was I really about to use the same exit strategy as some of those women just because I longed for Sally Stein in a more intimate environment, one that didn't require Braille or a Seeing Eye dog to locate a condom or, more pertinently, the salt-and-fucking-pepper shakers?

Because I had never faked an orgasm before, I did what I think any sensible man would have done in my position. I tightened my grip on each of their thighs, let go, curled my fingers inward a few times, let them quiver, yes quiver, took hold of their thighs a second time, and braced myself for the big-fake finale, which I triggered by collapsing slightly inward, bumping a leg of the table with my own leg, and letting out a soft, muzzled gasp. To the other guests, this probably sounded like I had burned my tongue on an arugula salad served at room temperature, but I felt it was important to err on the side of excess. I then grabbed the hands of both women and held them tight, preventing them from returning to the area that would have exposed me.

Head spaces are divided by a long hallway with doors on either side. It's not easy to pass through that hallway after you've been thinking about tag-team hand-jobs, and enter a more mundane space to review the balance of your checkbook, or remind yourself to send someone a greeting card. So, after another pairing of wines that accompanied fresh Maryland crab cakes, my mind snuck across the hall and ducked into a space suitable for contemplating the main course: cruelty-free veal in a rosemary apricot chutney.

Not that I could actually taste the lack of cruelty.

If eating in the dark gave people that particular skill, I imagine the world would be a very different place. Cruelty-free veal had become popular in some of the city's best restaurants, and it was the only kind Sally Stein would ever eat. I remember finding it odd the first time I saw it on a menu, because it made everything else seem incredibly cruel in comparison.

In the darkness that shrouded my veal in the Hollywood Hills, I found myself exploring the origins of other unusual dishes and the foodies who must have developed them. Was the Japanese foodie blindfolded when he or she invented the kinder methods that led to Kobe beef? Or did that person simply look up from dinner one evening and state to the person across the table, *"This steak is good and all, but it might taste a heck of a lot better if we fed the cows beer and gave them full body massages."*

And what about the Egyptian foodie who developed foie gras before it bounced over to the Romans, and eventually the French who made it the delicacy that it is today? Was that person at a dinner party when they decided that cruelty may in fact be the secret ingredient? Or did they just get impatient with the eating habits of their geese, and declare it was time to start force-feeding them figs to enlarge their livers?

Someone had to be the first person to suggest these things, and whoever they were, they definitely lived to eat; they did not eat to live. The blind clergyman in Switzerland was right about one thing. Dining in the dark was peppered with complexities, whether you ordered them or not.

By the time the blind caterers escorted us out onto the cantilevered deck at the conclusion of the meal and allowed us to remove our blindfolds, everyone in attendance smelled of twenty-year-old port or freshly lit cigarettes. The other guests all started speaking at once, recounting their individual journeys, claiming it was the best meal they had ever eaten. Sally Stein just smiled as if she prepared the food herself. I glanced around, looking for a leak in one of the other women—a smoker who didn't smoke, eyes that couldn't hold a gaze. The Second Woman did nothing to reveal her identity.

Every house requires a certain amount of detective work. In order to correct a problem you need to determine the source, otherwise the fix will be only temporary, especially when human error is involved. It's all part of the Garbage Disposal Syndrome. Garbage disposals do not have souls, and they do not have it in for you. They don't up and quit just because they would prefer eternal life in a landfill, even though they've displayed those traits when you are alone and there are no witnesses. No, the real reason garbage disposals die untimely deaths is because someone has been feeding them an improper diet of eggshells and chicken bones and other items that belong in the trash. When in doubt, always examine the homeowner. That's what my old man used to say.

I considered myself pretty damn good at retracing the steps of my clients until I locked eyes with Sally Stein. She took a long, sensual drag off someone else's cigarette and exhaled in my direction; a flirtatious, playful gesture that seemed to be asking me if I was up for something adventurous.

Once the other guests had left for the evening, I used nearly every room in the house to coax the woman's identity out of Sally, but my inquiries only aroused her. She got off on my need to know, and I got off on the power it gave her, a dangerous combination that led us to new places.

We christened the sandstone floor in the kitchen.

The bar in the living room.

The new steam shower in the master bath.

Rarely in my life has a long-awaited moment exceeded my expectations. When I was a kid I often found that the anticipation of taking a trip turned out to be better than the trip itself. This was not the case with Sally Stein. The months I'd spent undressing her in my mind each day as she liberated her sweet-smelling ponytail did not in any way prepare me for the sheer hunger that consumed me in the hours that followed her dinner party.

Sally's refusal to divulge any information about her mysterious friend, coupled with her desire to reunite the three of us once I figured it out on my own, was ultimately the reason I agreed to transform her garage into a guesthouse. At least that's what I wanted her to believe, that my motivations to solve the case of the Second Woman were purely physical, that I had never been in a threesome and therefore longed to be in one, when in truth, I found them to be overrated. When in truth, I was falling for Sally Stein.

Sally was not a Lakers fan. She didn't have a weekend retreat in Malibu, or the power to offer me a part in her romantic comedy. But no one had ever designed a better way to get me to accept a job I had no business taking.

THREE

had met Rebecca Paulson's husband five years earlier in the home of
Kirsten Janikowski, a young flight attendant based in Burbank.
Kirsten bumped me up to first class on my way back to L.A. from Montana, where I had done some consulting work for a former client, and
in exchange for the upgrade, I'd agreed to come over and look at the
house she had just purchased. Kirsten had a mini-mall tan and a chest
full of silicone, and when the seat-belt sign wasn't on she used the
center aisle as a catwalk to model a pair of legs that could run a man
wild if he wasn't careful.

In 2002, California real estate was starting to skyrocket, making it a
hot topic of conversation. Kirsten Janikowski used our cruising altitude of thirty-five thousand feet to explain how she was going to take
advantage of the boom by flipping houses when she wasn't attending
to the friendly skies. Her enthusiasm bordered on born-again. She
had seen the light, and she was ready to be baptized.

I explained to Kirsten that I didn't normally work for people who
flipped houses, because their desire to make a quick profit made it
difficult for me to do my best work. Kirsten assured me she wasn't
one of those people. A few days after I returned from Montana, I made
good on my promise and went out to the Valley to give her an estimate.

Derrick Paulson opened the front door.

He was Kirsten Janikowski's boyfriend, her source of motivation, her male muse who was going to oversee the project. He was a budding real estate expert at the time, filled with all the swagger that comes from being a budding real estate expert. Derrick's determination to convince me of his expertise suggested that he had failed miserably at whatever he was doing prior to this, something you *never* see in real estate. He looked different back then, the reason I wasn't able to place him until I saw that second photograph. He was thinner and had more hair, and his teeth didn't make me wonder if they had been spray-painted by a dental hygienist an hour before I got there.

I never would have remembered this first introduction, or my tour of the Spanish Colonial bungalow, if it wasn't for the kiss Derrick planted on Kirsten at the end of the tour. I had never been in love before, so perhaps my recollection of what happened will sound a bit callous. But the truth is, whether you are in love or not, public displays of affection become questionable at a certain point. When a kiss clears the two-minute mark in front of the only other person in the room (it's not like they were in St. Mark's Square, surrounded by Italians and pigeons and postcard photographers), it's a pretty good indication that at least one of those involved has an ulterior motive.

I forget what I said the following morning when I passed on the job. I probably claimed I was too busy, or that I threw my back out moving a water heater, an excuse I use from time to time when the truth isn't appropriate. I do remember this, however. Something significant was brewing out in the Valley that day, and I wanted no part of the house that was going to see those people through it.

It wasn't until five years later, standing in the partially demolished master bedroom in Brentwood, that I learned the man I had met in Kirsten Janikowski's bungalow was married at the time to another woman. Kirsten was the beast that Rebecca Paulson's husband was out hunting in The Land of Opportunity. The twisted little thrill of infidelity explained the length of that kiss back in 2002.

*   *   *

When I recalled this story for Hector and Miguel Bautista, the two lead men in my crew, Hector told me I was crazy for getting involved. We had gathered at The Shortstop, a bar in Echo Park, to go over blueprints and devise a plan to complete the Paulson project by Labor Day, while at the same time building Sally Stein her guesthouse.

Hector was thirty-seven and more opinionated than his younger brother. Miguel was thirty-five, quiet, and wore cowboy hats to church. Physically, it was hard to tell they were related. Hector was of medium height, rock solid from top to bottom, with a massive head and a chin as wide as your average kneecap, which he had been shaving daily since the sixth grade. Miguel was short and wiry, and didn't require the services of a razor until he was twenty-three. In the absence of noticeable facial hair, Miguel developed a sense of pride and machismo that pushed him to outdo his brother when it came to lifting heavy objects. If Hector was unloading sixty-pound bags of cement out of the truck, Miguel would jump in and assist him two bags at a time, on legs that wobbled but never went down.

Both brothers were hardworking, highly skilled craftsmen who could handle any task as long as it didn't involve dealing with homeowners. Neither of them wanted anything to do with my responsibilities, so they pretended they couldn't speak English whenever a client was around, which made them excellent sources of information. When things went south in the home of Dr. Rolland, Miguel revealed that the doctor was seeing a therapist twice a week (I personally would have bumped it up to every other day, but what do I know?). When we were remodeling the house of Allison Reed, Rebecca's coworker who provided the referral, Hector was the one who heard Allison's husband planning a weekend rendezvous with some guy in Santa Barbara.

Unlike me, Hector and Miguel had lives outside their occupation. They were both married with kids, and they were determined to provide those kids with opportunities they themselves did not have growing up in Mexico. Neither of them had read *The Bridges of Madison County* (perhaps the only two Mexican carpenters in all of Los Angeles who hadn't), but they loved their wives in a way that will never make it into one of those commercials for diamonds in December. The Bautista brothers expressed their feelings silently every time they got into their truck: they drove home to their wives faster than they drove away. And I considered them family, pretty much the only family I had left.

"What happened to fishing in Alaska?" asked Hector, speaking for both of them, which he did most of the time.

"The fish will have to wait."

"Why can't Sally Stein wait? Why not push her to September?"

I hesitated. It was a perfectly legitimate question, and all it took was a pause in its third trimester to betray me. "That's a little more complicated."

Hector leaned back in his chair. "You fucked her, didn't ya?"

"No. Of course not. It's her parents. They're coming to town in September and she wants them to, you know, have their own little place."

"Their own little place?"

"They're little people. They prefer little spaces."

Miguel smiled, finding this humorous. Hector did not. Both waited for the confession they knew was coming. "All right, so I slept with her, but that's not gonna change anything. We just need to work out a schedule. We can do this."

"Unbelievable. What happened to you learning your lesson the last time?"

"Last time was different. This was out of my control."

"There's no point in having rules if you break them."

"Agreed. The Paulson job is a shitty work environment, but sometimes you have to make an exception. And Sally, well, Sally wasn't a client at the time. Technically."

"Was she good in bed?" asked Miguel, finally speaking up.

"I'm not at liberty to say. Client confidentiality."

Hector shot this down two inches off the runway. "Bullshit. Come on, man. You at least owe us a few details. Who we gonna tell?"

"She got me to take the job, didn't she? Let's just leave it at that." To escape further questioning, I signaled to the waitress that we needed another round. When I turned back to the table, Miguel was holding out his hand in front of his brother. Hector shook his head, retrieved his wallet, and gave him twenty bucks. "You had money on this?"

"Hector didn't believe me."

"Believe you about what?"

"About Sally."

"What about her?"

Hector gave his brother a nod, "Go ahead, tell him."

Miguel paused. "Last week, when I went over to seal her kitchen floor, I heard her talking about you to one of her friends. It sounded like she was, I don't know . . ."

"Like she was what?"

"Planning something."

I pulled my chair closer to the table. "Which friend? What did she look like?"

"I don't know. They were on the phone."

"Did you get a name?"

41

"No name. I think she knew I was listening."

Was that possible? Had Sally figured out that Miguel and Hector understood everything she was saying, and this was information she *wanted* me to have? Providing me with a clue as only she could? "When were you going to tell me this?"

"I told Hector. He said I was high on fumes."

"Exactly what did she say that made you think this?"

"It was the way she sounded. You know, excited, like a *niña* with a secret. She kept walking around the dining room table. Then she passed by the kitchen and said something about a business card. Then she lowered her voice and took the phone into her bedroom."

Of the eight women who had dined at Sally Stein's that evening, all eight gave me their business card in hopes that I would come over and do something to their home. Fortunately only six of them were wearing dresses, including the one in question, but that was still five more than I had time for. If I didn't play my cards right, I could get roped into remodeling a few additional houses, and for all I knew, that was also part of Sally Stein's plan. Sally was an equal opportunity philanthropist. She wasn't just good to those who were less fortunate, she was also good to her friends.

I looked up from the blueprints on the table between us, and saw both brothers staring at me. "Did something else happen at that dinner party we should know about?"

Again, I waited too long before answering Hector's question.

"We ate in the dark. That was about it."

*   *   *

Over the years, I've worked on houses in Montana, Wyoming, Texas, Florida, New York, Michigan, and Illinois. These locations, while different from the landscape in Los Angeles, all had one thing in common: nothing epitomizes the American dream like a house. It is the reason renovation has become the most expensive drug on the market, and the reason some people can't stop doing it once they start.

My irrational commitment to Sally Stein days after inserting myself into the life of Rebecca Paulson—there was hardly enough time to pull off one job, let alone two—was an alarming indication that I was no longer impervious to the side effects of the drug I had been dealing. But like people under the influence, people needing their next fix, I couldn't hear the siren. I thought I had everything under control.

Our plan was this:

Once my blueprints had been finalized and approved by Rebecca (unless a client is working with a designer or an architect, I draw them myself) and the necessary permits had been pulled, we would spend the first couple of weeks deconstructing the Paulson house. Because Rebecca had a fairly limited budget, at least by Brentwood standards (her offer to double my rate was just a ploy to get me there), we would streamline the overall renovation, keeping it as clean and simple as possible, allowing us to concentrate on the areas where Rebecca would get the most return on her dollar. Aside from the termite damage, the original layout had good bones, a lost integrity worth restoring. Rebecca's friend Tess had pushed for more ornate improvements, but there wasn't time, and they weren't necessary.

A few words about designers and architects.

Designers, or friends acting like designers, can make or break any project. Good ones help you see your home in a way you never imagined. They become you, your surrogate taste, your power of attorney, your second set of hands and feet to help you manage all the things you have no time for. The inspirations of a bad designer may have nothing to do with your home, and everything to do with advancing that designer's portfolio. And because they are paid on a percentage of how much you spend—their markups on materials often reach thirty-five percent—they can cost you a fortune.

If you choose to go in this direction, make sure you connect with that person. Don't make the same mistake Amy Enghauser made when she allowed a designer, who shall remain nameless, to turn her Neo-Mediterranean house in Bel Air into a Persian palace. I may be difficult to work with at times. The Persians may have used the Mediterranean to import and export home improvement materials during ancient times. But there is no time when it's acceptable to cover the entire first floor of any home in periwinkle blue tile bordered by Persian mosaics. When I shared my feelings with Amy and her designer, and told them that I could not in good conscience implement this regrettable decision for fear that it would drive my crew into a state of madness, I was promptly replaced.

I've learned a great deal from the good designers I've collaborated with in the past, and even more from the bad ones. These days, I feel more connected to a house when I'm executing my own vision, even if that vision is at times just an amalgam of things I've learned, borrowed, or stolen from people I admire, both living and dead. It allows me to control costs and make improvements on the fly without having to wait and debate adjustments with a committee.

The personalities of the architects I've worked with can be categorized by their skill level, not uncommon in the trade. There were exceptions of course, but most fell into three primary groups. Decent architects were the warmest of the three and were typically open to the ideas of others. Good architects leaned toward the cooler side and preferred to talk in theory, not specifics. And the great architects were often dismissive and socially awkward, and wanted to be left alone to battle the limitations of gravity. I've never worked with a bad architect. Most of them fail out of school and go into real estate.

If you gave a representative from each of these three categories the choice to die in the arms of another person or in the entrance of a building he conceived, the great architect would reply, "Which building?"

The good architect would reply, "Which person?"

And the decent architect would ask, "What kind of question is that? I'm only fifty-five. Who said anything about dying?"

This, of course, is nothing more than a cheap anecdote contrived to make a point, but don't be afraid to ask that question during the interview process when you are searching for the right architect. If nothing else, their reaction will break the ice.

When things were up and running smoothly at Rebecca's, we would then head over to Sally Stein's and begin working on her guesthouse. Once we got that job to a place where I could split up the crew, Hector would return to Rebecca's with Juan and Alonzo, while Miguel would take the lead on the guesthouse with Marco and Eddie. I would bounce back and forth between the two jobs. We'd subcontract out major plumbing, electrical, and drywall. We'd hire masons and freelancers to help us with the foundations and the framing. And if we still got behind, we'd bring in day laborers as needed.

But first, we would need some additional insurance.

Before and After photographs are a crucial element to every job, never more important than when you inherit that job from another contractor who got in a dispute with the husband. They're evidence when things go wrong, and proof that you've delivered when things go right. Prior to starting, clients usually present me their ideas using pictures they have found in design magazines that depict a particular lifestyle they themselves envision. To protect myself from those susceptible to House Envy, an expensive disease people contract from looking at too many of these magazines, I always leave my clients with a set of pictures of their own house at the end of every job, bound in a leather album to look through in case of emergencies, those inevitable moments when their home suddenly feels inferior to the one on the cover of the new *Architectural Digest*.

Because I am not a photographer capable of competing with these monthly spreads, I bring in a professional. Or in the case of my friend Bill, someone who could be a professional if his life wasn't such a mess. Bill gave up shooting people a long time ago because, according to him, settings change, people don't. An interesting theory that might explain why people would no longer hire him. Bill was tall and comically thin, and he had an incredible eye. But when he wasn't shooting, that eye pointed inward into a mind that was constantly changing its own shutter speed. Bill also didn't have a car, so to get him over to Rebecca Paulson's I had to drive out to Eagle Rock and pick him up.

Morning on the 10 freeway is packed with people like me. Contractors, roofers, plumbers, gardeners, maids, nannies, exterminators—all headed west as our employers drive east into Century City, Beverly Hills, and downtown to earn the money to afford us. We are soldiers in different uniforms headed in opposite directions, providing the necessary counterweight to keep a city of this size functioning. And when the day is over, we will all turn around and switch back again as quickly as traffic allows. A game of musical chairs, if you will, everyone tuned to a different station.

On my first commute to Rebecca Paulson's, the traffic wasn't moving, and Bill was getting anxious. "How do you do this every morning? I feel like I'm gonna be sick."

"You get used to it."

"No way. I could never get used to this. I'd rather live on food stamps."

"So that's your plan. And here I was thinking you didn't have one."

"Do you have any idea how much of your life you spend driving back and forth to these places? Two hours a day, minimum, multiplied by six, sometimes seven, multiplied by fifty, maybe forty-eight—it's fucking mind-boggling is what it is. You should start smoking again. You'll last longer."

"Thanks for pointing that out to me."

"We should have taken side streets."

"It's the same amount of time no matter which route you take."

"That's even more depressing. You gotta move, dude." Bill punctuated this with a cough, then turned and stared out the passenger window. "I saw Gia last week."

I didn't respond.

"At this party in Los Feliz. She looked good."

"Gia always looks good."

"She asked about you."

"What did you tell her?"

"I told her you tried to kill yourself the day after she left, but you forgot to measure twice so the rope was too long."

"Did you rehearse that line at home or was that the maiden voyage?"

"I said I wouldn't know. You have no life. You're always working, and when you're not, you're too tired to get together. Nobody ever sees you anymore."

"I got a lot on my plate."

"He was there, too. They're a couple now. I think it's serious."

He was a guy Gia had met at Trader Joe's, a hip chain of grocery stores that started here in southern California. She called him Terrific, someone—in her words—she had more in common with. And since I was only transitionally terrific with a small "t," she started sleeping with him a few months after she moved in with me. I was never in love with Gia, and she was never in love with me. But I was always faithful.

"Good. I'm happy for her."

"I just thought you should know. In case you still shop there."

*   *   *

Couples speak to each other in an entirely different language, a hybrid of his and hers, a combination of broken sentences and unfinished thoughts, and questions that always seem to be asked whenever one of them is leaving the room. If other people are present, this form of communication often takes on a very different tone. For instance, when the Santa Monica Fugits threw a dinner party after their renovation, they spoke as if they had just fallen in love. But whenever the Fugits forgot we were working in a room nearby, they spoke back and forth to each other in unrelated statements.

"I won't be home for dinner Tuesday night."

"The dogs are eating too much."

"Phil Marshack is being transferred to New York."

"I think we should put them on a diet."

I knew Gia and I had become a couple the night I was describing a weekend getaway to some of my friends and she piped in with the little details I left out. I knew our relationship was doomed when she stopped providing those details and started correcting me instead.

The Paulsons didn't speak at all. At least to each other.

And they had it down to an art form.

Derrick Paulson answered the front door dressed in beige, pleated cotton Dockers, a light blue dress shirt, and a blue blazer with shiny brass buttons. To offset the power of that blazer with the shiny brass buttons, he wore new tennis shoes and no tie. He also had no recollection of ever meeting me before. "Let me guess. The new contractor?"

"Good guess."

"Come on in. She's in the kitchen."

I entered alone. Bill was still in the truck making fun of the exterior of the house.

"Where's your crew?"

"They don't start until tomorrow. I wasn't sure about your morning routine."

"Our morning routine?"

"When you eat. What time the kids have to be at school. Since you're going to be living here during the renovation, it's best to start slowly."

"Ahhh. Let me guess. You've done this before?"

"You could say that."

"Glad to hear it. The last guy was an idiot. Don't even get me started on him." Derrick walked over to the entrance of the kitchen. "Look girls, it's the man who's going to fix the house. Can you say hello?"

The twins, Kiely and Kira, both dressed for another day of kindergarten, responded in unison. "Hello." Rebecca was eating breakfast in between the girls. Derrick's eyes passed over her as if she wasn't even there. Kira got out of her chair and stood behind her mother, clutching the back of Rebecca's blouse for security.

"She's a little shy," said Rebecca with a smile.

"That's okay. I am, too."

"Thanks again for doing this. You have no idea how much we appreciate it."

"What's wrong with it?" asked Kiely, looking at her father.

Derrick had no idea what she was talking about. He let out a short, uncomfortable laugh and turned to me to explain that laugh. "And *she* asks a lot of questions. Don't feel like you have to answer them all. You'll never get anything done."

"The house," I offered, trying to help.

It still didn't register right away. Derrick was distracted. He wanted out of there. "Oh. That." Another laugh, this one rushed. "Nothing's wrong with the house, sweetheart, this man's just going to make it look better." He grabbed his briefcase off the counter and gave each of his daughters a kiss on top of the head. "I have to run. I'll see you two love-bugs later." He exited the kitchen swiftly, motioning to me on his way out. "Walk me to my car. There's something we need to discuss before you start."

Derrick pulled the door closed before speaking.

"Just so we're clear, I'm in real estate, so don't try and screw me, *comprende?*"

"You speak Spanish?"

"No. But I know what that word means."

I took as long as possible before responding. *"Comprendo."*

"Good. Now let's talk about your bid: $468,000? That sounds high to me."

"It's less than your last contractor. And you've got some structural damage. You won't find a more reasonable price in town."

"Excluding materials and subcontractors, what percentage of that money goes in your pocket?"

"Very little of it. It's all in the contract I gave your wife." Who, I wanted to add, wrote the check for my retainer fee, a check from a trust in her maiden name. For whatever reason, Rebecca was using her own money to launch this operation, and if Derrick Paulson was living in the present (or even the present-adjacent) he would know that I already knew this. Or maybe he did, and that's why he was over-compensating.

"Look, don't get me wrong. Do I want to do this on the cheap? No. I'm not that type of person. Do I want to increase the value of my house without spending an arm and a leg? You betcha. Who doesn't?"

The man continued jawing at me, about what I have no idea. I was too focused on his new way of communicating. In the years since I first met him, Derrick Paulson had become one of those individuals who speaks in questions so they can provide all the answers. I began wondering about his daughter Kiely, and how long it would take before she started doing the same. I imagined her kneeling in front of a dollhouse, holding her Barbie next to Ken.

"Do I want to get into your convertible? No. I'm not that type of girl. Do I want to increase the value of my dollhouse without spending an arm and a leg? You betcha. Who doesn't?"

Derrick must have picked up on the absence in my expression because that's when he noticed Bill snapping his Nikon on the sidewalk out front. Before I knew what was happening, Derrick took off after Bill as if Bill was some kind of gumshoe hired to track him down. Bill was using a long lens at the time, so he didn't see Derrick coming until it was almost too late. His survival instincts kicked in at the last possible second and he took off running as fast as he possibly could even though he had no idea who this man was, or why the man was charging after him, forcing me to do the same.

Bill was a smoker and didn't stand a chance.

When he realized this, he reduced the size of the circles he was making to throw off his predator until the circle became so small, he collapsed into a turtle position on a lawn at the end of the street, using his body to protect the camera from the maniac who had hunted him down.

"He's with me!" I yelled for the tenth time, finally catching up with them.

Derrick stepped back, chest heaving, confused, missing a shiny brass button. Bill was coughing too hard to speak.

"You . . . ?" asked Derrick incredulously. "Then why the hell was he taking my picture?"

"He wasn't. He was photographing the house."

This took a moment to process. "You said you were alone."

"No, I said my crew wasn't here. He's not a member of my crew."

Derrick suddenly looked angry. I think he was feeling foolish. "You should have said something." He glared at me for a moment before turning and marching back toward the house. "Not a good start," he grumbled, still within earshot.

Bill banged out another round of sounds that resembled the upheaval of a fur ball, then got to his knees to check on his camera. I tried not to laugh, failed miserably, pulled myself together. It's never really acceptable to laugh at the expense of a friend who has been traumatized to this degree, but Bill hadn't run anywhere since the Northridge quake in '94, and I'm pretty sure he had forgotten how to do it.

"Fucking Brentwood," he belted between coughs.

When I finally got Bill back to the Paulsons', Derrick was gone and Rebecca was loading the twins into her maroon minivan. She didn't have a nanny, which was highly unusual in these parts. Most of my clients who had children not only had full-time nannies, they bought cars for their nannies to use whenever they were transporting the children from one newfangled activity to another.

"What happened?" asked Rebecca, eyeing the grass stains on Bill's thrift-store pants.

"Small misunderstanding concerning my friend here." I opened the door of the truck and helped Bill into the cab. "He'll be okay. He just needs to lie down for a minute."

"Are you sure? He looks awfully pale."

"Positive. Pale is Bill's natural color."

The twins reminded their mother they were going to be late for school, ousting her from this line of questioning.

"Okay, well, I work part-time at UCLA Medical so I won't be back until this afternoon. Will you be okay here by yourself?"

"We'll be fine. You have nothing to worry about."

"That's what the last contractor told me, and he quit after the second day." The moment this left her mouth, she looked away, running her right hand through her curly black hair, as if trying to remove her response from the transcript. "Sorry. That's not your problem. I'm just a little overwhelmed, that's all."

There were, of course, multiple things to worry about. And Rebecca's reaction suggested that she was more aware of this than she wanted to admit, as did the manner in which she communicated with her husband, as did the Breathe Right caught in her hair. When I saw her in the kitchen earlier, I'd thought it was an oddly colored barrette. The adjustment with her hand proved otherwise.

Kiely grew impatient. "Mommy, the car isn't moving."

"I know, honey. One more minute."

I didn't want her to leave, and I always wanted the client to leave. It was easier to get things done. "May I?" I asked, moving my own hand slowly toward her. Rebecca's eyes narrowed, and her mouth parted slightly, yet she did not refuse the advance, letting me know it had been a long time since anyone had touched her face, her head, her hair. When I removed the Breathe Right, she cringed.

"Oh God."

"Happens all the time. They fall off during the night."

Then came a smile I hadn't seen before. Goofy, self-deprecating, always late for school. A smile that brought cohesion back to the beautiful imperfections that defined her. This was the response of a woman living moment to moment, some good, some bad, and some that allowed her to breathe again.

"I have allergies."

"It's that time of year."

"I should have looked in the mirror. I'm kind of a wreck that way."

Kiely honked the horn. Bill started coughing again. Rebecca turned and started back toward her minivan. "So now what?" she asked in transition. "You guys just start, or am I forgetting something?"

"Now comes the strange part. Now I ask you for a set of keys, and the code to your alarm system."

She thought about this for a moment, an indication she hadn't gotten this far into her relationship with the first contractor. "In case you have to leave before I get back?"

"Exactly."

FOUR

You should know a few things about the man Rebecca Paulson had given her keys to. I never had any intention of being the guy who received them, never wanted the responsibility. I had seen what they did to my dad, how they consumed his life until the day he dropped dead of a heart attack building cabinets for Fred and Margaret Drysdale, a couple of alcoholics who drank boxed wine because it came in bigger sizes.

My mom died of cancer when I was seven, and my dad never recovered. And while he was good to me and taught me many of the skills that led to my livelihood, her absence left a void in him that he could not fill unless he was gambling or immersing himself in the homes and the problems of his clients. I didn't understand it then, but I do now.

It's important to know people who are more messed up than you are. It gives you someone to measure yourself by, someone who takes the edge off your own shortcomings. My dad had the Drysdales. I have my friend Bill. And you, you have someone, too, whether you're willing to admit it or not. It's nothing to be ashamed of. It's the survival of the socially fit, the insidious formula behind reality TV. If you don't have that special someone, or if *you* are that special someone, you should consider taking time off to reinvent yourself. Or, if that's not an option, enough time to locate and befriend a person who fits this description, a person to stay just ahead of in the human race to the finish line.

My dad was a one-man operation until I was old enough to assist him. He was an old-fashioned carpenter who worked exclusively with wood—for wood, in his opinion, was the single finest material on earth. He marveled at the complexities hidden in every tree. The differences between birch and maple, the divine grain cathedrals that run through red oak. The darkness of walnut, the rich hue of cherry, the strength of mahogany. He appreciated the knots, the burls, and the bird's-eyes. He loved everything from simple pine to exotic imports like African blackwood, Purpleheart, Macassar ebony, Zebrawood, and Waterfall Bubinga. He never wore a mask because he loved the way they smelled, the way they tasted. He scoffed at people when they wanted him to stain light woods dark, and he refused to finish anything, no matter how simple it was, using man-made polyurethanes. His finishes had to be natural, something God intended. Beeswax for lower sheens, shellac—a resin secreted by the lac beetle—for harder, glossier surfaces.

When he wasn't working or betting on sports, he took me to lumberyards where he would spend hours searching for pieces the competition had overlooked, panning for gold in a river of wood, building a portfolio that would see him through his retirement. "No two patterns will ever be the same," he would say whenever he thought I was getting bored. "They're like fingerprints."

And when he found a piece he liked, he carefully loaded it into his truck and took it home and locked it away with the rest of his prized collection, knowing it would be of no interest to a bookie or a loan shark looking to settle up, regardless of how far behind he got. He took great pride in selecting wood for each and every job, but he never drew from his own personal stash. Those were his masterpieces, and someday he would assemble them into something that would last forever.

That day never came.

So when he died, I sold the house and paid off his debts. I loaded his tools into the bed of his Ford F-250 and left town with twenty-two hundred dollars in my pocket, pulling a trailer full of his favorite wood. My dad had always hoped I'd stay and take over his client list when the time was right, but I was twenty and itching to get out of the town I grew up in. I was ready to move to a bigger place where I wasn't Chuck Sullivan's only son, a place where all the houses didn't look the same.

Los Angeles seemed like an obvious choice.

From the pictures I had seen of the city, the topography was littered with houses. They were everywhere, in every style imaginable. Houses by Wright, Schindler, Neutra, Lautner, Gehry, and Meier. It was the land of all things unconventional. Surely I would be able to find a job working as a carpenter in L.A. Hell, once contractors saw what I could do, there would be multiple offers to join their crews.

My timing could not have been worse.

The year was 1991 and the real estate market had started to crash, a small, minor detail that I'd failed to research before loading up my naïveté and heading west. It wasn't quite as bad as my great-grandfather choosing to migrate in the same direction without a compass, but it sure felt like it when I arrived. Between 1991 and 1997 the value of homes in Los Angeles County would fall by nearly twenty percent, and people were leery of pumping money into an asset in decline.

Those first few weeks were a bitch. From the shitty little motel on Hollywood Boulevard, to the shitty, considerably hotter little motel out in Van Nuys, I nearly burned out right then and there, on the edge of a floral-patterned dreadspread hiding the DNA of a thousand transients. If you're a fugitive on the run, retrace these steps. This is where you go to feel invisible when people are looking right at you. And buy yourself the Thomas Guide, a book put out annually, filled with maps of

L.A. County designed to help newcomers navigate a city forty-six miles wide, comprised of neighborhoods looking to distance themselves even further. Because, let's face it, you're already a little lost or you wouldn't have fled here in the first place.

I had never rented an apartment, therefore I had no references. I tried to open a checking account, but the banks didn't want my money. They said I was a risk because I was under twenty-one and I didn't have enough to meet the minimum balance. And they wouldn't let me open a savings account unless I had a checking account.

I eventually found a landlord in Koreatown who let me pay him cash for a one-bedroom apartment as long as I worked on the other units in the building. Little did I know that people who performed these same services usually lived in their buildings for free. Once all of my dad's wood was properly stacked so it wouldn't warp, I bought a small futon at a garage sale and set out to find a real job on someone's crew.

The contractors I called weren't hiring, and to get in with the few who were, you had to know someone. Construction work was union and they were an even tougher crowd. I was so broke I would have gladly taken the work if it was offered, except I didn't drive all that way to work on buildings or roads or in a factory. I came for the houses.

The apartments I agreed to look after were crooked little places stained with nicotine and bad dreams and wrong turns that could never be righted. Loading zones for funeral homes occupied by pack rats who had no intention of leaving on their feet. Spaces only the occupant knew how to navigate, filled with piles and pillars of newspapers and books and clothes that no longer fit them. Their tables buckled under the weight of all the things they planned to have fixed one day: broken clocks, chipped knickknacks, car parts, lamps; junk by every definition of the word. I fixed the leaks in their ceilings and the faulty wiring in their electrical outlets. I unstopped their toilets and their showers, and listened to their stories—equally tattered tales, forgotten and piled high.

My most memorable encounter was with an old woman named Olive, whose skin had become so translucent you would have sworn you saw the blood moving to and from her barely beating heart. Olive's entire apartment was filled with Nativity scenes she made out of ostrich eggs mail-ordered from Africa. She had hundreds of them, all painted different colors, all hollowed out and cut in half to house her tiny figurines of Jesus, Mary, and Joseph, the Three Wise Men, and whatever barnyard animals she could cram into the small space left over.

If you ever find yourself in a discussion with someone who believes it's impossible to fit the birth of Christianity into a single ostrich egg, tell them about Olive in Koreatown. Give her that. She not only proved it could be done, she proved it over and over again.

Olive and I drank tea together most mornings I lived there until I realized she was suffering from what I now know to be Alzheimer's disease. At the time, I just thought she was getting senile. It began with her accusing me of stealing the Austrian Nativity scene, then the French crèche, then the glitter she sometimes sprinkled on top of the eggs. It ended with her in a rage, convinced I broke into her apartment in the middle of the night and relieved her of a Cornish hen she had in her freezer. I told the landlord about the episode and he told me not to get involved with the people I worked for. He said it was none of my business.

So I broke into her apartment. While Olive was out on her daily wander, I jimmied a window on the fire escape and rummaged through her address books—all six of them—until I located the phone number of her son back in Pennsylvania. Making the call to this man and telling him about the rapidly declining condition of his mother wasn't the hard part. It was handling his response. He was appreciative, yet totally unaffected, as if I was a neighbor who just called to tell him he had left his sprinklers on.

I tried again the following day, and the day after that. I dialed randomly through a schedule I imagined him keeping, until I finally got his wife on the line. I explained the situation to her, and she responded with a silence packed with all those things that hit you at once when news like this arrives on a telephone. The guilt, the distant grief, the dollar signs, the new responsibilities, the husband who never mentioned my previous calls. Twenty-four hours later, Olive's daughter-in-law showed up by herself to take Olive home, although I doubt that was the word either of them would have used to describe it.

Los Angeles is no place to grow old and poor. No matter where you place Jesus.

My afternoons in Koreatown were spent passing out flyers describing my carpentry skills to potential customers, complete with a graphic of a speedy little handyman who looked more like a tweaked-out elf on the run from a narcotics officer who had issues with Christmas. The computers you could rent at Kinko's back then had a limited selection, and I was too young to know any better. I practically covered the whole damn city with those stupid flyers, on foot, in the truck, east to west and back again, placing them under windshields, in mailboxes, under doors, in hardware stores, anywhere people would allow me to leave one behind. Days became weeks, and still the phone never rang.

When I wasn't out inadvertently letting the citizens of Los Angeles know that they would have to be insane to let the creator of this flyer into their homes, I milled around with the Latino day-laborers outside Home Depot, picking up occasional work mixing concrete, landscaping, and painting. I landed a job building a couple of walls on the set of a porno out in Chatsworth, only to be fired for taking too long. No one ever explained to me that movie walls, whether on a low-budget skinflick (not suitable for anyone under eighteen), or the feel-good movie of the summer (not suitable for anyone over eighteen), didn't have to support anything other than suspension of disbelief.

I considered selling some of my dad's wood. It was worth good money, and I easily could have pawned it off to one of the lumberyards, only I couldn't bring myself to do it. My old man had been down numerous times, spent most of his nights there just trying to get back to fifty-one percent, that little plot of real estate that separates the winners from the losers. If he was able to refrain from cashing in the wood, then I owed it to him to do the same. And the thought of using it to build furniture I could sell, well, that didn't feel right either. For one thing, I didn't have the space, and even if I did, I couldn't stomach the idea of putting all that work into something just to negotiate with people on the price of my father's life. His wood would have no meaning in their homes.

On my twenty-first birthday, I was ready to leave.

It was my cutoff date, the expiration of my poorly devised plan. It was time to accept my losses and head back to Illinois to regroup. I had put aside enough gas money to get there, which meant that if I slept in the truck and ate only lunch from that point forward, I had fifty-eight dollars left to blow on my birthday. And there was no way in hell I was leaving town without at least one night to remember, one good story to tell to my friends from high school even if I had to embellish it beyond recognition.

As the sun set on that warm August night, I laced up my favorite pair of Wolverines and walked north into Hollywood. After a steak at Musso & Franks, I drifted over to a little dive bar called The Firefly to knock back my first legal drinks as an "adult." I must have looked pretty fucking tired beyond my years that night because the bartender never asked me for identification. He just poured me a shot of whiskey and set it on the bar. I'm not sure why I chose The Firefly over the other bars in Hollywood; they all looked about the same to me. Proximity perhaps. The shortest distance between me and the last hour of my birthday.

Around eleven-thirty, the bar started filling up with hipsters and late-blooming *Breakfast Club* wannabes dressed in their vintage blazers and their skinny ties from Aardvarks. They bought drinks for the professional drunks. They jockeyed for position at the bar in preparation for something big.

When the hour of midnight arrived, everyone took a step back and watched in awe as the bartender lit the top of the wooden bar on fire, as he apparently did every night at this time. Orange and red flames leaped out of blue flames springing from the grain alcohol that raced toward my seat near the jukebox. The young guns cheered wildly and exchanged high-fives and ordered more shots. The drunks looked vindicated, like everything in their lives made perfect sense until the bartender extinguished what he started.

By the time they announced last call, I had my story, only I was less eager to return home and share it with those I had grown up with. The bartender had given me an idea, albeit a primitive one. He had found a way to lure patrons to him, something I was never going to accomplish passing out flyers featuring an elf on methamphetamines, or fixing apartments no one really cared about. The region was suffering from a five-year drought, and there were plenty of houses just waiting to burn. With the right sales pitch and a little blind luck, maybe it was worth one more shot.

The Hollywood sign is anchored in the hills because you can see it from pretty much anywhere in the city. The houses in that area have been built there for the same reason: it's the best place to remove yourself from the chaos below, while remaining just close enough to be featured prominently. These are the walls where architects hang their most interesting creations. But altitude isn't cheap in L.A., and there's only so much wall space to go around. So as the city grew, and the land became more expensive, builders began constructing seven-figure homes in places that once seemed impossible. If my new, potentially poorly devised plan was going to work, this was the place to do it.

Focus on exterior work, I told myself. It was less intrusive and right there for everyone to see. Select five different houses, all precariously built on cliffs, all sided with cedar shakes burning up in the hot sun. During the dead of night, climb to the base of those houses, through the bougainvilleas and the underbrush to check the soil around them. Look for erosion and exposed bedrock, places where the cost of securing proper scaffolding would inflate other bids. Then work on your sales pitch regarding the condition of those cedar shakes. Explain to the homeowners how the shakes would all have to be replaced in a year or two if someone didn't immediately strip, clean, and saturate the ones that were already there.

Once I felt prepared, I parked my truck outside these houses and waited until I saw the homeowner coming or going. I approached them respectfully, trying to maintain my composure when the first two told me to get off their property before they called their private security companies. The third was a renter, and told me to take it up with the owner. The fourth was a contenter who liked his house the way it was. "Rustic" was the word he used to describe it.

The fifth and final house was the home of Mrs. Bonderman, a graceful woman in her early sixties, who had deep lines of expression etched into her face, proudly displayed maps of everywhere she had ever been. I introduced myself and took her through the prognosis. Mrs. Bonderman nodded thoughtfully and studied her home. "You're right about that cedar. I've had four different painting companies up here in the last two months. They all said it's a real problem."

"Whatever you decide to do, don't wait too long. That's original siding. It'd be a shame to have to replace it all."

"We can't afford any of their bids right now. Not without refinancing."

"They're right. It's not any easy job. But there is another way."

Mrs. Bonderman sized me up for a moment. "I'm listening."

"Well, if I was gonna do it, I wouldn't waste all that time and money trying to secure the right scaffolding. I'd rappel down from the top. Using ropes."

"And you know how to do that?"

"Sure. I've done it a bunch of times."

Mrs. Bonderman remained skeptical, yet detectably amused. "How old are you?"

"Twenty-one."

"I see. And how much would that cost me? You rappelling down from the top?"

It's important to employ a sense of humor when looking back on your life. Especially if you're recalling one of those painfully green periods, a shade of green you might find among the paint swatches at Dunn-Edwards, or Sherwin-Williams, or wherever you buy your paint. The kind with those horrible names: Granny Smith, Grassy Knoll, Henry's Escape. The kind that make you ask yourself, *"Who's Henry? And what in the hell was he trying to escape from?"*

"I can do the whole thing, supplies included, for ten grand."

Long pause.

"That's awfully cheap for someone who's done it a bunch of times. Everyone else said they couldn't do it for less than twenty-five."

I rifled through a manual of expressions trying to locate one that wouldn't give me away. "If you like the work, you can tip me at the end. How's that?"

Mrs. Bonderman considered the offer.

"I'll talk it over with my husband. Do you have a card?"

As I reached for my wallet I remembered that I had thrown away all my business cards along with the leftover flyers. "No," I said, coming clean. "I don't work with a business card anymore. Truth is, I'm not really the type. I'm not even a painter. I'm just a carpenter who appreciates wood. But if you hire me, no one will do a better job of restoring the outside of your house."

By the time I got back to my apartment in Koreatown, there was a message on my machine from Mrs. Bonderman, asking me if I could start immediately.

I didn't know the first thing about rappelling, and it took most of the night, and a good portion of my gas money, just to figure it out. I purchased ropes, carabiners, and two different harnesses from Adventure 16 on Pico. Then, waited for the sun to set, and practiced by walking down the backside of my apartment building.

The following morning, I returned to Home Depot and hired Hector and Miguel Bautista, who I had worked with once before on a job digging trenches for a do-it-yourselfer. Even though we barely said a word to one another on that first outing—they were still learning English, and I was only starting to learn Spanish—I respected their work ethic; the way they always seemed to know the other's next move without having to communicate, a valuable commodity in this business, and one that can't be taught.

The Bonderman job kicked our asses in any language.

We worked in shifts out there on the end of those ropes, leaving one guy on the roof at all times to lower down supplies and make sure the knots held. We wire-brushed each cedar shake by hand, replacing those that were too far gone, then painted the house with three coats of opaque stain that burned and stained our skin almost as effectively as it treated the wood. We could have gotten away with two coats, and put a little more money in our pockets, only we wanted that house to last. We wanted to be able to point to it in ten years and say, "We did that. That's our signature up there on that hill."

In the end, I think we made around six dollars an hour, but the sacrifice paid off. People driving along Mulholland Drive two hundred feet below stopped to see what we were doing. Joggers and bikers looked up. People in need of similar repairs came to us with their phone numbers, just as I had hoped.

In many ways, the three of us grew up together in those early years, educating ourselves on the fly as the jobs got bigger and more sophisticated. We went from three guys who would do anything for a buck on the outside of a house, to a closely knit team that specialized in the unconventional within those same homes.

We took the field together each morning, accepting every challenge that came our way: tile, roofing, masonry work, you name it. We did anything and everything that gave us a chance to work with wood. We were bootleggers with an attitude, and we took great pride in doing it better, faster, and cheaper than the competition. And when someone finally blew the whistle on our little operation, I went out and got my own contractor's license. If that was what it would take to keep doing what we did best, then so be it.

We worked too damn hard to get in the door. We weren't about to give up the keys.

FIVE

Sally Stein looked as if she were about to pop the question I had been waiting for.

We were lying on her Swedish mattress, on her twelve inches of imported memory foam after another round of what we had started the night of her dinner party. If this mattress remembered everything, not just the contours of a body or two, it would tell you that it was a Friday, at the end of my first week working at Rebecca Paulson's. It would tell you about all the nights prior to this one, nights that often ended with me thinking about Rebecca long after Sally had fallen asleep. What was *she* like in bed? What did she see in her husband? What happened between Rebecca and Sally that ended their friendship?

"How are things going at the Paulsons'?" asked Sally, rolling over to face me.

There are no fonts to indicate sarcasm or irony. No one has gone in front of Congress and lobbied to have Bookman Old Style or Garamond 10-point converted to convey these things. And even if they did, and their proposal passed both the House and the Senate, I suspect it would have been *ironically* vetoed. It is with these limitations in mind that I will attempt to articulate the equally intricate tone that gift wrapped my response to Sally's highly anticipated question. The closest thing I can compare it to is the one used by teenagers when asked about things they don't want to discuss, that detached tone that backfires and makes their parents or their principal press them for more details.

"Good."

This hung there for a moment before Sally took the bait.

"What's her house like?" she asked. "Is it nice?"

Her, no longer plural.

"It will be when we're done with it."

"When will that be?"

"The end of August, if all goes well."

"Why wouldn't it go well?"

"Every job is different. And they're living there, so we have to do it in stages."

"Is Rebecca happy?"

"I wouldn't really know. It was a crazy week. I didn't get to see her that much."

Sally gave me one of those smiles that is intended to tell others you're being playful, when in truth, you're quite serious. "You didn't get to? That almost sounds like you wish you had?"

"She's married."

"So?"

"With kids."

"You've never ever slept with a married client?"

"She's not my type," I said, offering up a half-truth. Rebecca wasn't my type, at least the type I used to imagine myself with. But over the years, the property lines of that category had become less defined. The more women I worked for, the more intriguing I found each of them to be. Their complexities became nearly as appealing as their lips, their breasts, their legs. The seemingly irrational approach to the way they viewed certain situations wasn't the same as a nice ass, but the mysterious formulas that created these perspectives made their physical

attributes less important to me. A good body can be remarkably per-
suasive, but it can lead a man only so far. The real power of a woman's
sexuality lies within the engine that makes her body move. And like
fingerprints, and grain patterns hidden in every tree, no two will ever
be the same.

"What's your type?"

Sally had it all: the confidence, the compassion, the body that
floated and marched at the same time, a trio of steam that became even
more combustible with the emergence of what sounded like jealousy,
something I initially considered beneath her.

"You are. I wouldn't be here if you weren't."

She smiled and scooted back into the pillows. "Did Derrick Paulson
ask you to sign a nondisclosure agreement?"

Now we were getting somewhere.

NDA's are not that unusual in my line of work. They are no longer
relegated to celebrities and people the media considers worthy of attention. With divorce being the new marriage for the umpteenth year
in a row, people outside the limelight have started asking for them as
well, people gearing up well in advance for their bitter brawl over
money, assets, and the children they created while in training. Stock-
brokers, captains of industry, accountants, anyone who feels the need
to protect themselves from a potentially costly confession from someone working inside their home. When people ask if I will sign one of
these contracts, I always think twice about working in an environment
that requires one.

"No. Why do you ask?"

Sally wasn't the type to dish, and I respected that about her. She
shrugged. "Just curious. I read something in the paper about how
they're all the rage these days."

"Should he have?"

She pondered the conversation that would follow. Her response, my response to her response, where they would all lead us, and what we would do once we got there.

"Beats me," she said after she had taken herself through it. "I didn't really know him that well." And with that, she swung her legs over the edge of the bed and stood up. "I'm going to take a shower. Join me if you'd like."

Sally's disappearance into the master bath made me appreciate her even more. Whatever happened between her and Rebecca had just sent her through a kaleidoscope of hidden emotions. But in the moment before she closed the door on our conversation, on the little game we had been playing with each other, she gave me something to work with. A look of empathy for a life she did not understand.

Which got me thinking about the threat of a nondisclosure agreement.

One of the reasons things went as well as they did that first week at Rebecca's was because Derrick was out of town on business. But he would be back soon enough, and when he returned, I would have to begin justifying why I took the job, something I wouldn't be able to accomplish if he asked me to sign an NDA. If Derrick Paulson ever realized that he never should have let me in the door without one, I'd be reduced to merely working on his house, contractually banned from exposing the cracks in his façade.

I needed to come up with a way to get Derrick Paulson to trust me.

A way to make him think I was his friend.

* * *

Rebecca came home for lunch unannounced and caught me in the living room. It was a Wednesday, week two, and still no sign of husband Derrick.

I have two favorite moments during every renovation, and this was one of them. Standing inside a gutted room once it has been cleaned up, studying a blank slate full of potential. We had completed stage one of the deconstruction (we stopped demolishing things once we discovered the art of salvaging materials), which included the living room, the dining room, the master bed and bath, and the kitchen. Normally, we hold off on the kitchen as long as possible, but it was on the side of the house with the structural damage, and that needed to be addressed immediately.

Before starting, we'd built vapor-sealed walls to create temporary living quarters for the Paulsons in the back wing of the house, and turned one of the guest bedrooms into a makeshift kitchen by tapping into the plumbing in the adjacent bathroom. Miguel and his guys were busy working on the exterior of the house, removing the un-dulating scrap metal and loading it into a recycling roll-off in the driveway. Hector and his guys were in the master bedroom, framing in new walls.

"What are you doing?" asked Rebecca from the archway of the foyer.

"Tracking the sun."

"If it burns out, it'll be a while before you notice."

She was smiling when I looked over at her.

"It's too dark in here. I want to move the windows and make them bigger."

"How much will that cost?"

"I'll take it out of my contingency. I was a little distracted the day I did the walk-through. It's my fault."

"The room *is* kind of moody."

"The house was built in the winter and these windows face the southwest. The original architect didn't take into account how much the sun would shift off-season. Coupled with the low-hanging eave of the roof, you're sacrificing eight months of good light in favor of four."

Rebecca thought about this. "Okay. That makes sense."

"You'll be glad you did."

She held up a large paper bag. "I brought you guys lunch."

Hanging over Rebecca's other shoulder was a purse I hadn't seen her carry, a purse designed by Sally Stein. I had told Rebecca the week before that I had a prior commitment with Sally, and at some point I would have to divide up my crew. Rebecca greeted this news with understanding, aware that her own house had entered my workflow unexpectedly. But other than a slight buckle in her expression, she did not indicate that she was once friends with Sally Stein. She never brought it up in the days following this conversation, and I was beginning to think she never would.

Until the purse popped in.

How did I know this was a purse designed by Sally Stein? An excellent question that fathers an answer I'm not particularly proud to share with you. I went shopping for one. On Sunday. And I dragged Bill with me.

. . .

Bill was a purist who worked only with film. Except he still hadn't developed the pictures he'd taken of Rebecca's house after his run-in with Derrick, and I wanted to check in with him to make sure he wasn't staring longingly over the edge of a building. I also figured he'd make the shopping excursion more interesting.

The moment I pulled into the parking lot of The Grove, an outdoor mall on West Third Street, Bill became that guy in a horror film who always dies first. The one who gets a flat tire in the rain and is then stupid enough to get into the truck of a wild-eyed drifter who picks up people who get flat tires in the rain.

"What the fuck are you doing?" he asked.

"I just need to swing in here and look at something."

"At The Grove? You can't just swing into The Grove. A mall is not a place you can just *swing* into. You said we were going to Molly Malone's for beers."

"We are. This is on the way."

"This is on the way to Armageddon, dude. A suburban plague capable of wiping out entire cities before they even know they're sick."

"You can wait in the truck."

"I'm not waiting in the truck. No way. What if you never come back?"

"I'm not coming back. I brought you here to abandon you."

"Like an elderly grandparent?"

"No, like a photographer who hasn't developed the pictures I paid him to take."

"All right, okay, I'll do it first thing tomorrow. I promise. Just quit screwing around. Seriously. Get back in the truck. We need to get out of here immediately."

I closed my door and started for the entrance, counting the seconds until Bill came after me. Five, four, three, two, Bill: "What the fuck? I said I'd develop the film!"

"I still need to go inside."

"You're serious?"

"I'm afraid so."

"Listen to me very carefully. If we go in there together, we're no longer just a couple of guys going out for beers. We're on a man-date."

As I stood there in Barney's looking at the Sally Stein signature purse that recently had been re-released as a result of its success on eBay,

Bill paced back and forth behind me at a safe distance, his hands in his pockets, shaking his head. "What have these women done to you?"

"Don't be such a homophobe. You can learn a lot about a woman from the kind of purse she carries. At least that's what I'm hoping."

"Yeah? You can also learn a lot about a guy who goes to The Grove on his only day off just to buy one."

"I'm not here to buy it. I'm just here to see what it looks like on the inside."

"Oh, well that changes everything. Hey, maybe when we're done we can head over to the farmers market and pick out some fresh basil."

"I said you could wait in the truck."

"This chick better be one fine piece of ass, because you are in way over your head, my friend. Seriously." Bill popped a piece of Nicorette into his mouth (he smoked *and* chewed the gum, often simultaneously), then wandered off to look at a defibrillator mounted on the far wall.

Like Sally and the city we lived in, the purse was full of secret compartments. Some with zippers, some with pockets, some with pockets within pockets that had zippers. Layers and layers of leather that made me feel as if I would never get to the bottom of the woman who designed it, even if I studied it for the rest of my life. If James Bond ever got married, this would be the purse his wife would use to get them both out of trouble. If James Bond ever divorced her, this would be the purse that got him killed.

.   .   .

We ate lunch in the driveway with our backs against the garage, just out of the sun, Rebecca right there on the ground with us, perfectly comfortable with the setting. As expected, Miguel and Hector played the Spanish card. They raised their burgers a couple of times and said

"Muchos gracias," but other than that, they maintained their distance, letting me know they weren't comfortable with Rebecca's presence. Lunch was about hiding from the client, not including them in our routine. And the younger guys always took their cue from the Bautista brothers, so the meal was pretty much a fiesta of silence, which was unfortunate because I wanted Rebecca to experience the best half-hour of the day. She had a good sense of humor, and I was confident she could hold her own with the crew once we got bantering, something we did every day at this time to free the random thoughts that had been trapped in our heads all morning.

Rebecca was fine with the silence. She wasn't one of those nervous talkers who feels compelled to fill every gap, or one of those nervous laughers who can't end a sentence without attaching it to a runaway rickshaw. Rebecca just sat there, enjoying her meal, listening to the wind gliding through the trees.

The service industry is full of unsettling stories about short-order cooks and arrogant chefs who get diabolically creative when you send your food back for alterations. For this reason, you choose your restaurants carefully; your body is your temple, you are what you eat, you watch *Dateline,* you don't want your death broadcast on the news. You should apply that same level of caution to your renovation. If you treat a workman poorly, he will retaliate, whether malicious or not. Sometimes all it takes to create a nightmare-in-waiting is a simple distraction. Six months from now, when you're out on that Caribbean cruise you've always wanted to take (the one that makes you realize you're not built for cruising) and you get a call from your alarm company telling you your house is flooded, don't be surprised if it's the result of the little temper tantrum you threw on that day you were without water. Losing your patience with a plumber who is soldering pipes in one of the bathrooms is not the best way to get the most for your money.

What you should have done was feed him. Plumbers work in the bowels of a house where the wars of repetition are often won or lost depending on what they had for lunch that day. Their meals should stick even better than the welds you trust them with. Burgers, double meat sandwiches, something big enough to keep him company when he's in there all alone. Plumbers spend half the day thinking about lunch, and the other half thinking about dinner. A free meal is your chance to focus that plumber on your home.

Electricians consider themselves the most sophisticated of all tradesmen due to the ever-present dangers of electricity. If yours are anything like mine, they'll respond to a variety of things: Cobb salads, leaner meats, soups on cold days. They may pass in favor of their own menu, but the offer lets them know you're aware that nutritional needs directly affect their attention spans. If you think I'm exaggerating about the connection between food and concentration, just ask your insurance company about the top three fire hazards inside your home. Although they won't back me up on this for legal reasons, the first two can be attributed to empty stomachs.

1. *Distractions in the kitchen.*
2. *Electrical problems.*
3. *Chimneys and fireplaces.*

My crew's favorite lunch is Chinese food. They're all from Mexico and South America, but if given the option, they'll take kung pao chicken or cashew chicken over a burrito any day of the week. These bribes, or signs of goodwill, are by no means a requirement on your part. They are, however, a wise investment.

The guys ate unusually fast that day and returned to work instead of going into the backyard to kick around a soccer ball for ten minutes, which is what they would have done if they hadn't felt beholden to Rebecca for providing lunch. Up to this point, Rebecca and I had spent very few moments alone together. When I saw her in the mornings she was always busy with the twins, and in the evenings I was always scrambling to wrap up another ten-hour shift. And when a decision had to be made regarding the house, I never felt like we were truly alone because I was technically on the clock, and it would have been rude of me to drift off into my attraction to her, even though I ended up doing that about forty-nine percent of the time anyway.

"The girls really like you. Every morning they ask if Henry's coming today."

"They're great kids."

"It must be weird . . . getting involved in people's lives, then just . . . leaving."

"It can be. But most people bring me back for one thing or another."

"The people who can't stop?"

"You're familiar with them?"

"Tess warned me about turning into one of those people."

"I don't see that happening."

Rebecca didn't see this as a compliment, which it was. "Yeah. Me either."

"So what do you do at UCLA Medical?"

"I work as an administrator."

"Do you like it?"

"It keeps me busy. And I'm good at that kind of stuff, so . . ."

"Good at staying busy or good with paperwork?"

She smiled. "Little of both, I guess. What about you, are you married?"

An interesting transition considering I thought we were talking about her job.

"No."

"Because you haven't met the right person or because marriage isn't for you?"

"Little of both, I guess."

Her smile didn't last long. Something had entered her mind, or perhaps it had been there the entire time and it was just waiting to be introduced. "Do you think I might be able to get your opinion on something?"

"Sure. What do you need?"

I followed Rebecca through the garage into the wing of the house where they were living. She opened the door of her temporary bedroom and closed it behind us once we had entered. She said nothing to me en route to this location. She looked preoccupied with her decision to take me there.

Have you ever had one of those dreams where you encounter a stranger in an unfamiliar setting, on a street you don't recognize, a coffee shop you've never been to? You see that person has forgotten their umbrella or their newspaper or some odd item people don't usually carry around with them, like a toaster or a wagon wheel, and you go after them to return the item, but when you step outside into the next scene they've already vanished. Sometimes you speak to them briefly before they leave, other times they're just a background player, looking on as your subconscious runs around unsupervised. And when you wake up from that dream, you don't even really recall what the stranger looked like. You just remember the way they made you feel in that one moment you were in their presence. And that feeling lingers for days, and you hope you'll see that person again when you go back to sleep, but you never do. So you drive in to work imagining what would happen if you dropped everything and embarked on a completely irrational journey to locate them, because that feeling they gave you, that feeling that lingered for days over something as mundane as a forgotten toaster, has left you wondering if that stranger is the one you're supposed to be with.

Standing there with Rebecca Paulson behind the closed door of her temporary bedroom, I felt like I had found my stranger.

"Do you have any animals?" she asked.

"No. But I've worked for a lot of people who do."

"Our cat Clyde, he's not doing well with the noise." Rebecca opened up the closet door and moved aside some of her clothes, revealing a short-haired, gray-and-white cat curled up in the back corner, hiding behind her shoes.

"Yeah. Remodeling is no fun for the animals."

"He won't come out. He won't eat. I'm really worried about him."

"How old is he?"

"Fifteen. He's my oldest friend in the world."

"Is there someone he can stay with until we're done?"

"The girls would be heartbroken. They're madly in love with him, and they're displaced enough as it is."

"How was he on Sunday when we weren't here?"

"He still wouldn't come out."

If you don't have kids, your life most likely revolves around your pets, and you've already made arrangements for them during your renovation. If you're well-off, you might even be including them in your design plans. For some animal lovers, creature comforts are becoming as popular as childproofing in the homes of those who have procreated. And I'm not referring to dog doors and exercise kennels along the side of the house. I'm talking about window beds for cats and dog showers and $1,699 Jentle Pet spas, all of which I've built or installed in people's homes. Some of you may be rolling your eyes at the idea of placing a dog into a bubbling massage pool, so I won't go into great detail about the attic we converted into a playroom for Biscuit Davenport, a miniature schnauzer in Cheviot Hills. The soundproofed, mirrored window we installed is worth mentioning, however. It allowed Biscuit to look into the ginkgo biloba tree that shaded the back of the house, giving him an eye-level view of the squirrels that gathered to eat there. The reflective coating on the exterior of the window kept those squirrels from seeing Biscuit obsessing about their activities only a few feet away, an image I am quite sure they would never forget.

"Tell you what," I said, unable to think of a better solution. "Let's see how Clyde does this Sunday. If he still won't come out, we'll revisit it then. Some animals just take longer to adapt than others."

Rebecca mulled this over. "Okay. That sounds right."

I returned to the living room, and Rebecca went back to work at the hospital. There was nothing I could do about the noise. I couldn't tell the guys to take the edge off their sledgehammers and silence their nail guns because Clyde was going through changes. Yet I felt for the old cat. I really did. For a human being in Clyde's position, a renovation of this magnitude was the equivalent of living with a marching band that played the same John Philip Sousa song over and over again.

Bill called just as I was firing up the Sawzall. "Dude, I've got a problem."

"You're at Jamba Juice and the blenders aren't working?"

"I'm serious. None of the pictures came out. That pig-fucker broke my camera."

SIX

My first trilogy of bad decisions completed itself on Saturday, at the end of that second week at Rebecca Paulson's, at a time when there were at least five other things I should have been doing. I should have been driving over to Samy's Camera to see if I could salvage Bill's Nikon. I should have been driving to my temperature-controlled storage space to rotate my father's wood. I should have been at the grocery store buying food. I should have been at Sally Stein's washing off the day in her steam shower, buying myself more time on the guesthouse.

Five was a horrible estimate. Five didn't even come close.

This was a number I hadn't reached before. A number that just kept going and going the more I thought about it. One that included sleeping, laundry, an extension class on time management, reading, developing a hobby, opening an IRA, seeing friends. Hell, even just sitting at home on my couch doing absolutely nothing. That's what I should have been doing. Absolutely nothing. Worst-case scenario.

But I wasn't doing absolutely nothing.

I was driving to Bridget Campanelli's loft downtown to give her a quote on some shelves she wanted built. Bridget was Sally's friend who owned a restaurant, so, naturally, I was hoping to time my arrival with the dinner hour. I chose to begin my investigation with Bridget for a few reasons, starting with the fact that I wanted her to be the one who sat next to me at the dark dinner party. Like Rebecca and Sally, Bridget knew how to move. She had a good engine. She also knew both of them, as she stated the night we met. Bridget Campanelli was my link to their past.

I needed to know more about the falling out between Rebecca and Sally. Delays on both projects were inevitable, and I didn't want to get caught between two angry women competing for my crew. I also wanted to believe that my trip to see Bridget was definitely, without a doubt, work related, and it had absolutely nothing to do with me operating under the spell of both Sally and Rebecca.

The redbrick building where Bridget owned her loft once housed a small toy factory. Los Angeles was running out of room to expand, and lofts like these were a concerted effort to get people to divorce their houses and relocate here. Restaurants and shopping centers were springing up nearly as fast to sweeten the deal, to offset the countless number of homeless people who called these streets home: the dreamers, the small-town carpenters who never threw away their flyers, the fallen kings and queens of the prom from each and every state, who had their reasons for moving here, and even more reasons for never moving back.

On weekdays, downtown L.A. bustled with businessmen and businesswomen and misguided tourists on their way to Hollywood, beguiled and bemused, looking around as if to say, *"Is this all there is?"* At night and on the weekends, they fled for higher ground, leaving the area to the zombies who at some point fell out of a cab and into a bus that eventually dropped them off here, the last stop on the tour.

This is where those car commercials are filmed. The ones that make you wonder how they did that. The Lexus, the Mercedes, the Cadillac, driving through deserted, urban streets designed to make you feel like you are the only one on the road when you are in that particular automobile. There are no special effects involved. The people who should be on those streets have not been digitally removed. It's just another Sunday morning, downtown in the City of Houses. Not a single angel in sight.

The Thievery Corporation was playing loudly on Bridget's stereo, causing me to ring the buzzer on the outside of her security gate a second time in case she didn't hear me. A moment later, Bridget appeared in one of the large windows looking down at me from the third floor. She was wearing sweatpants and a black tank top, featuring a chest that was small and inviting, like the rest of her. The bio on her restaurant's website said she was thirty-eight, yet she looked closer to thirty. If she was lying upwards about her age, she was the only one in L.A. who dared to do so.

Before calling down to me, Bridget released a short burst of air to brush aside the dirty-blond bangs that were obstructing her view. "I'll buzz you in."

When I stepped out of the freight elevator and into the enormous loft, Bridget was absent. The kitchen sat directly in the center of the space, like a stage, elevated eight inches off the ground. The appliances were made by Gaggenau, the countertops were stainless steel with marine edges. In the middle of the kitchen, beneath a chandelier of copper pots hanging from the twenty-two-foot ceiling, there was an island of butcher-block maple. On her stove, a symphony of fresh herbs was simmering in a marinara sauce. Along the windowsills facing east, the rest of the crop was still growing.

"Sorry. I'll just be a second," Bridget announced from behind the frosted glass divider that separated her bedroom.

"Take your time."

I don't really know what I was expecting when I got to Bridget Campanelli's. As Hector pointed out that night in the bar, I had broken my own rules before, but not intentionally. I never made the first move.

And my past regressions never happened in ways the porn industry would like you to believe they did: the scenario where I'm working under a sink and in walk the legs; the problem in the bedroom and there she is on the bed. Never. Not once. Unless you include Sally Stein's dinner party, but again, she wasn't technically a client at the time.

When I did cross that line with a client, it happened in more emotional places, places that took some time to get to. And when I found myself in those places where loneliness meets trust meets availability, I always did my best to walk away from the touch or the embrace that led to the kiss that led to the regret. But as Sally Stein had proven, my best could use some improvement, some reinforcement, some retrofitting, a big red star on my list of things to do.

Bridget's furniture was modern, all very classy, including a few collector's pieces by Arne Jacobsen, my personal favorite in the Danish Modern movement, and Charles and Ray Eames, the yoga masters of wood who inspired Jacobsen by reshaping life in the American home in the middle of the last century. I was on my haunches admiring these chairs when Bridget finally entered.

"Sorry. I cut myself cooking."

"You're an Eames fan."

"I am. You?"

"Very much so."

Bridget looked down in frustration at the Band-Aid on her left index finger. "Why do they make Band-Aids this small? If a cut is this small, who needs a Band-Aid?" Bridget held up her left hand, perhaps the very hand that had shifted my gears under Sally Stein's dining room table, so I could see what she was talking about.

I'm not even sure if I looked at it. I was too busy scanning the convenience of this situation for a subtext that could only be written by the other participant. There was something slightly sexual in Bridget's body language, although nothing I was willing to bet on, nothing that stood out from that natural quality she couldn't get rid of. She was genuinely annoyed by this little Band-Aid on her left index finger.

"I think they're for kids."

"Then they should come in a separate box. With a warning that tells people who don't have kids that this is the only size you'll ever be able to find when you need one."

"You should write a letter to the surgeon general."

"I would, but I'd probably bleed to death before I got it in the mail."

"I might have some butterflies. Let me check." I walked back over to my tool bag, which I had left just outside the elevator, and retrieved a small first-aid kit from one of the side pockets. "You're in luck. I thought I left it at the job site."

"A man who carries around his own medical supplies."

"My hands take a beating."

"Worse than working in the kitchen of a restaurant?" Bridget held up both hands this time, proudly rotating them to model her own collection of scars and burns. Most of these marks were old and faded; the sign of a chef who became the owner.

"Probably about the same." I offered her my kit. "Here you go."

"Would you mind? I'm left-handed. I'm not very good with my right."

Positively genius.

How did I not even consider that? A lefty seated on my right? Christ, I'd been banging around down there since I was twelve, I knew the challenges of trying to rub one out with the opposite hand. But Bridget Campanelli just stood there, looking at me as if *I* was the one with the weird look on my face, as if *I* was the one reacting to the delivery of this line in a peculiar manner. "Never mind. I'll make it work."

"No. Allow me. Let's do it at the sink."

Bridget followed me into the kitchen area, still perfectly composed. She hesitated for a moment, smiled, then offered me her hand.

The cut was real all right, about a half-inch long on the underside of the finger, yet fairly deep, the result of a sharp knife—the only kind you'll find in the home of someone who cooks. Either this was one incredibly strange coincidence, or the smile that precluded the removal of the tiny Band-Aid meant Bridget also recognized the irony of the situation, and she was just better at masking her reaction.

"Did you clean it out?"

"I ran some water on it."

"Hold it over the sink." Her hand jerked backward as Mercurochrome trickled into the cut. She crinkled up her face, held it for a moment, let it go.

"I hate that stuff."

"It does the job." I dried off Bridget's hand, applied a butterfly bandage to the cut, then placed a larger bandage over it. "How's that?"

"Much better. Thanks." Bridget flexed her hand, pleased with the movement both bandages allowed. She ignited the burner beneath her marinara sauce and gave it a stir. "You hungry?"

"Nah. I should probably just look at the space where you want the shelves, and be on my way. I'll grab a burger on the way home."

"That's crazy. You just saved me a trip to the drugstore, you're not eating fast food. That stuff will kill you."

"Well, if you're gonna put it that way. But only if you have enough."

"I've got plenty. I always cook for too many people." She pointed at her stereo equipment in the open living area. "It's for over there. I need to do something with all my electronics."

"You're looking for an entertainment center?"

"Yes and no. I want something that'll fit in with my other pieces. Something along the lines of what you did in Sally's den."

"How much do you want to spend?"

"Money is no object. As long as Charles Eames and Arne Jacobsen would approve, you have license to do whatever you want."

An appealing offer, but there was no time even if I built the unit off-site, at night, in the wood shop in my garage. As charmed as I was by this woman, I had to turn her down. I had to study the space a moment longer, find something wrong with it, then open up my mouth and tell her that I was unavailable.

"I'm pretty busy right now, but I could probably have something to you in a month or so."

.   .   .

You've heard about those people who board the wrong airplane and don't realize it until they've arrived in the wrong city. The obese women who don't realize they're pregnant until they give birth in a public bathroom. The guy who brought a dancing bear into a nursing home to entertain the elderly, he was as surprised as anyone when the bear attacked a ninety-two-year-old in a wheelchair. That was a dance he had never seen before.

Every day, someone out there is pushing the boundaries of human behavior. When I was younger, I often thought about those people to distract myself in professional situations like the one I found myself in with Bridget. But after years of working in the homes of other people, my own encounters with human beings behaving strangely had left me desensitized to the antics that often make headlines.

There was the divorcée in the Pacific Palisades who decided that a renovation was the perfect way to reinvent herself after getting the house in a settlement with her husband. My memory of her was indelible. I'd taken the job as a favor to the Lamberts, former clients who were worried about their friend, and for good reason. Katherine

Whitlock-Webber had kept the hyphenate, a warning sign that she hadn't accepted the fact that her divorce was final.

The job started out innocently enough. Katherine was excited to have us around. She made pots of coffee and baked us bread, muffins, and cookies. She took pictures and printed them on her computer and asked us if there was anything she could do to help. When I said we were fine, she brought out little tubes of hand cream from different hotels she had stayed at, and gave one to each member of the crew. Apparently, our skin looked pretty darn dry, and she didn't want us aging unnecessarily.

And that was just the first day.

After a week of this, a week in which she never left the house once while we were there, she began sketching little portraits of everyone. When I politely told her she was slowing us down, she said she didn't mind, we could take as long as we wanted, she was in no hurry whatsoever. I made the mistake of telling her that I had a schedule to keep, and that was when she started chipping in, sweeping up behind us, organizing our tools, monopolizing our favorite game.

Time-check, or *que dice el reloj*, is something we play throughout the day for control of the boom box. When one of us is getting tired of the music, that person calls for the time and we all throw out a suggestion. No one on the crew wears a watch for this reason, and no one needs to because all of us can usually come within ten minutes of the actual time even if it's been hours since we checked in. Whoever comes closest gets to spin the dial or change the CD. Out of everyone I've ever worked with, Miguel is the best in the business. Bar none. But even he was no match for Katherine Whitlock-Webber.

The woman was psychic.

Hostages, that's what we became. Prisoners defeated right there on the battlefield, detained in a house in the Palisades and tortured by hours of soft rock, broadcast over one of those radio stations where the DJs make dedications to listeners who have submitted their feelings. Dedications that begin with phrases like: *Words cannot explain how much I miss you.* And end with phrases like: *Did you ever know you're my hero?*

Manu Chow, Flaco Jimenez, Los Lobos, Steve Earl, Wilco, Dylan, The Stones, Tom Waits—all dead and buried. Air Supply, Chicago, Lionel Ritchie, Streisand, Midler—alive and well and belting their hearts out. Katherine knew we did not enjoy this music, but she thought it was funny, which it was for about the first ten to fifteen seconds.

We found a way to fight off these love songs with power tools and earplugs, and Katherine got the hint and gave up playing altogether. Shortly thereafter, the pendulum of her manic depression swung deep in the other direction. She began flipping out about projects we had already completed. The one-by-six, tongue-and-groove maple we laid in her bedroom had to be removed; the wood was making her nauseous. The skylights we installed in the roof made her paranoid; they had to be closed and sealed immediately. The poor woman was like a windup doll winding down, leading me to believe I was going to arrive one morning and find her dead in the bathtub. I went to the Lamberts and told them about the fragility of their hyphenated friend, and they stepped in and got Katherine the help she needed. The job was thankfully canceled.

Thinking about people like Katherine Whitlock-Webber to keep myself from thinking about people like Bridget Campanelli made me think about Henry Sullivan. The names were starting to blend together, lost in all the other names I haven't even mentioned, lost in the measurements of an entertainment center I had no time to build.

*   *   *

Halfway through the manicotti stuffed with ricotta cheese and bacon, near the end of a bottle of Italian red, I had an epiphany. Bridget

Campanelli wasn't the Second Woman, based on the simple fact that I was completely convinced she was. If this sounds illogical, I have done a poor job of describing Sally Stein's purse.

In summation, the purse was a Rubik's cube of leather, a web of estrogen that a suspicious husband or boyfriend would never be able to navigate if he ever decided to go hunting for something in a place where he had no permit. That man would be better off looking for infidelity in the pouch of a kangaroo.

The mastermind behind that same purse was the architect of this fantasy, not me, I had to remind myself. My preference was irrelevant. I was just the conduit between Sally and the woman she was attracted to. The device that would bring them together.

"So how do you know Rebecca?"

"Rebecca Paulson?" asked Bridget.

"At the dinner party, I got the impression you knew her."

"We met through Sally. She was an FOS."

"FOS?"

"Friend of Sally's."

"Does everybody meet through Sally?"

"Not everybody. But almost everybody."

"How come they're not friends anymore?"

"I don't know. Sally doesn't talk about it. She's never been one to talk about people behind their backs. It's one of the reasons everyone confides in her."

"Nothing wrong with being able to keep a secret."

"She's the best. And believe me, we've all tried. It's too bad she has such a great eye for fashion, she would have made a great spy."

"How do you know she's not?" I asked. Bridget smiled, unaware that I was fifty-one percent serious. "What about you? Do you stay in touch with Rebecca?"

"No. We were never that close. I liked her, but everyone was always going in ten different directions back then. It was hard to keep track of who was doing what. Then she got involved with that guy, and no one ever saw her anymore."

"Her husband Derrick?"

"Yeah."

"Wonder what she saw in him."

"I have no idea. None of us could ever figure it out. I know she really wanted kids. She talked about that a lot." Bridget could see I was thinking about this more than a contractor should have been. "Why do you ask? Is everything okay with her?"

I suddenly felt protective of Rebecca and her situation. "Yeah. Far as I know."

Bridget leaned forward and poured the rest of the wine into our glasses. You don't become the owner of a successful restaurant unless you know how to read people. Bridget didn't have to look at the menu to see what I wanted, and she didn't ask me to explain myself once she realized it. "If you really want to know more about Rebecca and Derrick, you should talk to Laura. She took one of his seminars when she was trying to figure out what to do with her life."

"Laura?"

"Married to Silent Howard, the stockbroker who never speaks. They were at the dinner party."

Laura wasn't in Sally's living room at the time of the Rebecca Paulson conversation. We'd lost her to one of the guest bathrooms near the end of the tour, so I wasn't aware that she was also linked to their past. Laura presented me with her business card when she was leaving, and it went immediately to the bottom of the pile. Of all the women at Sally Stein's that night, Laura Married to Silent Howard was the last woman I would choose if I had a say in who was seated next to me.

At the end of the evening, Bridget walked me to the elevator. I thanked her for the meal and went to shake her hand as she leaned forward, having already committed to a hug. We did a little bit of both, awkwardly, then parted.

"I'll be in touch."

"Good luck. And thanks again for the bandages."

When I arrived at the spot on the street where I had parked, all I found was an empty space and a pile of glass that used to go up and down in the form of a window.

My father's truck had been stolen in my absence. This, one of the only material possessions that really meant anything to me. She was a rust-bucket on her last legs, no doubt about that, but I couldn't bring myself to part with her. She was an old friend who never let me down on a single job, and now she was in the hands of someone else.

As were my wallet and my phone. A realization that came to me as I reached for them both. Earlier in the day I'd made a supply run to the lumberyard, and when I took out my wallet to show my receipt to the guard at the gate, something they make you do before driving off the lot, I must have forgotten to put the wallet back in my pocket.

I quickly walked back to the entrance of Bridget's building. When I got to the place where the evening began, however, to the iron threshold I crossed over into this mess, I became engrossed in a series of failures that kept me from ringing the buzzer and asking Bridget for help.

I should have gone to Samy's Camera to try and salvage Bill's Nikon. I should have gone to rotate my father's wood. I should have gone to the grocery store, or to Sally Stein's, or directly home to my apartment to do absolutely nothing. Worst-case scenario.

SEVEN

t's time to see the doctor," said Hector, standing over the grill in the backyard of a duplex the brothers shared in East L.A., where we had gathered for his son's birthday party. "You need to make yourself an appointment."

"I've considered that."

"Who else would steal an '86 Ford F-250? The thing barely does seventy on the freeway. No chop-shop is gonna take that piece of shit."

Miguel nodded in agreement. "It's not worth the risk."

"The *pinche culero* is trying to get a reaction out of you. You never responded to the tires so he upped the stakes. You gotta put an end to this once and for all."

On my walk home the night before, I stopped at the Rampart station and filed a police report, but I didn't mention the doctor. Cops working the nightshift hear a lot of crazy shit coming out of people who have been victimized, and I wasn't about to put myself in that category by describing a feud that included double doors, faucets, and shades of Ralph Lauren white. Something told me that would not be perceived as probable cause.

"Can we go back to Bridget Campanelli for a second?" asked Bill, who couldn't stop going back to Bridget Campanelli ever since I told him about her on our way to the U-Haul place that rented me a pickup truck, a truck that informed anyone who could see straight that it was available for $19.95 a day.

The morning began with Bill pounding on my door at eight o'clock, eager to get to a barbecue that wasn't scheduled to start until noon. Bill didn't receive a lot of invitations to parties that served food because once he got to those parties he turned into a bear, stuffing himself in preparation for the long hibernation ahead. I tried to talk to him about it once, after he nearly choked on a deviled egg, only Bill didn't want to hear about it. He resented me for being able to eat for free in this town, and I was, according to him, the last person on earth who should be giving little speeches about food.

I could tell there was something different about him the moment I answered the door. His anger over the broken camera dissipated on Thursday when I'd paid him $1,500 to keep him from suing Derrick Paulson, and another $500 to remove the stupid neck brace he had been wearing. In the days that followed, my money had blossomed into something much bigger. Bill looked happy for the first time in years. There was even a little color in his face. He didn't care about the Before and After pictures, nor was he concerned about the theft of my truck. He actually called it a blessing, a word I didn't think he could pronounce. "You were too attached to that thing, anyway. You ought to get yourself a Moped like the one I just bought."

"That money was for a new camera."

"I don't need a camera. I'm done with photography. That idiot did me a favor."

"What are you talking about?"

"He freed me from the machine. I've spent my whole life looking through that lens. For what? What the hell was I trying to capture? Art? Immortality? Bullshit. It's passing us by, dude. While you're out there trying to leave your mark on a bunch of houses across town, life is happening all around you. You can't stop that with the click of a button and save it for later."

"You got all this from a Moped?"

"They're a fucking gas. It's like being a kid again."

A credit card you keep in your desk will hold you over until the stolen ones have been reissued. That credit card, in combination with a passport and a photocopy of your driver's license, will allow you to rent a truck or a car in case you find yourself in this situation. Membership has many privileges, but it won't do a single thing for you when you wake up on a Sunday morning and find yourself in a dead heat with the one person who has always been more messed up than you are.

"I've told you guys everything you need to know about Bridget Campanelli. It's not relevant to the story."

Bill, noshing on a plate of taquitos, turned to Hector and Miguel. "Come on, am I the only one who finds it weird that he was downtown giving some chick an estimate on a Saturday night? He's already getting laid, and he sure as hell doesn't need the work."

"Keep your voice down," I shot back.

"The kids are inside filling the piñata," said Hector, aligning himself with Bill. "They can't hear shit."

"Is she hot?" Miguel, getting straight to the point.

"She's a friend of Sally's. I was just doing her a favor."

"A friend from the dinner party?" Hector, strengthening his allegiance with Bill.

"A friend who's looking to commission a piece of furniture."

"Did you take the job?" Bill, talking with his mouth full.

"Of course not," me lying to Bill, not a good way to stay ahead of Bill. "Who needs another beer?"

It was no secret that I had become romantically entangled with Sally Stein. The details of the dinner party, however, remained closely guarded. They were beneficial to no one other than me and Sally, just like my feelings for Rebecca were beneficial to no one other than, well, no one. I wasn't about to give up any of this information, even to my friends, no matter how hard they hammered me.

The cooler wasn't far enough away to end the Spanish Inquisition, so I went inside under the guise of needing to use the bathroom, knowing the things they would share the moment I left. Bill would tell Hector and Miguel about the Sunday before, about how we went to The Grove to look at a purse that Sally Stein designed. Hector would tell Bill about eating in the dark at Sally Stein's dinner party, a detail I left out when feeding Bill just enough information to get him off my back. Miguel would laugh and encourage them both to ask more questions. And collectively, they would all question my objectives when they saw me inside talking to the women as the women prepared side dishes.

Spending time with Inez and Reina is always something I enjoy, and it has nothing to do with their expertise with side dishes. Inez, the older and quieter of the two sisters, married Hector in 1997. Miguel married Reina a year later. They are both strong women, emotionally and physically, and they're deeply dedicated to raising their children. The duplex they share with their husbands is in their names because Hector and Miguel, despite numerous efforts, haven't received their green cards.

The building trade, like agriculture and the service industry, would shut down without men like Hector and Miguel. But the fake green cards you can buy in MacArthur Park won't get you far. To keep your business up and running you need authentic ones, documents good enough to clear random checkpoints and keep ICE, the Immigration and Customs Enforcement agency (formerly INS before it was swallowed by Homeland Security), off the "wetbacks" of your two best men. You need someone like Bill who always knows a guy who knows a guy when it comes to predicaments that can be solved only on the black market. The man can't hold down a job, yet I'm confident he'd have no problem scoring an endangered species for a wildlife preserve if they took him seriously enough to return his phone calls. Bill handled our immigration problem back in the late nineties, and I have been indebted to him ever since.

The compound these couples shared in East L.A. was idyllic in many ways. Their kids were more than just cousins, they behaved like siblings, or at least the way I would want my siblings to act if I had any. It was my favorite place to spend a Sunday. It was an oasis that didn't need to be fixed.

After a meal of carne asada, cheese enchiladas, and beans that had been simmering since dawn, Hector put Flaco Jimenez on the stereo and raised a piñata for his young son Gabino. He blindfolded the boy, spun him around a few times, then cut him loose.

Gabino was patient. He didn't swing away wildly. He took his time acclimating himself to the darkness, carefully locating his target before giving it a whack. I used the distraction to approach Miguel, who I knew would ask the fewest questions.

"I won't be at the job site tomorrow."

"You going to see the doctor?"

"No, there's something else I need to do first."

Gabino struck the side of the piñata with a powerful blow and candy rained down on his brothers, sisters, and cousins who quickly swooped in to gather their bounty. Gabino dropped the bat and scrambled to remove his blindfold, discovering firsthand the real paradox behind every piñata: the kid wearing the blindfold is always the last one to reach the candy.

That's when Bill stepped up. His hands had been in his pockets, giving me the impression that he was hoarding a few enchiladas wrapped in tinfoil to sustain him until his next foray into the world. Bill removed his hands to reveal a stockpile of candy that he threw at the young birthday boy, tilting the playing field squarely in his direction.

. . .

San Pedro is home to the Port of Los Angeles, the largest port in the country. Just northeast of San Pedro, across the harbor, is the Port of Long Beach, the nation's second-largest port. Combine the two and they would become the fifth-largest port in the world.

You have a number of items in your home that came through here: furniture, cars, computers, clothing; if it was made in Asia, chances are it got off the boat in Pedro. This is not a harbor for water skiing, or a shoreline for making sand castles; it's a blue-collar section of the city, not the type of place you would consider if you're looking to attend a real estate seminar. In fact, if you saw on someone's refrigerator an advertisement promoting one of these seminars, you just might think to yourself, *"Huh. So the Holiday Inn in San Pedro is where I have the power to make all my dreams come true. Who knew?"* If you're a distant relative of the Sullivan family, and you decide to go to this seminar anyway, whether out of morbid curiosity, or because you have $799 slipping through a hole in your pocket, don't be surprised if it becomes the first mistake in a new trilogy.

I hadn't been to this area since the day I met Gia at the Long Beach Blues Festival. We were just two singles standing at the edge of a crowd, listening to Luther "Guitar Junior" Johnson. Gia caught me looking at her. I caught Gia looking at me. The next thing I knew she was sparking up a joint, offering me a hit. She was a redhead at the time, a phase that wouldn't last long, none of them ever did. She was promoting the seventies before promoting the seventies became the thing to promote;

the oversized Foster Grant's, the scarf in her hair, the hip huggers that barely reached the equatorial region that separated her lower back from her upper ass. Just above that line, in the equivalent of northern Brazil, Gia had a small tattoo of an arrowhead pointed south.

We passed the joint back and forth as the sounds of Guitar Junior drew us into a trance that lasted all of about three and a half minutes, the time it took for an undercover cop to locate the smell of the chronic she had twisted.

Undercover cops at a blues festival have one of the *hardest* jobs in the world.

Your chances of finding someone smoking pot at a venue like this are right up there with your chances of finding a sinner in church. Fishing for crab on the Bering Sea is an easier way to make a living. Putting out a fire at a gas station using a bath mat and a damp face cloth is a small task compared to this. The only way your commanding officer makes this job *more* difficult is by sending you to a gay pride parade immediately following the concert, with strict orders to turn that parade upside down until you locate someone who's not wearing a shirt.

The officer was surprisingly cool about it, despite the sarcasm he detected in my response. He confiscated the joint, then searched us both for a secret stash tantamount to a felony. Unable to locate one (Gia had another joint under the scarf in her hair), he escorted us to the exit and kicked us both out of the concert. Gia had gotten separated from her friends earlier, and they had driven, so I offered to give her a ride home. Feeling pretty good under the guidance of the weed, we took the long way, which included a stop at the Holiday Inn in San Pedro for a couple of drinks at the hotel bar.

Gia had a thing for hotel bars, or *zoobars* as she called them, because they were typically populated by people out of their natural habitat. Other than airports, zoobars were the best places to sit back and take in exhibits of people indigenous to Iowa, North Africa, and Rhode Island all at the same time. They were in every city in the country, and the exhibits changed daily, meaning you never knew what you were walking into, but you were always a little wiser walking out.

Six weeks later, Gia moved in with me.

I had avoided getting arrested in San Pedro, only to have that woman knock me off my feet.

*   *   *

Derrick Paulson was standing outside the banquet room in that same Holiday Inn, talking to some of the people who had already paid the $799 admission fee to attend his seminar. Derrick's young assistant was seated at a table in the lobby, signing up those of us who were running late. I gave her a check for the same amount, and she handed me a signed copy of the book Derrick had written, along with a starter packet filled with sample tests, questionnaires, and testimonials from satisfied customers—promotional materials that had taken the life of a tree. She then gave me one of those sticker name tags that normally read: *HELLO, MY NAME IS . . .*

Derrick's customized take on these tags: *SAY MY NAME, SAY IT WITH CONFIDENCE . . .*

I jotted down my name with very little confidence, slapped it on my shirt with even less confidence, and drifted down the hall toward the banquet room, thinking about Gia.

It's strange going back to a place you've been to with someone you've since split up with. If it wasn't, soft rock would have no forum. The dedications from DJs would begin with phrases like: *I can't believe how happy I am now that you're gone.* And end with phrases like: *I can't even remember your middle name.* Restaurants and movie theaters you frequented together—those don't even apply, they're a given, and usually avoided. It's the places you went to only once that torture you. A gas station off the interstate, a bowling alley, a dated hotel on the other side of town. These are the locations that feel haunted, like the footprints of that person are still there, and always will be.

Derrick was working on a short, heavyset woman in her early fifties, coaching her on how to say her name, two words that seemed to lower her self-esteem.

"Judith Crier," said the woman, self-consciously.

"Who is Judith Crier? A woman with bad credit? No, JUDITH CRIER is a woman who's ready to seize the day and become her own boss."

"JUDITH Crier."

"You're going to be poor for the rest of your life."

"JUDITH CRIER."

"That's it. Now say it with a smile."

"JUDITH CRIER!"

Derrick noticed me standing off to the side and excused himself from Judith Crier. "What are you doing here?" he asked in transition. "Is something wrong with the house?"

"No, the house is coming along just fine."

Derrick didn't respond. Seeing me outside the banquet room in San Pedro left him momentarily speechless, as if he had just been approached by his mailman in a foreign country with a certified letter that required his signature.

"I'm here for the seminar."

"Oh."

"I've been wanting to get into real estate for a while now, and, well, I saw the advertisement on your refrigerator."

Derrick just stood there, studying me.

"And I wanted to apologize. You were right. I should have said something about my friend with the camera. We got off on the wrong foot. That was my fault."

Derrick looked over at the other Judith Criers, the Merv Tchinskys, the Goran Hovats, the housewives, the bus drivers, the single mothers, the longshoremen defeated by the docks. He lowered his voice to keep them from hearing him. "No, I'm the one who owes you an apology. Rebecca and I got into an argument the night before, and we weren't speaking to each other. It was wrong to take it out on you. I acted like an asshole. I'm sorry." And he was sincere about it, that was the real kicker.

"Still, it's your house, I should have said something."

"What do you say we start over?"

"Sounds good. I'd like that."

This probably goes without saying, but if your contractor shows up in your place of business, unannounced, to apologize for something other than accidentally burning down your house, call security. Unless you're in a field where you're seeking new customers to dine in your establishment, or patients needing expensive dental work, your lives should never intersect outside your home. And even if your business does rely on expansion and word of mouth, your contractor isn't going to propel you into a higher tax bracket, so keep the two separate. When things go wrong in your house, and they will eventually go wrong to some degree, you don't want to have to couch your feelings because your contractor is scheduled to have a tooth capped and crowned the following day.

I made it through the seminar, hitting my marks, nodding thoughtfully, asking questions, and nodding even more thoughtfully as I listened to Derrick's motivated answers. While performing these nods, I scoped out the emergency exits in case Derrick asked me to say my name out loud. For Rebecca Paulson, I would wear a name tag and play the part of someone with credit problems, someone eager to buy a home with little or no money down through foreclosure, note buying, personal confidence, and the sheer will to succeed. I would make every effort to increase my cash flow within a few shorts weeks, and begin building my future *today*! But I wasn't about to stand up and say my name over and over again until it came out just right. That wasn't in my job description.

The plan was to leave immediately afterward. To thank Derrick Paulson for everything he taught me and head north to have dinner and dessert with Sally Stein. Groundwork, that was all I was looking to accomplish that day. Trust is like concrete, it takes a while to cure. But Derrick couldn't wait. He stopped me as I was leaving the hotel and asked if he could buy me a drink.

As we saddled up to the *zoobar* and took our seats in the exhibit featuring two species that shouldn't be drinking together, I continued my search for the seed Rebecca thought was a flower that turned into a vine that flourished in places like the San Pedro Holiday Inn, places where nearly broken people were willing to part with money they didn't have just to buy themselves a splinter of hope. Was Derrick Paulson the funniest guy in his class who became a comedian known for smashing watermelons? Was he the doctor who could save others but could not save himself? The father who could predict the outcome of any game until he began betting on them? Even our best qualities can turn against us, and when they do we are usually the last to know.

"Can I get your opinion on something?" asked Derrick, once we settled in. I waited for him to answer his own question. He did not answer his own question.

"Is it about Clyde?"

"Who?"

"Rebecca's cat."

"No. The cat's fine. It's Rebecca I'm worried about." He spotted the zoologist and flagged her down with the cocktail napkin he was holding. Then he turned to me for my order. "Couple shots of Jäger?"

I don't do shots of Jäger. I don't drink mudslides, liqueurs, schnapps, or anything even remotely frozen. I don't have sex on the beach or lemonade in Lynchburg. My fingers could be trapped in a car door and I would still try to one-hop a Jell-O shot into the nearest trash can. I drink beer, wine, and Irish whiskey. That's it. That's the depth of my glass, half-empty or half-full.

"Sure."

"Two shots of Jäger and a couple of Lynchburg Lemonades." The woman left to fill the order. Derrick continued. "I want the truth, Sullivan. Don't sugarcoat it."

"Fire away."

"Do you think renovating a house can make a difference in a marriage?"

This was the last thing I expected to hear coming out of his mouth. He could have asked me about the unemployment rate in Düsseldorf, and I would have felt more comfortable commenting on it. "I don't know. I'm not married."

"Professionally speaking."

"You're the real estate expert. I'm just a contractor."

"I specialize in investment properties. Foreclosures. I've never actually . . ." He stopped himself, thought about it for a second, then plowed forward anyway. "I've never actually tried to turn a house into a home."

This required a moment of silence. Even Derrick recognized how trite that sounded, and I didn't want him to forget it anytime soon.

"Professionally speaking?" I asked.

"Overall, in your experience."

"Overall . . . most couples struggle with the stress. Then there are the couples who can't decide what they want. The house becomes them in a way, their differences, the things they no longer agree on. Two couples I worked for got divorced before their houses were even completed."

"Have you ever seen a renovation bring two people closer together?"

Bar stools are known for eliciting unusual things from people (the reason they're not made out of memory foam), which had to be taken into consideration before answering this question. And the guy sitting next to me, the guy doing the soul searching, asking questions he didn't feel the need to answer, I had no idea what region of the world he was indigenous to. Granted, I gave him a $799 apology, but this wasn't the same mammal who liberated Judith Crier. "That could happen. But I'm usually gone at that point."

Derrick nodded.

I nodded back. I was getting good at that. I was on the verge of turning pro.

"That's what I thought."

"Why do you ask?"

Derrick downed his shot of Jägermeister. I kept waiting for him to piece it together, for him to suddenly remember meeting me in Kirsten Janikowski's Spanish Colonial out in the Valley, only it didn't happen; it was like it never happened. The old me was utterly forgettable. This new me was someone he wanted to talk to.

"We've had some marital problems in the past, and we wanted to make sure our relationship could handle it. It's the reason we waited so long to start remodeling."

"What was the argument about?"

"Argument?"

"You said you got into an argument the night before we started."

"Oh, that. I don't even remember. Just one of those stupid dis-agreements that become arguments before you have a chance to stop them. I'm sure it was my fault."

"Must be hard being on the road as much as you are."

"It's not easy. That's for sure."

More nodding. If this continued I was going to have to ask the zoologist to blast the hinge on the back of my neck with a shot of WD-40.

"I'd like to do something nice to make it up to her. Maybe you could put in one of those Jacuzzi tubs in the master bathroom. She likes taking baths."

"That's not a good idea."

"Why not?"

"Because they begin cooling the water the moment you turn the jets on. And they store water in the pump, algae starts to grow, a year later it's like bathing in a pond."

"She wouldn't like that."

"Nobody does. I try and talk people out of them, unless it's for their dog."

"Their dog?"

"Long story."

"What if you did something to the driveway? Like a mosaic using different-colored bricks. You could put her initials right in the center."

"I don't think that's what she wants."

"How do you know? Did she say something?"

"Just an observation."

Derrick shook his head and went to work on his Lynchburg Lemonade. "I'm not sure what that woman wants anymore."

"You should ask her."

"I can't ask her. If I ask her, she'll say I shouldn't have to ask her. She'll say after six years of marriage I should just know."

"Maybe it's your approach."

"What do you mean?"

If Derrick Paulson had truly reformed himself, and Rebecca was aware of the double life he was leading during her pregnancy, and had forgiven him for it, then he had no reason to sit there confiding in me, his contractor, an acquaintance at best. Unless he was playing me, artfully maneuvering me into a place of his own design. Testing his motive required a tactful response. I was there, after all, to gain his trust, to make him think I was his friend.

"You're different when you're not promoting yourself. You're less abrasive."

Derrick eyed me for a moment. He then looked away and lowered his guard with a sad little sigh. "Now you sound like Rebecca. She says I make some people uncomfortable." An earnest proclamation, delivered in a way that made his past feel closer to the present. Within this expression there were snapshots of his youth, a photo album that revealed his struggles to be heard. If this was a form of manipulation, I had seriously underestimated the man's skills.

"I can only speak for myself."

"Maybe you're right," he said after some thought. "Maybe I just need to slow down a little. Become a better listener."

If it had ended there, I would have felt like I had broken even, like the duel had ended in a draw, fifty/fifty. But Derrick Paulson was on to something, he was making a play to swing that decisive one percent. The percent that makes or breaks you.

"Maybe you could help me with that. You're at the house all day, you spend a lot of time with her. I bet you could get her to open up about things that would make her happy."

"I'm not the guy for that."

"Why not? You'd be doing me a huge favor."

"I've got my hands full as it is."

"I'm not asking you to go out of your way to get involved. I'm just asking you to keep your ears open when I'm not around. If you want the job to go smoothly . . ."

Derrick didn't have to complete his sentence. The alternative was clearly stated in his omission. He stood up abruptly and tossed a twenty on the bar. "I have to run. We'll do this again real soon. Let me know what you come up with."

EIGHT

May 15.

Sally and I were sitting in the breakfast nook of her home in the Hollywood Hills, going over the plans for her guesthouse, sipping cups of kopi luwak, coffee that runs $600 a pound. There are only two ways to produce and sell coffee for $600 a pound. The first way is the easiest. You buy a pound of French roast from one of the eleven Starbucks in your area, then repackage that coffee in a bag made out of fifty-dollar bills.

The alternative involves freakish, feral little beasts in Indonesia.

Asian palm civets look like a cross between a mongoose and a house cat. They're nocturnal mammals—no surprise there—known for gorging themselves on ripe coffee cherries they pluck from the trees. In the stomachs of these creatures, the beans soak in gastric juices and enzymes and whatever else happens to be down there at the time; a natural, bizarre process that makes the coffee beans less bitter. Once the fruity exterior has been digested, the beans are shipped out the back door in small piles of dung, which people then sort through to retrieve the beans for roasting. The civets are not in a union, nor have they been taught how to do this.

And this wasn't a dream. Sally Stein wasn't naked, and Willard Scott wasn't knocking on the window. The coffee was not a figment of my

imagination; it was the same coffee the queen of England has been ru-
mored to fancy.

"What do you think?" asked Sally, peering out over the lip of her cup.

"It's good."

"I know, right?"

"It's not worth six hundred dollars a pound though."

"It was a gift from Bridget. For introducing you guys."

Sally's morning routine was already quite familiar to me. Unlike
the Paulson job, there would be no need to acclimate myself with her
schedule. I had already taken a few Before pictures with my digital
camera—Bill's expertise was neither available nor necessary. Sally
Stein's old garage was coming down.

On average, renovation is around $50 a square foot more expensive
than new construction. As opposed to trying to incorporate the original garage in some way, it would be faster and more cost efficient to
build a two-story structure from the ground up, in the same style as the
main house. We had delayed the start of the project until the following
week, and I considered asking for a longer extension, but Sally had
been patient, and I needed a break from Rebecca and Derrick.

Things were going well as far as the renovation was concerned.
Hector and his guys were increasing the square footage in the kitchen
by extending it into the old laundry room. Miguel was building window seats in the master bedroom. And Marco and Eddie were unearthing the water main in the front yard in advance of the plumbers who
would repipe the house with three-quarter-inch copper, a procedure
that won't necessarily solve your water-pressure problems unless
you also replace the galvanized main running out to the street.

I had finished moving the windows in the living room, and was in
the process of building a new walk-in shower in the master bath. Overall, we were making good progress. Clyde, however, was not. He wasn't

adapting to the noise. And I don't think he was comfortable with the reconciliation that was under way between Derrick and Rebecca. The listening, the dinners at home, the eye contact, the happiness the twins felt when their parents were getting along—all developments ostensibly brought on by a couple of shots of Jägermeister at the Holiday Inn in San Pedro, following Derrick's return from a business trip to St. Louis. Clyde didn't trust any of it. Or maybe he wasn't even aware of it, and I was just projecting my own apprehension onto a cat that remained hidden in a fort made of Rebecca's shoes. Either way, I decided to step back from the situation.

Sally told Marianna she would handle the breakfast dishes.

Marianna took this as a cue for privacy and left to straighten up another area of the house. Sally waited for separation, then addressed my ambivalence toward Bridget's gift. "You okay? You've been in a funk lately. Is it because they haven't found your truck?"

"What are you looking for?" I asked her flat out.

"What do you mean? With the guesthouse?"

"You know what I mean. The little treasure hunt you've sent me on. What are you hoping to find?"

Sally got up and replenished our coffees, using the activity to cultivate her response, to create a moving target. "Does it matter?"

"Maybe."

"What, you're not having fun anymore?"

"I understand the thrill of the chase. I get that. I'm just wondering what it is we're chasing. What you're chasing."

"Don't complicate things by overthinking it, Henry."

"Then simplify it for me."

Sally didn't like talking about her motivations. She threw me a bone anyway. "Life is short. What's so wrong with doing some of the things you think about?"

"Nothing."

"Then why can't we just leave it at that? Why can't we just be friends with benefits, without all that other stuff that complicates relationships?"

"So that's what we are? Friends with benefits?"

This surprised her. In her mind, the terms of our relationship had already been laid out, notarized, and signed by both of us in three different places. "Do you have a problem with that?" she asked.

"No. I'm just glad I know where I stand."

"I'm not saying it won't become more than that. I just want to have fun right now."

"Even great sex gets old at a certain point."

"Then we'll deal with it then. Let's not ruin it prematurely by talking about it."

"Fine. We'll talk about something else. What happened between you and Rebecca Paulson?"

Sally started clearing the table, putting the breakfast dishes into the sink. "You're a guy. You wouldn't understand."

"Did you have a thing for her?"

"*Pfft.*"

"It's just a question. You're obviously attracted to this other woman."

"Because I'm attracted to one of my friends, you think I'm attracted to all women?"

"You're right, I'm just a guy. What the fuck do I know?"

Sally dropped a plate into the sink. "No, I never had a *thing* for her. We were like sisters. We had a falling out, and now we don't speak to each other anymore. That's it, end of story. Satisfied?"

"I'm sorry I brought it up."

"I need to get dressed."

The problem with friendships that end is that they never really end. We often think about that person more when they're gone than we did when we were actually speaking to them. We imagine ourselves placing a call to that person, and we wonder what the response would be if we did. But in the end, we realize it would be awkward, and we would have to try and pretend like it wasn't, and that would only make matters worse.

So the phone remains in its cradle.

.   .   .

"When do you start working on that other house?"

Rebecca was standing in the new shower in the master bath, sipping some kind of latte concoction from Starbucks, which she had purchased for the crew on her way home from work after dropping the twins at a playdate. I was setting the levels for two glass sinks that would sit on top of a floating vanity I was building, marking where I wanted the pipes to go in preparation for the plumbers who were due to start phase one of their work in the morning. "Monday."

"So I won't be seeing you as much."

"I'll be going back and forth for a while. You should probably come out of there. It was just hot-mopped yesterday."

"Sorry," she said, stepping out of the shower, which would eventually be faced in split travertine and clear glass. "It's weird being in a shower that isn't finished. It feels so much bigger."

"It is bigger. I extended it outward in both directions so you'll have room for two shower heads."

Rebecca already knew that. She knew exactly what I had done, and what I was going to do in the space. The kitchen, the master bedroom, and the master bath are arguably the three most important rooms in a house. This was not a place where we were looking to save money. This was just small talk.

"Remind me again what we're doing over here?"

"That'll be the sitting area that looks out into the courtyard garden."

"Wouldn't it make more sense to put the tub there?"

"No. The tub goes here, on the platform I built. By raising it and setting it back from the window you'll be able to look outside into the garden without having to worry about your neighbors looking in from their second-story windows."

"We've already had this conversation, like, three times, haven't we?"

"Yeah. Maybe four."

She hadn't even asked me about the thing that was really on her mind, and already she was nodding. "What did you think of Derrick's seminar?"

I knew Derrick Paulson had something to do with the falling out between Rebecca and Sally. This, however, was the first time I saw Derrick and Sally standing in the same place, across from each other in the eyes of Rebecca Paulson, who still hadn't referred to Sally by name.

"It was educational. I learned a lot."

"About Derrick or about real estate?"

"I don't know. They're kind of one and the same, aren't they?"

It was nice to see someone else nodding like that for a change.

"Sometimes he tries too hard. He's not always like that. It's just been a rough couple of years. Some of his investments went bad when the market changed."

"Not the best time to be renovating a house."

"My parents are helping us out."

"He's lucky to have you."

"It was now or never. We couldn't go on living the way we were."

Admissions like these are fairly common on the job site. People often feel more comfortable confiding in strangers. It's like screaming into a pillow: you know the pillow isn't going to turn around and tell all your friends, or worse, write a book about it. There's no real pattern to determine when or where they will come about. The kitchen is no more of a confessional than the living room. I wasn't in the master bedroom when Deidre Mueller told me her husband had lost his confidence, and I wasn't in the garage when Simon Feldman told me he hit a cyclist with his car. And it didn't matter what we were talking about prior to these declarations, they just happened. They were dress rehearsals, and I was the reaction those people needed before the play opened, or closed in previews due to extreme exhaustion, or creative differences between the two leads. Renovating a house to save a marriage is much like having a child for the same reason. It happens every single day. Rebecca Paulson just needed to say it out loud.

"Then I'm glad I took the job. You won't recognize this place when we're done."

Rebecca smiled for a moment, reminding me why I had been avoiding her gaze since stepping away from her and her husband. The smile faded back into a nod. "Did something . . . unusual . . . happen at the seminar?"

"Like what?"

"I don't know. Derrick's been different lately. It's been nice. The girls are happier. I'm just wondering if it had something to do with the seminar."

The only person Rebecca failed to mention was herself, which was the problem with Rebecca Paulson. I wasn't wrong about her apprehension. It was all over the place. In her posture, her voice, her arms folded and pressed against her chest. It seemed as if she wanted to believe in her husband's attentiveness, but those arms that were holding her together were the same arms that were holding something back.

"I wouldn't know. I've never been to a seminar before."

Rebecca didn't nod. She looked right through me.

Jägermeister has altered the behavior of millions of people. It has led men to profess their love all over the world, around kegs on-campus and off, in ski lodges, beanbags, and hot tubs in the Poconos. But it's not a truth serum, and it never lasts until morning. You don't down a shot of it in San Pedro while having a heart-to-heart with your contractor and wake up cuddling with your wife in Brentwood.

Even though Derrick sounded sincere the day he shared his troubles with me, this was a mighty quick turnaround for a motivational speaker who specialized in foreclosures. Rebecca's inquiry validated my suspicions. Something must have happened in St. Louis, where Derrick had traveled on business prior to the change in his behavior.

"Well, I'll let you get back to work," said Rebecca. "Thanks again for everything you're doing to the house. If there's anything I can do for you, I hope you'll let me know."

"Actually, there is something you could do. You work at UCLA Medical, right?"

"Yeah."

"I'm having trouble getting an appointment with an oncologist who works there. Maybe you could help."

Rebecca's entire face got smaller, lighter, whiter, making me aware of just how wrong this sounded. "Are you . . . sick?" she asked.

"No, not physically. I remodeled the man's house. I just need to speak with him."

. . .

The renovation network is oftentimes the best way to get things accomplished. If I'm working for good people, I have no problem opening up the Rolodex and calling in a favor with a former client. I've helped kids get into private schools, and golfers get into country clubs. Nannies looking to move to a different family? I could name three of them during your backswing. Need an exterminator to come over to your house at three o'clock in the morning to trap a fruit bat in your bedroom, take down this number. Ancient artifacts sold on the black market, I've got just the guy for you.

Using this network for my own benefit is something I avoid unless I get myself into a real pinch. Dr. Rolland wasn't taking my phone calls, and you can't get an appointment with a cancer specialist unless you have cancer, which can only be confirmed through another doctor's office. I wanted to confront Rolland away from the house where our feud began. I wanted to catch him off-guard in a location where he was accustomed to telling people the down and dirty truth.

Rebecca made that happen by placing a call to someone she knew in the office of a general practitioner. She got me an eleven-thirty under the name of Roger Herpolsheimer, a guy who was being treated for cancer over at Cedars-Sinai. Before doing this, she wanted to know everything about my falling out with the doctor. How it started. What his wife was like. What I was going to do if he confessed to stealing my father's truck. She was particularly interested in the doctor's wife, and my theory that Mrs. Rolland said we were sleeping together to remind her husband that she was a sexual being capable of attracting another man. Rebecca looked at me differently at the end of this story. She said she found it admirable that I stuck it out to the end of the job. She needed no convincing. There was excitement in her eyes, giving me a sense of her own secret desire to be involved in something more adventurous. It was, in a way, an activity we could do together.

I entered Dr. Rolland's office at UCLA Medical, carrying the one item that had been purchased with my stolen credit card before I canceled the card. The thief bought this item the night of the crime at a pawnshop downtown, then waited a few days to mail it to me, prompting me to place my visit to the doctor at the top of my list of things to do. Any second thoughts I had about overreacting, about being irrationally accusatory over the disappearance of my father's truck, vanished the moment I opened that package. The thief wanted me to spend hours trying to figure out the meaning of this item. He wanted me to know there was nothing random about it.

When I was done filling out the new-patient paperwork, answering all those questions about my genetic history, I parked myself in the corner of the reception area and waited to be called, the item that was sent to me concealed in a bag at my feet.

Non-hodgkin's lymphoma, the disease I didn't have, is a cancer that starts in the lymphatic system, and is usually contracted by people over sixty, people like Roger Herpolsheimer. But like all cancers, there are no constants. It can gun you down anywhere, at any time, and it's nothing to mess around with. Not even for a day, a morning, an early afternoon.

Bill disagreed. He believed there was a constant. He said everyone who comes down with the disease spends years hoping they don't come down with the disease. According to Bill, that was the real problem with cancer. Somebody should be researching *that*. That's where all the big money should be going. He also warned me that I'd be the only patient in the waiting room who had any hair, and he encouraged me to shave my head so I wouldn't make anyone feel uncomfortable. I told him the other patients wouldn't care. People fighting for their lives don't sweat the small stuff.

I knew this because my mom and I talked about it when I said good-bye to her, when I didn't know I was saying good-bye to her. As a seven-year-old boy, the wisdom she gained through her illness confused the hell out of me. I understood what she was saying, to a degree, about how we shouldn't worry about anything that can't worry about us. That wasn't what I struggled with. It was my mom's decision to warn me about this worrying in our last moment together. It felt like an explanation, as if her own inability to stop sweating the small stuff was the reason she got sick and had to leave.

The most troubling aspect of losing someone at that age is when you begin to lose the sound of their voice. You think you've still got that voice up there in your head, and to prove it to yourself you play it back whenever you think about the person. But through time, the voice becomes less recognizable no matter how often you play it. Then one day you're down to just a phrase or two, everything else has faded away. And then those phrases fade as well, and all you have left are pictures.

These thoughts of my mom turned my attention to the faces that would rise or fall based on Dr. Rolland's evaluation. I wanted to tell them to record their voices. I wanted to tell them it wasn't their fault, as inappropriate as that would have been coming from a hairy Herpolsheimer hoping to end a feud that had nothing to do with life or death. A contractor who was looking for closure on a truck, not a tumor. To bolster my position, I tried to tell myself that it wasn't just a truck, it was my father's truck, and this was about principle, defending the family name. I tried to make the truck bigger, less small, more justifiable to sweat. The family name wasn't even on the appointment sheet. I had to do something.

A nurse came out and called for a Mrs. Granger, who got to her feet with the help of her husband. When they shuffled through the double doors that led to chemotherapy, the doors swung back and forth and came to a stop with the finality of a heartbeat I could not ignore. If it wasn't for Mrs. Granger calling my attention to these doors, I would have been able to walk in and out of that office with conviction regardless of the doctor's response. But those doors got me thinking. If I was the guy waiting on the other side of them, greeting those same faces every day, I would have made a stand on my front lawn as well, even if the domestic doors were made out of mahogany, and didn't swing back and forth making that awful noise. Forget about scale or aesthetic harmony, the doctor was right. Double doors belonged in a hospital, not on the face of his home.

"Mr. Herpolsheimer?"

I stood and followed the nurse into the belly of Rolland's practice and took a seat in one of the examination rooms at the end of the hallway.

"There's been a mix-up with your chart," said the nurse. "We haven't received it yet, so this will only be a consultation. When he's done, I'll be back to take some blood."

Dr. Rolland entered the room five minutes later, looking at the paperwork I filled out. He offered his hand without looking at me. "I'm Dr. Rolland."

He turned to find out why I hadn't shaken his hand.

Aside from the people who have become so good at lying they can no longer separate the truth, and the people who've received so many Botox treatments they look the same at gunpoint as they do watching a robbery on TV, aside from those people, and maybe a handful of players on the poker tour, there are a few simple ways to determine if the rest of us are lying.

It all begins with the element of surprise. If you suspect your significant other has become someone else's significant other, do not wait up for that person on the couch with your arms crossed. In the time it takes that person to walk across the room, he or she will have enough excuses to fill up your voice mail. They've been preparing for that moment. They had an alibi in the chamber before they even entered the house.

Take them out for dinner instead. Wine and dine them, make them feel like you are the last person on earth who would ever suspect something dubious. Then ask them point-blank if they're having an affair. You should have your answer in the first few seconds. If they repeat the question, they're guilty as charged. They're trying to buy themselves time. It's not like they didn't hear you, and it's not like you proposed the question in Latin, or Sanskrit, or one of the other dead languages.

"What did you do with my truck?" I asked Dr. Rolland.

The doctor's head jutted forward for a moment, then dropped downward for a second look at the clipboard that held my paperwork. "You're not Roger Herpolsheimer."

"It was my dad's. I want it back."

Rolland opened the door of the examination room to check the number, to make sure he hadn't walked into the wrong room. "Where's Roger Herpolsheimer?"

"I'm Roger Herpolsheimer."

"Your real name is Roger Herpolsheimer?"

I had my answer, only it wasn't the one I was expecting, and it would take a few more minutes to accept that. Unless the doctor was one of those people who could no longer separate fact from fiction, he neither stole my truck nor hired someone else to do it for him. There wasn't a trace of deceit in his movements or his mannerisms. He wasn't angry. He didn't call for the nurse to get a security guard to have me removed. He was just flat-out confused, a condition that increased exponentially when I pulled out the one item the thief had purchased for me using my stolen credit card.

"What is the meaning of this?" I asked, holding up a used trumpet. "What in the hell are you trying to say to me?"

Let's just pretend the man was a professional liar hiding behind the confusion over Roger Herpolsheimer. It wasn't like that trumpet was suddenly going to expose him, or hypnotize him into telling me what I wanted to hear. Rolland, however, didn't appear frightened or even fazed by this behavior. He looked like he actually felt sorry for me, like he'd seen this type of insanity before in some of his patients, once the disease had moved into their brains.

The doctor's innocence did not absolve his behavior during the renovation of his house. He was horrible to his wife, to me and my crew, and probably to many others who had crossed his path. But my visit, which left me feeling ashamed and humiliated, provided some closure. I was able to walk out of there knowing my father's truck was not in the hands of a cancer specialist, it was in the hands of someone else who had an entirely different reason to be angry with me.

NINE

Laura Married to Silent Howard was day-trading karma.

She bought and sold this intangible commodity using words, not currency, and she spoke as if she could not stop. While she was talking negatively about someone or something, whether at Sally Stein's dinner party or during the walk-through of her home, her husband stood quietly beside her looking like he did his best thinking during these periods of loquacious liquidity. In the corners of Howard's eyes, where forty becomes forty-five, crow's feet marked the days when he probably made more of an effort to be heard. But somewhere along the line Howard had laid to rest all of the buffering mechanisms that might have taken the edge off his venomous wife. As Laura deconstructed people only to build them back up again, Howard just stood there with the distant gaze of a public official who had authorized the various zoning permits.

But I'm getting ahead of myself.

As much as I would like to fast-forward through the events that antedated my visit to Laura's home into Hancock Park, there are some things you should probably know before we get there. Of all the days and all the decisions that defined that fateful summer, the week following my confrontation with the doctor is the one I look back on the most. It was the fulcrum point on which everything took a turn for the worse. A line of demarcation you can see only in hindsight, one you'd rather leave out when recalling the story for others. For continuity purposes, and for those of you who are in real estate, consider this full disclosure.

Following our conversation about the relationship we weren't having, I noticed a slight shift in Sally Stein, my friend with benefits. If mentioned, this shift would have evoked a response like *"You're just being sensitive,"* or *"Now you're just imagining things."* Except it was there all right, just like it was there in me when I said those exact same things to a few of the women in my past. Now I was the one whose desire to talk about the "relationship" had put an unfortunate damper on things. The one who revealed his feelings too soon, which in the arena of friends with benefits was tantamount to hanging a state-of-the-art relationship-detector over the main entrance in Sally's head. The sex was still good, and she still enjoyed spending time with me, but I could feel the presence of that little red light ready to sound the alarm if I ever got too close.

Ironically, the guesthouse faced a similar barrier.

When we got into breaking up the concrete slab at the base of the old garage to replace it with a foundation that would support the weight of a two-story structure, we found that the soil beneath it had started to sink. As a builder short on time, I would have preferred unearthing a woolly mammoth, or the skeleton of a five-thousand-year-old Homo sapiens who died while searching for a better cave. Factor in all of the television crews and archeologists who would have descended onto the area to investigate either discovery, and that still would have been easier to deal with than erosion on Sally Stein's hillside.

The soils engineer ($$) was the first entry in the parade that came marching up the hill to deal with this problem. He drilled some exploratory holes and conducted an extensive soils report that confirmed my worst fears before handing me off to a structural engineer ($$$). I knew we were going to have to bring the hillside up to code—the house was built in the early sixties and the laws had changed after the Northridge earthquake in 1994. But I did not anticipate that we would have to build a new retaining wall, and bring in a crane to drill fifty-five feet down until we hit bedrock to insert six additional caissons just to support the new structure. To give you a broader scope of this image—in case you are unfamiliar with the word—caissons are pillars of concrete and steel used to build things like bridges, as in the Golden Gate, as in the Brooklyn, as in the bridge that spans the bay of You've Got to Be Kidding Me.

For those of you currently in the middle of a renovation, you've probably been faced with an obstacle of your own by now. The rush of a new beginning has faded into a hangover of repetitive noises, and things are taking longer than expected, which you now know is to be expected. Your old roof wasn't built to code and has to be replaced. There's dry-rot in your floor joists. The workmen haven't been there in days and your contractor hasn't returned your phone calls.

If the problem is within the house itself, you may be taking it personally, as if you should have done a better job with your inspections before purchasing that home. If so, you are not alone. Some people have a tendency to view their houses the way they view their relationships. Their vision of what the other person *could* be keeps them from seeing that person for who they really are—until something goes terribly wrong. Aside from opening up all the walls of a house in escrow to get a good look at the bones, full disclosure is an impossibility. Every house has its secrets, and you should embrace the ones that are found, as difficult as that can be. It's better in the long run.

Sally Stein handled the news gracefully.

She agreed it was a good thing we uncovered the problem on the hillside, and said the money to fix it (in the end, an additional $85,000) wasn't an issue. Sally had no interest in seeing a budget for the guest-house. She said she trusted me, an acknowledgment that should have put me at ease but instead only complicated what I was feeling.

The key to contracting is often knowing when to do the job yourself and when to bring in someone else. The caissons that needed to be drilled and filled were definitely a job for someone else, so I hired a company that specialized in hillside engineering. The problem was they couldn't start right away—usually the case with anyone good. They were jammed on another job, held up by the bureaucratic backlog that often delays the approval of certain permits. I called in a favor with a woman I knew in the permit office, and she got what they needed pri-oritized and pushed through. In exchange for my help, the contractor agreed to send over a crew with a crane the following week, a virtual blink of an eye in this trade, but still enough time to create a work stoppage that carried over into the Paulson house, where I was facing a more unconventional detour.

The delay at Sally's meant we could focus our attention on Rebecca, and while that was good for the house, it wasn't necessarily good for our friendship. The day after Dr. Rolland's innocence was established, Rebecca took her daughters to school, then called in sick and spent the day at home, talking to me as I worked. She started a list of potential suspects, and asked me questions about my past. She wanted to know about other clients I had gotten into disputes with, workers I had fired, subcontractors I withheld payment from over shoddy workmanship; any little detail that might constitute a clue. She felt compelled to help me in the same way I felt compelled to help her when I took the job.

As the days wore on, Detective Paulson created little opportunities to continue talking about the case, domestic opportunities that sud-denly required the services of a rent-a-husband, an aspect of my job that often came with the territory. Simple, everyday tasks she had no trouble with before, now required my assistance while Derrick was in Florida conducting his how-to-be-your-own-boss seminars. Unloading the groceries out of her minivan. Filling the tires on Kira's starter bike. Anything to give us a moment alone.

Once I stepped away to assist her with one of these tasks, Rebecca would share her thoughts with me as if they were impure and required privacy. "I figured out the meaning of the trumpet," she said on one occasion. "The thief is telling you stop blowing your own horn." Then she'd hit me with that smile of hers. It didn't matter that we were outside or in the garage. None of these moments went unnoticed by Hector and Miguel.

I could have said I wasn't comfortable talking about my past, which was the truth. I could have let Rebecca's phone calls go through to my voice mail after I had left for the day. But I answered every single one of them, waiting until the third or fourth ring to make sure I didn't come across like a sophomore in high school. Her questions became more and more personal as she inched her way closer to the one she asked me on that third night we spent chatting on the phone. I was down in my wood shop working on the piece for Bridget Campanelli. Rebecca was reviewing our rather short list of suspects, convinced we were overlooking someone.

"Have you ever slept with one of your clients?"

She sensed my apprehension and quickly clarified the question. "You don't have to answer that. I was just thinking out loud. Jealous husband, that's always a good motive."

"Yes."

"More than one client?"

"Yeah."

"Are you sleeping with Sally Stein?"

Prior to this, Rebecca hadn't even referred to Sally by name. It was always "that other house" or "that other job." The element of surprise had worked in her favor, whether intentionally or not, and my hesitation betrayed me. Unlike the question that painted me into this corner, she made no effort to retract it. I didn't want to lie to her, but I also didn't want the truth to distance her in any way.

"That's what I thought," said Rebecca while I was still debating this. "She seems like your type."

"How would you know that?"

"Sally and I used to be friends."

With all the time and effort I had invested just to get to this juncture, you'd think I would have been a little more prepared for our arrival. But the moment Rebecca inquired about Sally, I suddenly felt like I had done something wrong, like I was a rent-a-husband having an affair on his rent-a-wife, as ridiculous as that sounds.

"What happened?" I asked. "How come you're not friends anymore?"

"Does she know you're working on my house?"

"She knows I'm doing another job. But it's nothing we talk about."

"What do you talk about?"

"Stuff. Stuff people talk about."

"Is it serious?"

"Not really. How come you're not friends anymore?"

Rebecca thought about this, then thought about it some more. "That's kind of hard to explain."

"Try me."

"I'd rather not. That's a chapter in my life that I don't care to reopen. Especially now." There was nothing subtle about the shift in Rebecca Paulson. Her voice slipped away fast, the way water falls through fingers. "I hear one of the girls crying. I need to go."

"Rebecca . . . ?" She didn't reply, and I had trouble thinking of something that wasn't awkward to put in her place. "The electricians are coming tomorrow."

"It's okay, Henry. Your personal life is none of my business."

•   •   •

The Sunday before Memorial Day.

Laura Married to Silent Howard prided herself on being environmentally responsible, and it was time for her house to express those values. Although these weren't the exact words she used on the phone when describing her plans to me, that was basically what she said. When I cross-referenced this information with Bridget Campanelli's comment about how Laura had taken Derrick Paulson's seminar when she was trying to figure out what to do with her life, it became clear to me that Laura Married to Silent Howard was in need of a project.

When I arrived at their two-story, Tudor Revival in Hancock Park, at the wheel of my new-old truck—a '91 Ford F-250 that I bought out of *The Recycler*—Laura was out front planting impatiens, working on her curb appeal. The truck had a burnt umber finish with good dents and a reinforced tailgate. In its previous life, it was used to haul machinery for an irrigation company. It had experience. I didn't have to break it in. Laura was wearing gardening gloves that went with her gardening outfit that went with her garden, an ensemble that caused me to linger inside the truck.

She was in her early forties, neither heavy nor thin, with cropped, butter-yellow hair that looked like a hasty departure from her natural color, perhaps a knee-jerk reaction to a bad driver's license picture, or a comment from her hypercritical mother. I'm no expert, but I've found that people who talk negatively about others do so because they assume others are talking that way about them. Fight fire with fire. Get them before they get you.

So why was Sally Stein, a woman who never said a bad word about anyone, friends with Laura when she was no longer friends with Rebecca Paulson? What was their emotional connection? And was that connection *really* strong enough to have grown into something physical? The trowel in Laura's right hand was doing all the work. Her left hand just sort of hung around like a groupie, lacking the dexterity it took to lead.

"You're late," said Laura as I got out of the truck. "That's okay. I'm sure there was nothing you could do about it."

One down, one up and I hadn't even closed my door.

Hancock Park is one of the oldest, wealthiest neighborhoods in the city. It's located south of Melrose, north of Wilshire, between Rossmore and Highland, a historic community once fertile with oil wells before it was subdivided into residential lots in the early 1920s. The houses are big and well preserved, featuring some of the finest local architecture of that era. The streets are lined with sycamore and jacaranda trees and divided by speed bumps. Fences of any kind are discouraged by the Hancock Park Homeowners Association.

If you live in a place monitored by one of these associations, do your architect and your contractor a favor and befriend that group before presenting your renovation plans. Send them gift baskets with wine, not fruit. Have them over for a lavish dinner and compliment them on their commitment to the community. On a good day, they'll keep that loner down the street from painting his house orange and lining his driveway with mixed-media sculptures by Robert Mapplethorpe. On a bad day, they might just come after you.

Laura spoke into an intercom box in the foyer. "Howard, Henry is here."

"It's fine if he's busy."

"Please. He's in his reptile room watching the Indianapolis Five Hundred."

"He has a reptile room?"

"It's his sanctuary. It's filled with lizards and snakes and God only knows what else. Go look by the gazebo in the backyard; you'll see the rodents he feeds them thawing in the sun."

"I'll take your word for it."

"I honestly don't understand it. But he works hard, he deserves a place to relax."

Even from a distance you could see that Laura had found her calling. She had a natural eye for design, one with iconic sensibilities, and a real understanding of the light within the space she was working with. The hickory floors in the living room just beyond the foyer had been stained a dark espresso to highlight her use of varying shades of cream found in the natural stone around the original fireplace. The cornice moldings had all been stripped and whitewashed to bring out the surprisingly airy shade of taupe she chose for the plaster walls. She didn't try to fight the simple, linear lines of the room. She accentuated those lines with a large, handwoven rug that provided a neutral frame for her antique furniture. Each table and each chair was artfully mixed and matched, combining the beauty of Eastlake and Renaissance Revival with the simple functionality of the Depression Era.

And I had Laura pegged for a fan of paisley prints, and tables littered with knickknacks and dried flowers and porcelain giraffes varying in height. The type of person who would buy a canopy bed without consulting her husband on the belief that he would eventually get used to it. Laura Married to Silent Howard was not that person. She not only had good taste, she had the foresight to give her husband a room all to himself when she remodeled the house the first time.

It never ceases to amaze me how many of my clients overlook this important detail when we get together to discuss the job. Granted, there is a natural domino effect in renovation. You know this if you've ever bought new furniture. Once it arrives you realize that certain items in the room no longer look good, so you move things around, and buy new lamps, and paint the walls to provide cohesion.

For some of you, it ends there and you go on with your lives. For others, you can't stop until the entire house has been remodeled. Which is fine as long as you remember to remove at least one of those rooms and put it aside for your husband. A den, a study, the garage, the basement, a reptile room, any place he can call his own. At times you will have to compete with this room, but it will pay dividends more valuable than any stock in your portfolio. Whenever I see that a wife hasn't included one of these spaces in her renovation plans, I always bring it to her attention.

The only time I didn't was in the home of Rebecca Paulson.

Laura pushed the button on the intercom a second time. *"Howard?"* Still no reply. She used the delay proficiently. "So, rumor has it you're doing the Paulson house. What's it like? Is it horrible and tacky? That's not fair. I'm sure it's perfectly lovely."

"It's like any house that's being renovated. It's a work in progress."

"You have to tell me all about it when we're done. You know Rebecca and Sally used to be best friends."

"I think I heard that."

"Howard!" she yelled into the intercom. "We're starting without you!"

"I'm right here." Howard had appeared out of nowhere, smelling like cedar chips.

"There you are. You remember Henry."

Howard gave me a nod and looked away, leaving the conversation to his wife.

"Where would you like to start?" she asked, turning back to me.

"The kitchen."

"That's a problem. The kitchen is full of dirty dishes. We had a Cranium party last night, and the maid never showed up this morning."

"I don't mind."

"I do. We'll have to save the kitchen for another time. I love her to death, and Sally swears by her, but between me and you, I think Marianna is taking us all to the cleaners. The Guatemalans are the best. The Salvadorians, they're all lazy."

"How about the master bedroom?"

"That we can do."

When the kitchen isn't available for harvesting information, you need to have a backup plan. Mine is the master bathroom, which can be appropriately accessed only through the master bedroom. You can't fake a stomachache or a hyperactive bladder in another area of the house or you'll be directed to one of the guest baths, which will tell you little to nothing about the homeowners other than what they want you to know. If the homeowners have a problem with you using their master bath, most won't say anything if you're standing only six feet away from the door. If they do, and they still try and lead you away to one of the guest bathrooms, just keep walking until you reach the driveway. They have no understanding of the things you will see in the months ahead.

Laura was nonplussed by my request and even turned on the light for me. She had gotten so enthralled in her plans to go green, I'm not even sure my request to use the master bath registered until I closed the door behind me.

The medicine cabinet is off limits. Opening that door is a violation of privacy and against my personal code of ethics, as flawed as that code may be at times. It's also one-dimensional in comparison to a magazine rack, a far better source for determining the hidden landscape of any work environment. Laura's was located next to the tub and contained the last three months of *Architectural Digest*, each swollen with earmarks; one Gigi Levangie Grazer novel; two issues of *People*; a Tiptionary (how to save money and time every day); and a book of baby names, some of which had been highlighted in pink, others in baby blue. Howard's magazine rack was next to the toilet and contained nothing but *National Geographic*s in chronological order.

On the back of the toilet was an ovulation kit and a fertility monitor.

· · ·

Green renovation was once viewed as a movement started by tree-hugging extremists who built houses out of old tires and drank rainwater out of recycled tuna fish cans. But now that people have discovered the financial benefits of conservation—usually the tipping point in any industry—a wealth of new products and technologies has been developed to meet the growing demand. Being a proponent of green, I am constantly forced to reeducate myself on these new advancements to implement them for clients looking to renovate on the cutting edge of this revolution.

Laura was not a Stealth—someone like Sally or Rebecca who incorporated green elements into their designs without advertising their decisions. Laura was what I call a *greensleeve*, a rare breed of people who renovate houses in mint condition just to be recognized as environmentalists, which in my opinion is both environmentally irresponsible and just flat-out crazy.

Before leaving, I would encourage Laura to cancel her remodeling plans and focus on conservation: solar tiles for the roof, a tankless water heater, a sprinkler system that uses gray water collected from the showers and sinks to water the yard. I would try and dissuade her from ripping out eighty-year-old floors just to replace them with salvaged materials that may have been taken out of another house where someone might have been suffering from the same condition. If my sales pitch proved ineffective, I would look her in the eye and tell her the truth about the stress she will have to endure if she gets pregnant during her renovation. Whatever it took, I would not go quietly.

But first, I would accept the beer she offered me at the conclusion of our tour.

Howard had retreated to the bosom of his reptile room, and Laura needed a glass of pinot grigio to wet her worn-out whistle. Who was I to let her drink alone? She did some of her best talking after a couple glasses of white, and I was under the impression she had one before I even got there. We reconvened out by the pool away from the gazebo where Howard's rodents were indeed thawing in the sun. Laura wasted little time.

"So, before we talk about the house, you have to fill me in on Rebecca and Derrick. I can't believe they're still married. None of us thought it would last a year."

"Why's that?"

"You've seen them together. They're totally wrong for each other. Not to mention all the rumors that were floating around at the time."

"Rumors?"

"About how Derrick had a girlfriend when they got married, and Rebecca was just too desperate to see the signs. I personally thought she was really sweet, but when it came to guys, well . . ." Laura stopped to refuel. "You know how this town is. Rebecca didn't exactly have the looks to compete, and it's not like she was getting any younger. I think she saw Derrick as her last chance to land a husband. It's so sad when a woman settles for less just because she wants kids."

She waited for Rebecca to flatline before attempting to resurrect her.

"But who am I to judge? If her girls are healthy and happy, I'm sure that's all she cares about. It's not easy being the black sheep of a family."

"For you or for Rebecca?"

"Rebecca. Please, my siblings are a total mess compared to me. Rebecca's, on the other hand, are all ridiculously successful. And her parents are loaded. I think that's why Derrick sticks around."

"Do you still stay in touch with her?"

"Sort of. We're L.A.-close. I keep up with her through other people."

"People like Sally?"

"No, God no. Sally never talks about Rebecca."

"How come?"

"I have a theory on that, but I can't share it with you."

"Why not?"

"Because she's your client. I can't talk about her unless we make a trade."

"A trade?"

Laura had grown so accustomed to surviving on the "mmh-hmns" Howard mumbled whenever he sensed it was time to let her know he was still breathing, that she found nothing odd in all of these questions. She fed off them. She was a binge talker. A domesticated ninja with a tongue for a sword.

"You know, I tell you something juicy, then you tell me something juicy in return. That way we can never use it against each other."

"I wasn't aware that's how it worked."

"That's because you're not a woman. It's an unspoken agreement we have. I'm just forthright about it."

"Okay, you go first."

"Do you want another beer?"

"I'm good, thanks."

"Well, I need another glass of wine," she declared, pouring herself a healthy topper. "Look at me. You probably think I'm an alcoholic."

"It's the heat."

"I hadn't thought of that." Laura studied the amount left in the bottle, as if there was a spot on every label that marked the boundary of what was socially acceptable. "Where was I?"

"Sally and Rebecca."

"Right, Sally and Rebecca. Let me just preface this by saying I totally adore Sally. She's like one of my best friends. Only she's not as perfect as everyone thinks."

One more sip of wine for good measure.

"The short version goes like this. It started back at UCLA. Sally wasn't into sororities, so when Rebecca, who was a couple years younger, had trouble getting into one, Sally took her under her wing. Sally doesn't have siblings, so she's always looking to play the big sister. Cut to 2000 or 2001, whenever Rebecca started dating Derrick. I forget how they met, traffic school maybe, somewhere odd like that. Well, it was pretty obvious to everyone except Rebecca that Derrick was a player. The kind of guy you have a fling with, not that I would ever do something like that. But if I was that type of person, I'd probably seek out someone like Derrick. He's a safe bet. He won't get attached and start talking about the relationship."

Yeah, I hate when that happens.

"Anyway, Derrick and Rebecca got engaged, and Rebecca asked

Sally to be her maid of honor. But Sally thought Rebecca was making a huge mistake."

"She said no?"

"That's not even the best part." Laura leaned forward and lowered her voice, either for emphasis or out of habit. "I can't confirm this, but I think Sally took it a step further. I think she fooled around with Derrick just to prove to Rebecca that he was a womanizer. But it totally backfired. Sally could get any guy she wanted, so Rebecca saw *her* as the predator, not Derrick. Which, I think, in a weird way, just made Rebecca more determined to go through with it."

It was hard to know where to begin.

The setting made sense. Weddings have the potential to divide and conquer just about any friendship among women. Derrick was as consistent as ever, I'll give him that. But the descriptions of Sally and Rebecca didn't sit right with me. I had trouble seeing the same women Laura saw, even after taking into account the six years that had passed since then. And by Laura's own admission, her version couldn't be proven.

"Your turn."

"What?"

"The trade." Laura smiled and sat back in her chair, clutching her glass of wine. "I'll make it easy on you. Who's this new guy Sally is seeing?"

"What makes you think she's seeing somebody?"

"She has to be. No one's seen her except Annabelle, and Annabelle's never been a good source of information. She gossips even less than Sally."

"Annabelle? The lawyer who was at the dinner party?"

"Don't feel bad if you have trouble remembering her. She's the bland, silent type who totally blends into the background."

TEN

When things go wrong on a job, the experienced go out of town.

That's what Sally Stein did on the first Friday in June once she fully realized the extent of the work that needed to be done to her hillside. She pulled a few strings with a senator she knew in Washington and flew to eastern Chad to visit a refugee camp that was housing thousands of people who had fled war-torn Darfur. I offered to drive her to the airport because trips to and from the airport were things people offered each other if they were in a relationship that was going somewhere. Sally kissed me and took a cab.

While Hector and Miguel kept things moving along at Rebecca's, I oversaw the subcontractors at Sally's and lined up a freelance framing crew to help us make up for the delay once we had been cleared to start construction. The new garage we were building would be detached from the main house, placement the LEED—Leadership in Energy and Environmental Design—considered an element of green design; however, they didn't advocate sleeping quarters over any garage due to compromised air quality and general safety. A lack of space left us no other choice. The homeowner needed a place to park.

Sally spent the week assisting humanitarian workers, volunteering in a makeshift medical ward, and teaching displaced children how to play games she played as a little girl. Kick-the-can was their favorite. She chose not to include capture-the-flag, a game that was still struggling to transcend the suburbs of America and find a niche in refugee camps around the world. Before leaving Chad to share her experiences with some high-powered friends in London's music scene, Sally wrote the Red Cross a plus-sized check, which I ballparked at around a hundred grand. Big enough for her to exclude the amount when she was telling me about her travels on the way home from the airport, a ride she requested while waiting to board her plane at Heathrow.

If eastern Chad is too far east for some of you to fit into your summer travel plans, pick another destination. A trip of any kind (barring those that involve cruise ships) will give you a chance to step back from your renovation and put things into perspective, and it will give your contractor an opportunity to deal with all the things he's been hiding from you: the gouge in the new hardwoods beneath that tool bucket in the dining room; the cracked tile in the shower; the feelings he's developed for your former friend.

At the Paulson house, phase one of the renovation was moving along nicely, notwithstanding a few minor problems. We installed the new Caesarstone countertops in the kitchen, but Rebecca appeared to have lost interest in the truck thief, maintaining her distance whenever I stopped by to check on the house. The new lighting design had been implemented by the electricians to brighten the mood in the house, but Derrick was back in town and doing his best to leave a shadow. He returned from his seminars in the southeastern part of the country with snow globes of St. Louis for the girls, claiming he had a layover there on his return flight, an explanation that prompted Rebecca to finally confront her husband. Miguel, who was more receptive than Hector in regards to my friendship with Rebecca, provided the update, only he wasn't able to decipher Derrick's response to the one question that made it through the vapor-sealed walls before Rebecca closed the door to their temporary living quarters.

"Are you having an affair with someone in St. Louis?"

Derrick's reply wasn't needed. Rebecca should have wined and dined him first.

The next morning I received calls from both Derrick and Rebecca while I was waiting for the inspectors up at Sally Stein's, nibbling on the *empanadas de leche* that Marianna began making me after I tipped her off about Laura Married to Silent Howard. "Watch your back," I told her after my walk-through in Hancock Park. "She's a talker. And she's talking about you."

Derrick called to tell me how pleased he was with the job we were doing. He shuffled around the silence, asked a couple questions, and quickly followed them up with answers he wanted me to have. *"Have you exceeded my expectations? You better believe it. Would I recommend you to other people? In a heartbeat."* Before hanging up, Derrick coughed up the real reason he was calling. He had tickets to a Dodgers game on Saturday and he wanted me to go with him. I had already made plans with Bill that evening to see a performance artist he was trying to bed. The show was at some tattoo parlor on Santa Monica Boulevard, where the woman was going to read haikus that had been tattooed onto grapefruits she would be juggling. But Derrick's invitation was work-related, I told myself. I would have to call Bill at a carefully selected moment when I knew he wasn't home and cancel in favor of Derrick's show of thanks.

Rebecca called half an hour later to apologize for her behavior.

She didn't say anything about my mistress in the Hills, except that she thought we were good for each other, a statement I would scan repeatedly for hidden meanings. She blamed her mood swing on the stress of trying to manage the household in the absence of her traveling husband. The girls were getting claustrophobic in their temporary living quarters, Clyde was losing weight, and her friend Tess was pushing her to use some glass tile she saw at Walker Zanger for the backsplash in the master bathroom. Rebecca was unsure if the tile would be compatible with the split travertine we were using on the face of the shower. "They're just these little glass tiles," she said in a voice rising in pitch, cracking under duress. "Why am I having such a hard time deciding what to do?"

Other than shop class, the only thing I was very good at in school was stating the obvious, so I will revert back to that strength by saying Rebecca's tiny little meltdown had nothing to do with the tiny little tiles Tess found. She accepted my offer to go with her to Walker Zanger to look at the tile, with the caveat that she got to drive. She was adamant about that, and it took me only a couple of miles to understand why.

*   *   *

In science, a controlled environment is essential for a hypothesis to become a theory, for a theory to become a fact. Experiments must withstand an extensive barrage of testing to prove or disprove even the most obvious working assumption. For instance, when the government was conducting tests on soldiers under the influence of LSD back in the fifties, they compared the behavior of those soldiers attempting to perform routine military operations with the behavior of sober soldiers in those same situations. The experiment, however, fell short. They never sent those same groups of soldiers out to the desert to watch the sunrise, and listen to Thelonious Monk, and make falafels for all their friends. If they had, they might have witnessed the soldiers on LSD functioning at a higher level than their sober counterparts, a level that would have contradicted their analysis of human beings tripping in formation.

My drive back from the airport with Sally Stein and my drive to Walker Zanger with Rebecca took place within a few days of each other. Although it wasn't technically a controlled experiment because Sally was the passenger and Rebecca was at the wheel, it was educational just the same.

Sally told me to pick her up at departures instead of arrivals to bypass the general chaos of passengers happy to be back on the ground again. When I got out to help her with her bag she kissed me long and hard, then held me close after the kiss was over. "I have so much to tell you," she said against my shoulder.

You know you've got it bad when someone is sharing their experiences of being in a refugee camp, and you're still thinking about that hug back at the airport. I couldn't believe I was even at the airport with Sally, there in the white zone, the zone reserved for the loading and unloading of relationships that were going places. The booming voice in the tin speaker above was talking about me for once, letting everyone else know that real couples were protected as long as they were holding each other. Friends with benefits, they would be ticketed or towed.

Descriptions of flies buzzing around the heads of children in Chad made me shake my own head on La Cienega Boulevard. I wanted Sally to know that I was also disturbed and moved by her images, that I wasn't just sitting there wondering if those children were the reason my ex-friend with benefits didn't want to take a cab home from the airport. And I *certainly* wasn't wondering what would happen to us when time reduced the potency of those images, as it eventually would even in the mind of the most compassionate.

Sally Stein wasn't comfortable outside the driver's seat. She made all of the routine checks I made, mirroring my movements without missing a beat in describing her stories. She checked my blind spot when I made a lane change. She leaned forward and looked both ways whenever we passed through an intersection. She made eye contact with oncoming drivers before we made left turns, her posture alert and on edge, her right hand clutching the handle on her door. Sally didn't give me instructions on the best way to get home, and she said nothing about my driving other than the occasional "You're clear."

At Morton's, where we stopped to satiate her craving for a good steak, Sally ordered a Grey Goose martini, an iceberg salad with blue cheese dressing, and a double Porterhouse loaded with cruelty for the two of us to share. Sally was seated close. There was no sign of the little red light in her head waiting to sound the relationship alarm.

"I did a lot of thinking while I was gone," she said, digging into the bread. "The trip was good in that way."

"I bet."

She chewed her bread carefully before speaking again. "I really like you, Henry."

"I really like you, too."

"I don't think I've done a very good job of showing you that outside the bedroom."

"That's not true."

"Yes it is."

"What about the shower? And the floor in the kitchen? I'm still having trouble bending my knee."

"You know what I'm talking about. Before, when you asked me about us, about what we were doing, I was . . . a little cold."

"No you weren't."

"Stop trying to make me feel better, Henry. I've been taking every-thing for granted, including you." She pushed the bread aside. "I guess what I'm trying to say is . . . I missed you. . . . And I wasn't sure if I would."

"And now you're feeling guilty."

Sally gave me a look. "You don't have to be so smug about it."

"I'm not smug. Just surprised. I didn't know what to expect when you got back."

"Did you start seeing someone else?"

"Would it bother you if I did?"

Sally shifted in her seat and freed her ponytail. "I don't know. Maybe."

Unlike the other times she pulled her secret weapon on me, there was nothing sexual in her intent. In fact, it looked like an act of sur-render, something an elderly bank guard might do during a heist, or a kid with a crayon caught in the act.

"No," I said, offering her one of my patented half-truths—my affair with Rebecca wasn't physical, but affairs don't always have to be.

She studied me for a moment, digesting the response. Then she took a mischievous pull on her martini. "You know what I think? I think we need to have fun tonight. I think you need to take me dancing."

Just so we're clear on this, allow me to briefly address the two main selling points of this activity so there is no confusion about where I stand.

1. *Dancing is great exercise.* So is being chased by a mountain lion, except when you're being chased by a mountain lion you're not surrounded by mirrors, looking at yourself being chased by a mountain lion.

2. *Dancing is fun and sexy.* Subjective on both accounts (see:
   Irish contractor running from cougar). Not really that much
   fun, not really that sexy. Do not allow your friends to encourage guys like me to partake in this dancing you fancy. Whatever chemistry you had cooking between you and your partner
   will suffer as a result of our neighboring movements. And
   don't think you can out-sexy our non-sexy. Our presence on
   the dance floor will be felt, and not in a good way.

Sally pulled me onto the dance floor of some club in Hollywood
where whiskey neat was fifteen bucks a pop and the bathrooms were
about ingesting substances into your body, not excreting them. Because I considered myself a friend to those who dance, I broke out my
less-is-more technique. Sway-snap, sway-snap, slide, and repeat.

"You look like you have motion sickness," she said with a laugh.

"What?!" I yelled back, trying to compete with the music.

"Motion sickness!"

"Ocean thickness?!"

"Motion sickness!"

You get the point.

Sally Stein wasn't much of a dancer either, or she was just sup-
pressing her go-to moves to keep me from feeling even more out of
place. But it was good to see her laughing like that again. So good, I
eventually lost myself in all that swaying and snapping and repeating
myself. Something was happening to us out there on that dance floor,
and whatever it was, it would carry over into the end of the evening.

Sally didn't even stop to look at the new foundation for her guesthouse. She led me straight into the bedroom, past all the hard surfaces
she usually thrived on, and pulled me down on to her Swedish mattress, where we remained for hours, fucking, but that wasn't the right

word for it. If it had been, I may have been tempted to inquire about her friend Annabelle once we stopped for a breather. But it never entered my mind. For the first time since we began engaging in this thing you should not engage in with your contractor, it felt like we were finally alone.

"It's good to be home," she said falling off to sleep. "It's good to be home."

. . .

Rebecca began our journey by changing the memorized seat setting from number one to number two, a typical adjustment if someone other than herself had been driving the minivan, which wasn't the case. The seat moved away from the dashboard and tilted back into a more relaxed position. The mirrors moved accordingly. Rebecca then fired up her engine and threw it into reverse in one graceful motion. The twins were at a playdate; Rebecca looked behind her anyway. As we accelerated down the driveway, her fingers glided over the arc of the steering wheel and landed in the nook between the wheel and the horn. Using only two of those fingers, she whipped the wheel around clockwise, and barreled into the street. In the split second before dropping the van into drive, she changed the radio station and cranked up the volume.

Although I have never been in an automobile with Jeff Gordon or Danica Patrick, I am willing to wager they are no more confident than Rebecca Paulson when driving through residential streets, merging into traffic, or backing into parking spots. Toll booths on a turnpike, Rebecca would never pick the wrong lane. A blowout in the rain, Rebecca Paulson is the woman you want in the driver's seat. She was a rare breed, an undiscovered talent who seemingly could tame any road in any machine.

I had seen her drive down the street with the twins buckled into the back, her hands firmly on the wheel in the ten-and-two position, looking like any other mother navigating a maroon minivan. Without the girls, Rebecca drove to exercise her thoughts. Once she got the minivan up to forty-five in a thirty-five, she placed her left hand out the window, expanding her fingers as if she was trying to air out her wedding ring. She then brought her fingers back together again, and dipped her hand up and down through waves of oncoming wind, like a dolphin leading a boat and its captain out to sea.

Initially, it seemed as if Rebecca Paulson played Van Halen that loud to avoid any form of communication. But as we drove onward, I realized that seat setting number two wasn't just for thinking, it was also for dreaming. And eighties rock was her own personal sound track, her lyrical time machine that took her back through memories good and bad.

Her dream ended abruptly when Rebecca shut off the engine and got out of the minivan. "Do you mind if I have a cigarette before we go in?" she asked, fetching a Parliament out of her Sally Stein purse.

"Go ahead. I didn't know you smoked."

"I don't. I did. I just bought a pack recently."

"For old-time's sake?"

"I don't know. I guess to deal with the stress." The desperation that was in her voice the day we met had returned, much heavier than before. She held the Parliament between her teeth without letting her lips touch the filter, and caressed the opposite end with the flame of a lighter.

"I'll take one of those."

"You, too, huh?"

"I haven't bought a pack in years, but I still bum occasionally."

Rebecca handed me a smoke. "Safety in numbers?"

"You're a good smoker. What can I say?"

"There's an oxymoron if there ever was one."

"What's the party for?" I asked while she was giving me a light. She didn't seem to understand the question. "At the end of August."

"Oh. That. I'm hosting my family reunion. Labor Day weekend."

"That'll be nice."

She laughed; didn't find it funny. "I guess."

"You're not close?"

"Not really. But we pretend to be."

"Family politics?"

"They don't really understand me . . . some of the choices I've made."

"And this is your chance to show them you're okay."

Rebecca dropped her cigarette on the ground and picked up the butt after crushing the cherry with her foot. "Theoretically. We should go in."

.   .   .

If you're working with a designer, do not ask your contractor to go shopping with you. Your designer will be offended, and may even think you're having an affair. Your contractor will think you're either hitting on him or taking crazy pills. Shopping is an acceptable topic of conversation only if your contractor is also helping you with the design of your home. We're a minority, a subculture of opinionated bastards who don't always play well with others, and at some point we just gave up trying. And we don't shop for rugs, or vases, or curtains that will help you pull the room together, unless we're having sex with you. That's a job for you and your decorator.

We will, however, provide you with choices regarding tile, flooring, lighting, hardware—things of that nature, things that will be firmly attached. If the design is right, and the plans are well executed in the right color palette, we don't feel like curtains should have to pull a room in any direction. We'd rather you kept that room empty.

It's perfectly fine to ask your contractor for his opinion on things as long as you bring those things to him. But again, I can't emphasize this enough, if you ask him to take time out of his day to go with you to look at bedroom furniture or a piece of art for the dining room, you might as well throw in an invitation to catch a movie and a light bite at a fondue restaurant afterward.

All you have to do is spend an hour at a store like Walker Zanger, and you'll understand how some people get addicted so quickly. Places that sell high-end, pharmaceutical-grade tile should only be visited prior to starting your renovation. Don't even think about entering one of these stores if you've already selected and ordered your materials. Don't drive past them on your way to work. Don't look at their catalogs. If you begin questioning yourself and the aesthetic strength of your materials halfway through a project, you're finished.

The two couples who got divorced while I was working for them both made this mistake. The fall of the Odenkirks stemmed from Mrs. O's inability to stop upgrading. One example in many involved a dinner she went to at some big producer's house in the Holmby Hills section of the Platinum Triangle. The following day, Mrs. O wanted the same chestnut Poggenpohl cabinets the producer had in his kitchen.

I explained to her that she had three options. She could order those cabinets, but they would take months to build and deliver, and they would cost around $75,000. We could rip off the style, and build them ourselves, something we did frequently, but that would also take more time and money. Or we could just continue on with the birch cabinets we were already building, which were better suited for the original design.

Mrs. O chose plan B.

Mr. O eventually became suspicious of my accounting reports when he noticed they didn't align with the work he was witnessing. When he confronted me about this, we both discovered that Mrs. O had been importing my reports into her computer, and doctoring the figures before passing them on to her husband. To compensate for these upgrades, she was using money she laundered out of the monthly household budget, and the savings account for their daughter's college fund. Their story did not end happily.

The dagger that castrated Carrie and Jerry's nuptials wasn't really a dagger; it was a tile sample from Walker Zanger. Carrie and Jerry were already in trouble, and I was too inexperienced at the time to realize it. They couldn't agree on anything, including who was going to be the alpha renovator. It's important for each member of a couple to be heard; however, only one of you can be the liaison to your contractor. Otherwise, you'll end up pulling your contractor in conflicting directions, resulting in time delays, scheduling conflicts, and borderline heavy drinking.

Carrie and Jerry were fiercely competitive with each other, and their daily chess matches only got worse throughout the process, escalating to the point where I wondered if each was secretly keeping score on tablets kept hidden in their respective glove compartments. That would have explained the fight at Walker Zanger, an incident that helped me recognize the importance of developing a set of rules for taking any job.

We all arrived separately, Carrie and me both under the impression we were going to look at slate Jerry had found for the pool area. Instead, Jerry used the meeting to lobby for some metal tile he liked for the kitchen, fully aware their original choice—glazed, terra-cotta pavers—was already in boxes in their garage.

Carrie finally snapped. "You want to change my *one* contribution? My *one* contribution to this entire house? Are you fucking serious?"

"The terra-cotta wasn't your idea. It was my idea."

"How are we ever going to raise a child together? We can't even agree on tile!"

"What does that have to do with anything?"

"I can't do this anymore."

Carrie marched out of the store without looking back.

Jerry turned to me and tried to explain his wife's public display of outrage. "Sorry about that. *Tom*'s in town. She'll be fine in a few days."

"Tom?"

"That time of the month."

Carrie wasn't fine in a few days. She was at a friend's condo in Marina del Rey.

◦ ◦ ◦

Rebecca's experience at Walker Zanger was more internalized. She drifted through the store, marveling at the selection, at the possibilities each tile sample presented. You could almost see her trying them on as if they were dresses or shoes sought after for similar purposes, wondering how she would look in them. Without the benefit of a fitting room, it was easy to get lost in all the ceramic, porcelain, listello, and glass; the stone tile, old and new, decorative or tumbled from all over the world, in every size for every makeover. If marble leaves you cold, like it does me, if it reminds you of the inside of a mausoleum in central Illinois, you will still appreciate the way it looks at Walker Zanger.

We slowly made our way over to the tiny glass tile that Tess recommended, Rebecca looking hopeful, empowered by the visions that came with each sample. We were in a dangerous place, moving at a dangerous pace. Rebecca's temptation could lead to more changes, more urges to upgrade, more stress on her already troubled marriage, and yet I did nothing to hurry her along.

Acacia Matte was indeed beautiful, and priced accordingly. A translucent blend of sea-salt green and chamomile with a spectacular range of color that spanned both water and sand, with hints of bluish gray. The greener, lighter tones induced feelings of health and well-being, while the cloudier earth tones left you feeling grounded, a perfect match for the travertine on the outer face of the shower. And I'm not just saying that because I wanted Rebecca Paulson to get divorced. The glass tile really was a better fit than the River Rock ceramic I'd already ordered for the backsplash.

At a little café on Beverly Drive, where Rebecca insisted on taking me to celebrate the fortuitous change in her bathroom—the tile was actually in stock, a rarity of such proportion it was hard not see it as some kind of omen—she revealed a renewed interest in her investigation. "What's happening with your truck?" she asked, closing her menu.

"Nothing."

"Have you heard from the police?"

"Not a word."

"I still think it was a jealous husband."

"You're probably right."

"I know I'm right. A woman is more likely to take a man back if he cheats. Men can't handle it. It's a double standard. They don't want to think we're capable of the same things they are."

"Sounds like you speak from experience."

Rebecca leaned her head to the left, then back to the right. "No, just something I read."

I said nothing. All there was to say.

"Were the affairs worth it?" she asked.

"I wouldn't really call them affairs."

"I mean for the women."

"I don't know. You'd have to ask them."

"Why'd they do it?"

"We should probably order."

"I'm not hungry. I just stopped here because it's a good place to talk." Her eyes made the table feel smaller. When standing, this was one of those looks that got me into trouble. "You took time out of your day to help me. I want to return the favor. That truck was your dad's."

I did that thing where I sigh, then follow it with a nod. I was so entranced by her scrunched-up face, and that hair, that twisted mop of black Easter basket grass framing those dimpled cheeks, that I had no idea if I was starting a new trilogy of mistakes, or ending one that was launched by this same face weeks earlier.

"Only two of them were married, unless you count the woman who was separated."

"Start with her."

I hesitated, giving myself a chance to change the subject.

"She lived in a two-story Craftsman out in South Pas. She and her husband, both professors at Pasadena City College, had grown apart, but they still cared about each other, so. . . When he was offered a six-month fellowship at a university up in the Pacific Northwest, they decided to separate instead of getting a divorce."

"Kids?"

"One. A freshman at NYU. They had him when they were young."

"What were you doing to the house?"

"Restoring some of the woodwork. About a six-week gig."

Rebecca leaned closer. "Go on."

"After a few months, they both realized they missed each other. They were in their early forties and they'd seen how much some of their friends struggled after a divorce. The idea of starting over was pretty damn scary. Even if they weren't in love anymore, at least they still liked each other, and that was better than being alone."

"Hmh."

"But, as hard as it was for this woman to imagine herself out on her own again, she also struggled with the thought of going through the rest of her life without ever being with another person, without experiencing that feeling at least one more time. She still had a couple of months before her husband came home, so . . . she decided to act on it."

Rebecca waited to see if I was done. "I think a lot of people feel that way."

"I think you're right."

"But they were separated. Her husband has no right to come after you. He was probably sleeping with someone, too."

"People see things the way they want to see them."

"Still."

"If we're not going to eat, I should get back to work."

"What about the other two women?"

"We'll save them for another time. We're getting behind at the house and Hector's not happy about it. I need to make an appearance."

Rebecca looked down and opened up her menu again. "I guess I could eat a little something."

ELEVEN

When you decide to stay home instead of, say, going out dancing, or to a dinner party, or to a baseball game with your new faux-friend, you are choosing not just one location over another, you are choosing a part of yourself over those other locations. If someone tells you something you can relate to, you might say, *"That really hits home with me."* You wouldn't say, *"That really hits the dance floor with me,"* unless you were looking for a fight or another dance. When you're waiting for a connection at an airport, you are traveling in one of two directions: home or beyond. And when you're finally headed back to that shelter from all of those other places, other people, other things, it should feel different from everywhere else in the world.

If it doesn't, it might be time to leave.

My commute home after going to Walker Zanger with Rebecca was the longest on record. One hour and forty-seven minutes to travel nineteen miles. Although in the end, it was probably more like twenty-five miles due to all of the bobbing and weaving through routes that weren't working. An accident on the 10 freeway shot me north on side streets that were equally packed and confused and choking with congestion. It didn't matter which way I turned, it was the wrong way. There was an armed robbery in Koreatown, which I timed perfectly, that closed down half the neighborhood. At one point I pulled a U-turn and began traveling south to go west to go north to go east just to get around the mess, and ran into a funeral procession near Hollywood Forever Cemetery. My advice to anyone willing to accept a burial slot in rush-hour traffic? Even forever isn't worth that kind of wait.

During this commute of all commutes, I tried to figure out how I was going to get Rebecca out of town before things got completely out of control. A break for Sally Stein had brought us closer together. Maybe a break for Rebecca Paulson would move us further apart. Unlike Sally, Rebecca was the mother of two young girls whom she adored, and she would be reminded of that when she tucked them into bed that night, relieved she had escaped the regret of infidelity. But how long would that feeling last? We still had another ten weeks inside Rebecca's house, and she was only getting lonelier, more eager to run. As badly as I wanted to see her free from her husband, as badly as I wanted to hold her in that way, an affair was not the solution.

I wasn't completely devoid of restraint.

I proved that to myself in the café when I managed to get out of there without telling Rebecca about the other two married women I had slept with, women whose husbands were far more likely to come after me than the professor with a fellowship. And I didn't have to lie to her either. Hector *was* frustrated with me, and he made sure I knew about it when I got back to the Paulson house after my three-and-a-half-hour trip to look at tile for an area where tile had already been purchased.

Hector aired his grievance in Spanish, out in Rebecca's driveway, as the guys were wrapping up for the day. "If I'm gonna be the one who has to cover for you, you're gonna have to pay me more. I'm not a fucking project manager. That's not our agreement."

"I've been dealing with the guesthouse all week," I barked back, matching his aggression. "This is the first chance I've had to connect with the client."

"We shouldn't even be doing that fucking guesthouse."

"What the hell happened? Where is this coming from?"

Something had to have happened. We'd been in too many houses together for Hector to confront me like this right there at the job site. He knew my responsibilities pulled me in different directions that he himself avoided for that very reason.

"The husband came home. He started asking questions."

"What kind of questions? You don't speak English."

"No shit. That's why he called up some chick and had her translate for him. I had to stand there like a fucking idiot handing him the phone."

"What'd he want to know?"

"Where his wife was. Where you were. When you'd be back."

"What'd you tell him?"

"I said I didn't know."

This was a first, Derrick showing up concerned about his wife's whereabouts. "What did the woman sound like?"

"Who gives a shit what she sounded like?"

"I do. Was she old, young, ethnic? What was she?"

"Young. White. Good Spanish accent."

"Anything else?"

"He doesn't like the color of the kitchen countertops."

"He told you that?"

"He told her that. Once he was done with me, they started talking about the house. He also doesn't like the window seats we built in the master bedroom."

"That's not what he told me."

"I'm just telling you what I heard him say to her."

"Did he use the home line, or his cell?"

"Home."

I made my way to the front door of the Paulson house.

"This is the kind of shit I'm talking about. It's not your job to fix them."

Hitting redial only revealed that Rebecca had called Tess in the interim. Probably to tell her about the tile. I had circumvented breaking a rule in that quiet café, only to break another one back at the house, with no sense of direction on what I would have done if I had discovered something incriminating. I had to get Rebecca Paulson out of town.

When I finally pulled up in front of my garage, bleary-eyed from the commute, Gia was waiting for me on the steps out front, sporting a new look. I hadn't seen her or spoken to her since she moved out months earlier, and I wasn't completely convinced she was real. Had someone died? Could that someone be me?

Neo-western with New York sensibilities was the first description that came to mind. Her shoulder-length hair was dyed punk-black, crested by a small, fitted cowboy hat that had never been anywhere near a horse. At the other end of this ensemble, cowboy boots gave way to red fishnet stockings that eventually disappeared beneath cut-off jean shorts. On top, a white baby-doll thin enough to hand the eye over to a black lace bra, nicely and naturally filled. In Gia's left earlobe, a fishing lure hung in place of an earring.

"Hello, Henry."

"What are you doing here?"

"I've come up with a way to keep you from going to Hell. All you have to do is say yes." Classic Gia. She had overthrown Purgatory, and I was her first assignment.

"How did I die?"

"Very funny."

Nope. That tone was real. It was alive and kicking.

. . .

Our relationship lasted about five months, three of which were good, one that was fair to middlin', and one that ended with Gia leaving with my answering machine. Here's a quick overview of each. You'll need them.

Months One and Two: *Why Yes I Do.*

We were compatible in many ways. We had the same taste in music and food, and we went out in search of both when I came home from work in the evenings. There was an energy about Gia that gave *me* energy, a spontaneous curiosity that drove her to live each day as if it were her last. After six weeks of this, this eating, fucking, getting high and listening to music as if we'd be dead in the morning, I took some of my stuff over to the storage locker where I kept my dad's wood, and made room for Gia's stuff back at the apartment. I put her name on the mailbox and made her a set of keys. I didn't care that none of her stuff looked good with my stuff; it was just stuff. We clicked on the inside and that was the only stuff that really mattered.

During this honeymoon period, I learned a few things about Gia that intensified my attraction to her. For instance, she legally dropped her last name when she was a junior at Cal Arts, and she didn't feel stupid about it when she got into her thirties, when she had every right to. She had a photographic memory, the kind that made me wish I had a mere fraction of that recall every time I was looking for my phone or my car keys. And it wasn't just her memory that made her a lot smarter than me. Her mind operated at a different speed, a higher frequency, one that required constant stimulation to stave off boredom, Gia's only real nemesis.

Month Three: *The Nesting Period.*

We stayed home and cooked. We read aloud to each other in the bathtub. We moved the furniture around to make room for the new stuff we bought together. We talked about getting a new shower curtain. We tried hard to fall in love.

Month Four: *Fair to Middlin'.*

Gia was getting bored. The new stuff looked as bad as the old stuff. The stuff was starting to matter. The only thing that seemed to occupy Gia's restless mind—a mind that had a way of accelerating both time and space at nearly ten times the speed of an average person—was the Internet, where she spent more and more time with each passing day.

Gia had been open with me from the start about her many ambitions, just as I'd been open with her about my lack of them. This was never a problem until we entered month four, or year four in Gia time. She was an idea farmer who used the Internet to cultivate her various crops. She built websites and wrote her own HTML and bought up domain names in preparation for the big idea that would put her on the map. To supplement her income, she got up early on Saturday mornings to comb garage sales for items she could turn around and sell for a sizable profit on eBay. She started *Gia's List* to compete with Craig. On her MySpace page, she had thousands of friends I would never meet.

If she ever learned how to stay focused long enough, I was confident Gia would leave her mark in some way. I just didn't anticipate it would involve me. Gia thought I was wasting my time in the houses of other women, and she had just the idea to help me reach my potential and eliminate those women from my life. She saw me as an artist, not a carpenter, and she encouraged me, then pressed me to quit my job to help her with her latest big idea. Cats had eclipsed dogs as America's pet of choice, and with more than 90 million little felines running around in 37.7 million households, it was a billion-dollar industry just waiting to be tapped into. Gia had the website all built. She just needed me to design and build a few prototypes, exact, miniature replicas of classic American homes that people could purchase to fit over their litter boxes. Functional art. A house within a house. Cat lovers would pay big money for that. Gia could feel it in her bones.

Month Five: *The Death of My Answering Machine.*

We weren't compatible at all. Each day really did feel like it would be my last. Gia moved most of my stuff down to the garage to make room for the big idea that sprang out of my lack of interest in her litter-box scheme. Her resentment toward me inspired her to turn the apartment into a small bottling plant to make and package *Gia Juice,* her own brand of hot sauce that had generated interest from a buyer at Trader Joe's, a buyer who would eventually become known to me as Terrific with a capital T.

Gia reentered my apartment the way she had left it months earlier. With conviction.

I went straight to the fridge and popped open a beer. "You want one?"

"I don't think that's a good idea."

"You would know."

"It wasn't easy coming here, Henry. I don't want anything to cloud my judgment."

"You don't have to worry about that. I think we've passed our window for breakup sex. Although, I gotta say, love the cowboy getup. You should have put that on the label of your hot sauce."

"You're still angry with me."

"What makes you think that?"

"It's okay. I'm still angry at you, too. That's why I'm here."

"In the future, just leave it on my answering machine. Oh, that's right. I don't have an answering machine anymore."

"We bought that machine together, Henry. And I paid for it. Besides, you don't need an answering machine. You never get the messages."

"I'm glad we cleared that up. Now if you don't mind I need to shower and get myself a hot meal."

"I think we should go into couples therapy together."

I waited for a punch line that never came.

"Couples therapy. Right. Last time I checked, we're not a couple anymore. We haven't been a couple since you started banging the buyer at Trader Joe's."

"You're having trouble moving on."

"You're giving yourself too much credit."

"I'm struggling with it as well. That's why I think this could be good for us. I need closure, and so do you."

"You're high out of your mind if you think I'm going into couples therapy with you. You've entered a whole new world of crazy."

"That's it, Henry. Make fun of the things you don't understand. Just let it roll right off your back like you don't care, like you're invincible. But at some point you're going to have to take a closer look at yourself. You're going to have to stop looking for homes in other people's houses. You're going to have to deal with your life out here, Henry. Because until you do that, women will only see you as a temporary fix, in their temporary kitchens, and you'll end up spending the rest of your life alone. And there's nothing temporary about that."

"Is that what I was to you?"

"No. But that's all you're capable of."

. . .

Derrick Paulson picked me up for the Dodgers game in his '99, hunter green Jaguar, a public statement of his financial problems. In Los Angeles, you can't drive a once-expensive import for eight years and expect to get away clean. You need to get a *new* expensive import during years when leases typically expire: two, three, four, five at the most, and even then you're pushing it. Or your car has to be at least twenty-five years old, an antique defined by the Antique Automobile Club of America. Auto enthusiasts might cut you a break at fifteen and call it a classic if it's a limited edition and in great condition, but that still leaves a seven-year window where you might have some explaining to do to your neighbors. L.A. isn't kind to people whose best years are behind them. Aging imports connote images of sadness: a guy down on his luck with a trunk full of scripts and a habit in each pocket. His story, like every other story in this town, has been heard before.

I was chewing on Gia's proposition from earlier in the week when Derrick arrived. The nerve of that proposition, the audacity, the fact that I actually agreed to it for no other reason than to prove her wrong. I was capable of a commitment, she'd see that about me, and when she did, she'd realize she was the one who had made the mistake. I was the sane one. I'd show *her* which one of us needed couples therapy.

Derrick invited himself up for a "brewski," which I quickly side-stepped by saying I didn't have any, an absolutely preposterous lie as outrageous as anything that had ever left my mouth. If it wasn't for the beer I would have turned off my refrigerator months ago.

"Not a single flipping brewski?"

"Afraid not."

"How about the hard stuff?"

"I don't keep it in the house."

"You're a bachelor. What do you do when the ladies have a request?"

"I stop and pick something up."

There was no shortage of beer at the stadium, and Derrick Paulson took full advantage. The Dodgers were playing St. Louis, the beer seemed to steady his nerves. Our seats were located in the best spot in the park to take in a game: five rows above the visiting dugout on the first-base line, raising the possibility that our tickets had been secured through a connection in the Cardinals' organization. But even if they were comps linking Derrick to a woman in said city, he did a hell of a job rooting for the home team. We bonded over The Bigs that night, high-fiving our way to a new level of faux-friendship. On his third stadium beer, Derrick told me to call him D, the nickname he gave himself in high school. "That's what my friends call me."

And that's the problem with nicknames. When someone comes right out and asks you to address them by one, you sort of have to oblige or risk hurting their feelings. Although I did not extend a similar invitation to D, he took it upon himself to call me Sully. Beer number four brought out the heckler in D. *"You couldn't hit a baseball with a tennis racket!" "Pitcher's got a rubber arm!" "Open your eyes, ump. If that ball was any closer to the plate, it'd be in your scrotum!"*

I'm sure there were other comments as well—I tend to forget things when I'm trying my hardest to look autistic, like the mentally challenged brother who makes the heckling brother slightly more tolerable. If they had been serving shots of Jägermeister, there was no telling the things I would have had to do to offset those remarks. A seizure perhaps, authenticated by a rolled-up program stuffed into my mouth.

And to think, I could have been hanging out with Bill, listening to haikus.

D eventually lost the part of his voice that allowed him to heckle with the stamina of a twelve-year-old, and when he did I steered him over to a subject I wanted him to address. He was properly lubricated by then and in the process of ordering another round.

"I'll just take a water," I said, retrieving my wallet. "I gotta work on Sunday."

"*Water?* You're hanging out with the client. You think Rebecca's gonna mind? Hell no. That woman loves a bad boy. Look at me."

"At the other house we're working on."

"Awww, horseshit. Come on, Sully, they'll understand. You want me to give them a call? Talk some sense into them?" Derrick took out his phone. He was a lousy drinker determined to prove that point by attempting to outdrink an Irishman.

"She wouldn't appreciate that."

"She's a she is she?" Not even sure how he got that out of his mouth. "You gettin' a little of that *she* on the side?" He smiled and seesawed his eyebrows up and down in case I really was mentally challenged and failed to recognize what he was referencing.

"No."

"Come on, a guy like you? I bet you've had more than your share."

"It's not like that."

"What's she look like? She got a name?"

I followed the sound of a bat back to the field. "You wouldn't know her."

"I know everybody in this town. That's why you should listen to me. I could be good for your business. I could set you up with all the right people."

"Sally Stein. She lives up in the hills."

The man's reaction belonged on a T-shirt, or a laminated place mat that Gia could sell on the Internet to people who have grown tired of the yellow smiley face. If you took that same smiley face, zipped its mouth shut, gave it a full bladder miles from the nearest bathroom, and added the threat of electrocution, you would be looking at D the way D looked when he tried not to look like that.

"Stein . . . Is that . . . Jewish?"

"I believe so."

"You're right. Don't know her."

D changed the subject and proceeded to get more and more drunk until the good folks at the stadium cut him off during the seventh-inning stretch, at which point D decided it was time to stop stretching and leave immediately. His laminated lie had brought me closer to the truth; narrowed it down, so to speak; cut it in half.

Scenario #1 wasn't pretty. Sally had indeed slept with D to save Rebecca from future heartache, failing to take into account the same joie D vivre that had charmed the pants off Kirsten Janikowski. Sally fell hard for D, and he for her, and they had a torrid affair that didn't end well because it was just so damn passionate, and it stills pains D every time he thinks about her or hears her name.

Scenario #2 wasn't pretty but it had a great personality. Something had happened between Sally and D years back that produced a mutual distain, except both fighters were fully clothed at the time. D lied because Sally had something on him that might impede his new hidden agenda, one that involved taking me to a Dodgers' game.

Derrick tossed me his keys long before we got to the car.

"I'm too drunk to drive. You're gonna have to take me home."

This caught me by surprise. He handed them over far too quickly. I'd been out drinking with big-talkers before, and you practically had to pry the keys from their fingers, especially after they spent most of the evening fishing for friendship dollars.

It also struck me that someone leading a double life would have known to be more cautious with his alcohol intake around someone working in his house. But this was the same man who had returned home from Florida with snow globes of St. Louis, so I decided to play it out and see where it would all lead me.

Around the Crenshaw exit on the 10 freeway, Derrick's head rolled off the passenger window, snapping him out of his drunken state. He sat up and rubbed his eyes. "You're a good man, Sully. Rebecca will take you home."

"I can take a cab."

"Not after driving me all the way to the Westside, you won't."

"It's fine."

"It'll be good for her. She needs to get out of the house."

"I'd rather not. Appreciate the offer though."

He gave me a befuddled look. "I thought you guys were friends."

"We are. That's why I don't want to inconvenience her. The girls get up early."

"I'll take care of the girls. She's always saying how we never go out anymore. You can stop at Starbucks and get her one of those specialty coffees she likes." Derrick said this sounding less intoxicated than before, making this push to send his wife out the door with another man all the more odd.

As tempted as I was to jump back in that maroon minivan and head east into a humid Saturday night, I was in full-retreat mode. I was pulling away from the Rebeccas, the Bridgets, the Lauras, and the Annabelles. The Second Woman, whoever she was, could have her anonymity; I just wanted my Sally Stein. The truck thief could have my truck; the meaning of that trumpet wasn't getting any more of my time. I was a bachelor going into couples therapy. I was a contractor in charge of my own destiny. "All right. You win."

"Good," said Derrick. "Cuz I'm a lousy loser."

I pulled out the only card I had left to play.

"At the hotel bar in San Pedro you asked me to keep my eyes peeled for something that would make Rebecca happy." I handed him the brochure I had retrieved from my back pocket. "You're looking at it. Eight days and seven nights at one of the best spas in Napa Valley. Over the Fourth of July. Very kid friendly."

Derrick studied the brochure, squinting through the beer in his belly. "Nice," he said, impressed by the setting, the pampered amenities. "Too bad I can't swing it."

"You've already got plans?"

"No, we'll be around. We've decided to put the kibosh on spending until the house is done. The market being the way it is right now."

"It's complimentary. The owner's an old client."

"Yeah, right. All we have to do is go to one of those seminars where they try and sell us a timeshare."

"There's no catch. I called in a favor. Consider us even for the Dodgers tickets."

Derrick cocked his head. "A week in Napa Valley? We can't accept this."

"I insist. You need to clear out that week anyway so I can make the turn into the other side of the house. You'll be doing me a favor."

Derrick looked out the passenger window and never came back.

The rest of the drive was dictated by silence.

In the driveway, Derrick spilled out of the car after a brief scuffle with the seat belt. I followed him as he swayed into the house, and watched as he passed Rebecca exiting the bedroom they were occupying. "You're drunk," she said, dressed in a transparent, cream-colored nightgown with nothing on underneath.

"Nope. Just a little tipsy. I need you to drive Sully home."

Rebecca turned and discovered me standing at the entrance to the hallway. As soon as I saw her head swing toward me, I looked down at my boots to give her a chance to put on a robe. I listened for her to do so, for the sound of her feet entering the bathroom. Her feet did not move. There was only the sound of Derrick passing out on their bed.

"He was in no condition to drive," I said to the floor. "I'm gonna call a cab."

Rebecca didn't respond.

I could feel her eyes upon me the same way I could feel the rest of her. Before looking away, I saw that her nipples were raised from the fabric of her nightgown brushing against them when she got up suddenly to greet the noise. The ache in my gut started to grow, and I could no longer hold myself down, below her knees, her thighs; the tuft of hidden black hair between long and shapely legs. I swallowed hard somewhere between her hips and the supple curve of her breasts, just trying to siphon the swell that had turned my mouth into a watering mess.

Neck, long and lean, to the point of her chin.

Lips full and red with life.

Eyes locked on mine.

We just stood there, twelve maybe thirteen feet apart, staring at each other, for how long I couldn't even begin to guess. Time left the moment I saw her. Our breathing settled into the same rhythm, and stayed that way until Derrick started to snore, reminding me where I was.

"Say something," I quietly begged her, my chest pumping to get out of its cage.

"I think about you," she said softly.

"You shouldn't."

"I know . . . Just tell me you don't and we'll leave it at that."

"It's not that simple."

"Tell me."

She waited and waited as the words crawled up through my throat. It was a long haul that started years before we ever met, back to and through all those nights when I went to sleep just hoping to see my stranger again, through all those days when I never thought I would.

"I don't think about you."

Maybe she heard the sound these words made on their way up, the friction of their resistance, the fight they fought when I told them to get

171

out. Maybe that's why she didn't speak another word. Why the corners of her lips curved upward into the infancy of what looked like a smile, before she turned around slowly, allowing me to run my eyes up and down her backside as she reentered the bedroom and closed the door behind her. Maybe that's why I stood there as long as I did, thinking about her, waiting to see if she would return.

TWELVE

At the end of the day, the success of every job relies on scheduling. If you book drywallers for the twenty-fifth and the walls aren't quite ready to be closed, the chances of them having an opening two days later are pretty unlikely, a delay that also affects the painters who are scheduled to start after them. But you've done this before, so you stagger your subs to provide room for human error, to give yourself a cushion. Whether it's a big job that spans the length of spring and summer, or a small job that should last only a week, you always have a contingency plan.

As we barreled down on the celebration of our nation's independence, my schedule looked like it had developed a thyroid problem. My daily planner was bursting at the seams with all of the Post-its, drawings, supply lists, and receipts that were jammed between each page, making it impossible to close without the giant rubber band I was using as a tourniquet. Nothing thins the blood like love, and I was hemorrhaging time and money on both jobs. So I gave myself a pay cut to stretch each contingency as far as I could, to ensure a little leeway on the backstretch. It didn't seem possible, falling for two women in one summer after seventeen years on the job. That was something I would have to ask my couples therapist about during my couples consultation with Gia, which was on the books for the following week, wedged between the inspectors and the return of the plumbers and the electricians. If I lasted that long.

First, the houses, since this is technically a story about contracting.

The drywallers never showed up at Rebecca Paulson's on Monday the twenty-fifth. No phone call, no lame excuse, no false promises about how they would get there as soon as possible. By late afternoon, they still hadn't returned my calls and I was well into a third revision of the fantasy-argument I'd been composing in their absence, ready to lay into them once I got them on the phone. They never gave me the chance.

When night falls, and the drywallers are still AWOL, it usually means they've contracted the construction flu, a virus that infects subcontractors looking for a shot at the big time, a bug they purge from their systems by simply cutting smaller clients loose, sometimes without notice. In many cases, the construction flu can be traced to commercial real estate, the same sector that claimed the ambitions of my last drywall crew. When subs get in the door with a big developer they can make twice the money in half the time without having to crisscross the city juggling houses. If another crew gets fired from an office-building job or a large condominium complex, and your subs get the call to replace them, you're shit out of luck.

I dialed around, looking for a miracle on a day's notice, came up empty, and went to my backup plan: we'd have to wall in stage one of the Paulson house ourselves to avoid losing the painters, which would delay everything after that. There was still a good amount of work left to do to complete phase one, but I wanted to paint early and touch up later to make the house look more habitable. The tile setters I brought in to help us with the master bath were almost finished, and they would then move into the powder room in the hallway that led to phase two. We hadn't built the bar, the fireplace mantel, or the custom bookshelves in the living room. Those projects, however, would all originate in the garage before we moved them into place and trimmed them out, therefore the intrusion would be more contained. Once the painters were done with each room, we would go in behind them and finish the floors. The concrete floor in the kitchen needed to be burnished and polished. The Unicork floor in the master bedroom still had to be laid. We would salvage the oak floor in the living room/dining room, and give it a clean, floating feeling by sanding it down and bleaching it twice before staining it white. When we'd set the schedule, I told Rebecca we'd still be working on that area of the house after they moved back in. We had no other choice. If we didn't make the turn into phase two in early July we'd be vulnerable to the unknown. We had opened up a few of the walls in the other end of the house back in April and inspected them for termite damage, and while they appeared clean, we wouldn't know for sure until the rooms had been gutted.

The ceiling in Rebecca's temporary bedroom had become a concern, and it had nothing to do with the amount of time she spent staring at it. Nor was it related to the unsettling suspicion her husband left me with the night he was too drunk to drive home from the Dodgers' game. The old plaster had started to pull away from the lathe, perhaps due to a slow leak in the roof. I debated replacing the roof when I bid the job, but at the time it appeared to be in pretty good condition, and that was all Rebecca needed to hear to save the money and use it elsewhere. The ceiling made me think otherwise.

Installing and plastering blue board—plain Sheetrock looks cheap in my opinion—would have been a hell of a lot easier if I hadn't already split up the guys and booked a four-man freelance crew to help us raise the walls at Sally's that same week. Miguel, who was originally slated to join me up in the hills with Marco and Eddie, stayed behind with them to run point at Rebecca's and finish building the upper cabinets for the kitchen and the walk-in closet in the master bedroom. Hector wanted nothing to do with the developments brewing at Rebecca's, so it made the most sense to swap out the brothers and have him, Juan, and Alonzo help me frame and sheathe the guesthouse with the freelancers.

Skilled, experienced freelancers have an attitude unmatched in the trades. They know they've got the goods to keep their phones ringing, and they know how much you need them or you wouldn't have brought them in. The guys I usually hire are a motley band of renegades who love to talk pussy. They never tire of it, and they never run out of names. Cupid's cupboard, pootenanny, spasm chasm, covered wagon, twatchel, mousetrap, chin rest, toolbox—the list goes on and on and gets longer with every job. If one of these guys contributes a euphemism that doesn't sound right to the other three, they vote on it. If the majority doesn't buy the explanation, that person is ejected from the game and has to buy lunch for the others.

It's no secret the female anatomy is a popular topic of conversation in the construction business, yet it's not as derogatory as you might think. Some guys just work faster when there's competition at stake. If you outlawed these verbal Olympics, those same guys would probably just start throwing hammers at each other, and nobody really wants to get caught in that crossfire, no matter how politically correct they think they are.

That being said, if you have to talk about pussy all day long, chances are you're not getting any. Kind of like porn. Nothing paints a more vivid picture of you not having sex than you watching footage of other people having the sex you're not having. But if you're a good carpenter, and I don't have to tell you what to do, I don't care what you talk about as long as you're respectful to the client and their neighbors.

Sally's neighbor Bertram was waiting for me on Tuesday afternoon when I returned from taking Juan and Alonzo back to the Paulson house to help Miguel and the others handle the additional work they inherited. Rebecca, Derrick, and the twins had already left to visit Derrick's parents in Sacramento before driving on to Napa, so I stuck around and helped Miguel with the blue board. Then I turned my attention to the ceiling above Rebecca's bed. As soon as I began probing the area with my pry bar, a massive hunk of plaster came crashing down, scaring Clyde, who was under my care until Rebecca got back. I followed his meow into the closet and tried to comfort him. Clyde did not appear well, even for an old cat in the last chapter of its life. His eyes were cloudy and he was developing a strange smell unusual for an animal known for fastidious grooming habits. I had successfully avoided Rebecca and the little smile that had been on her face since I saw her in that transparent nightgown. If Clyde continued to decline, I would have to call her and get the name of her vet.

Before starting every job, I go around to the client's neighbors and introduce myself. I leave them my cell phone number and tell them to let me know if the noise becomes a problem, a somewhat hollow gesture at best because the noise will become a problem and there is very little I can do about it. As long as we don't start work before seven in the morning, and we stop before nine at night, we are within our legal rights in most areas of the city to make the noise that drives the neighbors crazy. We do our best to quit by five, which occasionally turns into six or seven. If it goes any later than that we at least power down the saws so no one has to listen to us during the dinner hour. Most folks seem to understand that the sound of home improvement is nothing personal. Every once in a while I come across a Bertram.

Bertram was a writer who worked out of his house.

He was different from my last neighbor with a grudge, Mrs. Vandenbosh, in that his frustration was attributed to a lack of time, while Mrs. Vandenbosh had too much of it on her hands. We were working on a Mission-style house in the Mulholland Corridor across the street from Mrs. Vandenbosh, a woman in her early fifties who, when she wasn't heading up her local Neighborhood Watch program, spent her days watching me. She called parking enforcement claiming our trucks were more than eighteen inches away from the curb. She took down my contractor's license and verified it with the state, twice. She told my client that I was using my trade as a front to sell drugs to all the riffraff she saw coming in and out of the house every day. The gift basket I sent her was thrown into the back of my truck. The tickets I got her to the L.A. Philharmonic were torn in half and placed under my windshield wiper. And yet those reactions felt warm and almost fuzzy compared to the phone calls I received throughout the day. Sometimes she wouldn't even say anything; she'd just hold her phone up to a blender and punch the various speeds. Grate, grind, liquefy, ice crush. It was hard not to compliment her on her creativity.

For those of you in the middle of your own renovation, I wish I had something wise to offer you that might alleviate any tension that has formed between you and your neighbors. Other than the afore-mentioned bribes, the only thing I would say is this: make sure your renovation doesn't compromise the value of the houses around you. Don't cut down a hundred-year-old tree because some misguided contractor or landscape designer tells you it's disturbing your foundation. There are other ways to save both the tree and the foun-dation that won't throw off the entire balance of light in your neigh-bor's backyard. Plan ahead and avoid time-consuming upgrades. The better prepared you are, the better it will be for your neighbors. And most important, make sure you appear more frazzled and frustrated than they are whenever you feel them watching you. Double that behavior if you've moved into the tranquillity suite at The Four Seasons until your house is finished. After months of listening to *your* contractor and his crew pound away for hours on end without a single moment of silence, your neighbors don't need to see you sashaying up the driveway high on design magazines and chocolate pillow mints.

Bertram zeroed in on my truck, still in his bathrobe, per usual.

"How's the writing coming?" I asked.

"You're killing me, that's how it's coming. The guys who built the Panama Canal didn't make this much noise. First you renovate the house, then you bring in cement trucks and a crane, a fucking crane that takes up the whole bloody street, and beeps every time it moves around with that . . . giant fucking auger bit. But does it end there? No. Now I have to listen to these idiots all day long with their saws and their goddamn nail guns!"

"What happened to the noise-canceling headphones I bought you?"

"They're too quiet, they accentuate my thoughts."

"Your thoughts about the crane or your thoughts in general?"

"My thoughts about everything! Did you get my message?"

Bertram's weapon of choice was the eight-to-ten-minute message on my voice mail. Rambling monologues that had no beginning, middle, or end other than the resolution of him getting cut off once he'd filled up my mailbox, which I then kept full as a safeguard against follow-up messages. He was too neurotic to be a truck thief. And even if I had misread him and he *was* the perpetrator, he would have left me a message about it. The reason for this visit was Bertram's four o'clock conference call, a call that had to take place on speaker phone so he could walk back and forth. I told him that wasn't a problem, we'd take a break. Bertram responded in a victorious tone that would come back to haunt me.

"Good, because the call is going to last a long, *long* time. "

. . .

Balancing the two jobs was easy compared to managing my personal life. Sally was turning forty-two on the fourth and she wanted me to invite some of my friends to her birthday party. We had entered that stage in the relationship—the relationship formally known as the relationship we weren't having—where the friends of one come together with the friends of another and mingle hard for the first time. This decision was preceded by one epiphany in eastern Chad, two outings to Pinkberry (yogurt and fruit, yogurt and chocolate sprinkles), three trips to the movies (two Indian, one horror), and a couple of evening walks around the Hollywood reservoir holding hands and drinking bottled water.

You know this party.

The one where the woman puts her arm around the waist of her new boyfriend and says, *"Laura, you remember Henry,"* and Laura responds with an uncomfortable look and figures out only then why this guy Henry had nothing to offer in the trade she requested. The party where a Bridget Campanelli tells a guy named Bill about the new piece of furniture in her loft downtown, and the guy named Bill nods and offers her one of the deviled eggs he's been hoarding. *"Was that in your pocket? It's covered in lint."* A party where that new boyfriend might just find himself face to face with the woman who sat beside him the night those arugula salads came with caramelized pears.

Hector turned down the invitation without having to think about it. He and Miguel were throwing a barbecue on the fourth and he said, only half-jokingly, that I was a pussy-whipped *pendejo* for choosing Sally's party over theirs. I said I would try and make an appearance before heading west. Hector told me not to bother.

If the status of each woman had been reversed, if Sally had been the one who was married with two young girls, and Rebecca had been single, I would have pursued Rebecca in the same manner. I was wild about both of them, and craved them equally. But only one was technically available. Only one didn't feel forbidden.

Rebecca still found ways to thwart the retaining wall I had built around my imagination. She entered in her transparent nightgown with that look in her eyes that said she knew I wanted her despite my attempt to convince her otherwise. When I felt one of these visits coming on, I did whatever I had to do to hold her back until I found a moment alone, away from Sally. Then I embraced her in ways I'd rather not mention. Only this system of mine didn't always work, and once Rebecca got in she was tough to get out. Like the evening Sally and I went to an art opening to look at the paintings of an artist whose work was vaguely reminiscent of Stephen Hannock. We had finished our tour of the gallery and were back in front of a canvas Sally gravitated to the moment we arrived, a 40 x 60–inch landscape of an endless bridge at sunrise.

"Do you think people buy art based on substance, color, or a combination of both?"

"Color, sadly. But no one wants to admit that."

"You're probably right," said Sally.

"I need to ask you something."

"I guess it's like anything else. It has to fit in someone's life."

"It's about Derrick Paulson."

Sally looked over at me. We were definitely behaving like a couple because even though she found the inquiry out of place, she appeared more receptive.

"I know that whatever happened between you and Rebecca is none of my business, and I respect that. But I need to know who I'm dealing with."

Sally returned her gaze to the painting. "Why? What'd he do?"

"Nothing definitive. But I'm starting to think he's smarter than he looks."

"If by smarter you mean more calculated, I wouldn't disagree with you."

"Did Rebecca make him sign a prenup?"

"No. She thought it would taint the marriage."

"So if they ever got divorced, he could make a play for part of her inheritance."

"Rebecca would never get a divorce. Her parents are die-hard Catholics, they'd disown her if she did."

"Even if he divorced her?"

"He's got too much baggage. The only way he'd get a settlement is if he could prove she was the one who undermined the marriage."

"Like infidelity. Evidence she was having an affair."

"That would probably do it. But I think she'd get divorced before she'd do that."

That son of a bitch. I wasn't reading into my interactions with him, making something out of nothing. I was right all along. I *was* being played. The drinks in Pedro. The free-flowing stadium beers. The keys that practically flew out of his hand. Derrick Paulson wanted me to see his wife standing there in that nightgown. She was on to him. She'd confronted him about it the night before he invited me to the game, and he responded by fast-tracking his nefarious plan. Christ, was I that predictable?

My head began to spin backward through the timing of the renovation. The contractor who didn't work out. Derrick's reaction to Bill taking his picture. The man's career was in a nosedive, bad investments had bled him dry. Any money he did have was probably tied up in the house, which Rebecca would get if she left him before he had the proof to secure his share. That was his motivation to try and reconcile their differences. Derrick Paulson was trying to buy himself time.

Yet there was no way to present these observations—because that's all they really were at that point, observations that couldn't be proven—to anyone, let alone Rebecca, without sounding like a delusional madman.

"Henry?"

I turned back to Sally, away from the painting I was staring at.

"Don't get involved. Don't make the mistake I made six years ago."

It wasn't appropriate to ask her to elaborate on that mistake. Not then, not there. Sally had corroborated the missing piece of the Paulson puzzle, and she deserved a response that spoke of my appreciation of her. So I bought the painting of the bridge that never ended, for her birthday, for her guesthouse, for the future I could not see.

THIRTEEN

Dude, I'm not going to a birthday party in Malibu Colony unless you pick me up. PCH is no place for a Moped. I'm not gonna let some chick you're screwing turn me into an organ donor. You'll never recover from that."

It was good to hear Bill's voice. It made me feel grounded again.

"Fine, but you might have to get yourself a ride home. And if you line your pockets with tinfoil you're not going inside."

"How many bathrooms are we looking at?"

"Plenty. But those bathrooms won't do you any good. If you're feeling rundown, we can hit a gas station on the way."

Bill had this thing about germs.

He was on a mission to expose himself to as many as possible to increase the power of his immune system in preparation for the epidemic he knew was coming. An epidemic where only the smokers would survive, and if the smokers were chewing Nicorette at the same time, they would be the cream of the crop. The breeders. The diplomats. This was Bill's version of a health-insurance plan.

Following the exploration of Sally's purse at The Grove, Bill had hit the bathrooms on his way out. He preferred seedier places where homeless people went to clean up. Restaurants where he knew the employees didn't wash their hands. Rest stops just across state lines were his favorite; those germs were well traveled. But he wasn't about to leave The Grove without *surviving* The Grove, and that meant hunkering down on a toilet seat without the layer of toilet paper that has become customary in public settings.

He embraced the germs, taunted them, dared them to make him stronger, more equipped for the day when scientists would pay him handsomely just to observe him. And it would be just like Bill to live to be a hundred and ten. I could see him on the morning show telling the world, or what remained of it, his dirty little secret. The saints never live as long as they should; it's the sinners, and the twisted, who are built for the long haul.

Sally Stein's birthday party was at Jonathan Bloom's house, the trust-fund baby who poured a good drink. Things were already contentious enough up at Sally's with Bertram monitoring the decibels in his bathrobe; a birthday bash was not the best way to pacify him. She also didn't want him there. Sally had invited Bertram to a couple of parties in the past, and all he did was provide his usual dose of too much information, then hit on her when the rambling details of whatever it was he was writing about at the time had driven away all of the other guests.

I pulled over to the side of the road when I saw the valets parking imports out in front of Jonathan's place. The sun was an hour from setting. The air was salty and thick. Clouds had moved in.

"What are you doing?" asked Bill. "The party's up there."

"Do you smell rain?"

"*Rain?* It's July, dude. It hasn't rained in July in over fifty years."

"Nineteen eighty-seven."

"Well there you go. Twenty years. It's just the marine layer."

"I smell rain. And it wasn't in the forecast."

"It's probably your deodorant, or your detergent. Everything has to be scented with rain these days. They do it to keep us from noticing the whole goddamn planet is drying up. It's like clusters. You can't find a box of cereal anymore that doesn't have clusters in it. And before long, those will be scented, too. Rain-scented clusters, that's where it's all headed, dude." The progress Bill had made on his Moped appeared to be wearing off. "Let's go. I'm starving to death."

"You should have a cigarette first. You won't be able to smoke in the house."

"Oh Jesus. Another one of those parties?"

Bill fired up a Winston.

The truth was, I wasn't ready to go in. I wouldn't be able to hang back on the perimeter and watch it all unfold. This was Sally's birthday party, and I wasn't just her contractor, I was the guy she was dating. I didn't want to let her down in front of her friends. I wanted it to be a night she would remember. And just what did that entail, this night to remember? Was this the night Sally had in mind all along when she'd served me that erotic appetizer? The rendezvous point where the three of us would all head back to her place and finally indulge in the main course? If so, it would explain why she had been behaving like she had lost interest in experimenting with that friend of hers. She didn't have to encourage me to resume my search for the Second Woman if she'd already decided when and where she wanted us to reunite.

Play it cool, I told myself. Let her come to you. Don't overthink it.

Similar directions were needed when I dropped my truck off at the valet stand. "It's a four on the floor. Start her in second. First gear's for towing equipment." I repeated this in Spanish to one of the valets working the party, but he ignored my advice and lurched away loudly, making a spectacle of himself as he joined the automatics.

Bill chuckled and used a bad mid-Atlantic accent to announce us. "Ladies and gentlemen, the Sullivans have arrived."

Sally was at a charity event the day Bill came up to take the Before pictures of the main house, making this their first introduction. For all of Bill's quirks and eccentricities, he had your back when you needed him. On our way to the party, he made me stop at a flower shop—great bathrooms for exposure; any germs encountered there had already survived an onslaught of pesticides—and when he reemerged, he was holding a giant bouquet of flowers. That was how Bill operated. If I had called him on it, he would have said it was an afterthought; they were practically giving them away. He would never admit the flowers were his motive for stopping there.

Sally looked dynamite in a sexy little black cocktail dress that enveloped her like a warm breeze on a cool afternoon. Her hair was already down and I picked up her scent at eight paces becoming seven, getting stronger at six. When she saw us approaching, her smile guided me in.

"The magnificent Sally Stein," said Bill, accelerating forward, taking hold of her hand. "At last we finally meet." He then kissed her hand, actually gave it a kiss that only someone like Peter O'Toole could get away with. Sally smiled, half amused, a little leery, seventeen percent undecided. "Don't worry, I'm not hitting on you. I'm just hoping you have a cold."

A terse laugh shot out of Sally's mouth. The tall, lanky man standing there in his thrift-store blazer with sleeves three inches too short, smelling of cigarettes and mothballs and a hint of rain, had won her over. "Bill. And here I was thinking Henry made you up."

"Nope, it's all true." He presented the flowers. "These are from both of us."

"Thank you. They're beautiful."

She gave him a hug, and Bill responded by taking the flowers back from her and saying: "Make yourselves at home. I'll put these in water."

We both watched as Bill sauntered through the party, stopping at the first caterer who offered him an hors d'oeuvre. Without missing a beat, Bill took the tray from the male server and handed him Sally's flowers, mouthing what appeared to be specific instructions on what to do with them.

"*Where* did you meet him?" Sally asked, impressed by the maneuver, unaware that Bill had every intention of consuming the remainder of the tray himself.

"Years back. At this bar his band used to play in."

"Don't tell me. The bass player."

"And not a very good one at that. He just did it for the free drinks."

"I love it. I'm so glad he's here."

"Miguel and Hector send their regards. They had another engagement."

"It's okay. I know they're not exactly happy about this. About us."

"What makes you think that?"

"You're not the only one who has their sources."

Sally garnished this confession with a smile that took me back to her dark dinner party. The longer she held that smile, the more I realized this was exactly where she wanted me to go. It was her way of reminding me that she hadn't forgotten about the chase. Before I could formulate a decent response, she moved in and gave me a kiss to officially welcome my arrival. A few seconds into this kiss, she stopped and whispered, "Is Laura watching?"

I glanced up just long enough to see Laura Married to Silent Howard standing across the room, Howard tethered to her purse like a

weather balloon six hundred feet above the conversation she was pretending to have with someone whose back was to me. Laura's eyes were
indeed tripping all over us, flashing the expression I was waiting for.

"Yeah, she's watching."

"Perfect," said Sally, kissing me again to ward off any doubt. "Let's
get a drink. By the time we're done, the whole party will know you're
the guy I'm dating, and we won't have to spend the whole night talking
about it."

"Works for me."

The house was your typical nineteen-million-dollar, shingle-
styled Cape Cod on a fifteen-thousand-square-foot lot on the beach. A
trophy house with a fuck-you kitchen and a master suite that makes
you think you might just live forever. A Robert Rauschenberg hung on
the wall in the living room, while a Jasper Johns centered the study.
Out on the sun deck overlooking the Pacific, Sally led us to the bar and
ordered us both a Jameson and soda. When our drinks arrived, she
toasted my glass and alluded to the night ahead.

"Did Bill drive with you, or does he have his own way home?"

"He came with me. But he won't have trouble finding another
ride."

"So you're spending the night at my place?"

"That's the plan, isn't it?"

Sally raised her glass to her lips to try and keep me from seeing the
coy little curl on both ends. I felt as if we were back in her Pebblestone
hallway on the threshold of that tour for her friends, when this same
expression let me know I was about to experience no ordinary dinner
party. "That's the plan."

Jonathan Bloom stepped in off the beach where he had been wooing
some young ingenues with a kite he was flying. "Henry, right?" I turned

to him as he approached us, dressed in white from bald head to shoe-less toe. He was around forty-five, lived like he was thirty, looked good without hair. It suited him. He had the skull for it.

"Right," I said, shaking his hand. "Good to see you again."

"Likewise. Hey, you're a contractor . . ."

"Don't even *think* about asking him to look at something," said Sally, playfully. "That's beyond tacky, even for you."

"The man's a professional, Stein. I just want to get his opinion on a window that keeps getting stuck. It'll take fifteen seconds."

Sally took hold of my hand for emphasis. "Sorry. He has the night off."

"Ahh . . . so this is the guy we've all been wondering about. Nice, Stein. About time you found yourself an honest man."

They both turned to me. Sally got there first.

"Jonathan's been proposing to me for years. He wants to get a divorce under his belt before attempting to settle down with one of his bimbos."

"She won't do it. She's determined to see me fail on my own."

"He also has an affinity for dating women who look like him."

"That's my little birthday girl. Good to know you brought your A-game. Now if you'll both excuse me, I need to go find a loud, crowded place to continue hating myself. Enjoy the party, Henry. Later on, you, me, and a couple of Cubans. I'll tell you everything you need to know about her."

"He already knows. Why do you think he's here?"

"Because you drugged him. It just hasn't worn off yet."

Sally smiled and shook her head as Jonathan entered the house. "Such a freak. The brother I never had."

"I can tell. I like him."

"Come on, you have some mingling to do."

"You go ahead. I'm gonna hang here for a minute. Take in the view."

"Everything okay?

"Everything's great. I'll see you in there."

The sun wanted nothing to do with me. It was fading fast on the horizon, hidden behind swollen clouds with disfigured edges, in no mood for those personal moments of reflection we often put forth when it begins to set. It was just me and a Jameson with a hole in the bottom. I had done an adequate job convincing myself that I'd lost all interest in the woman Sally was attracted to. But the moment I walked into that party I was overtaken by a sudden urge to unveil her, to unhitch the hunch I'd been pulling around for weeks, to leave it in my rearview mirror, a desire that only became stronger and more reckless when Sally hinted we were almost there. And sometimes you have to get that close to finally recognize why you were keeping your distance to begin with.

I spotted Annabelle, Sally's quiet friend—the lawyer—across the living room where I eventually went to scope out the party. She was standing along the same perimeter where I always felt at home. According to Laura, Annabelle was a lousy source of information, and it was easy to see why as I watched her watching everyone else. She was an observer who got others to talk about themselves by listening and putting them at ease.

The party began to develop that strange sound found in a crowded restaurant or the head of a schizophrenic. That noise that comes from a large group of people conversing individually, yet the sum of their statements comes across like the distorted, staccato voice of one. I slipped deeper into this sound, making it difficult to separate everything that transpired in the moments that followed. I remember the way Annabelle looked when Sally, who was talking to a group of people near the kitchen, looked at her across the room. Their eyes never met, but in that one glance that wasn't returned, I knew Sally's friend Annabelle was indeed the Second Woman.

It's amazing how a person's appearance changes when lit by a gaze like the one from Sally Stein. I didn't consider Annabelle a strong candidate the night we met because she didn't strike me as someone who would pursue any type of fantasy, let alone one that involved a friend. She was somewhat ordinary-looking, a woman in neutral, neither feminine nor masculine, with straight brown hair of medium length, the color of dishwater after a hearty meal. Her body was disguised in clothes that were a size too big. Her mouth was hard to imagine on the lips of another woman. Blinded by my own vision, or my own lack of it, I initially viewed Annabelle as a mere bystander, a quiet passenger who kept her desires closely in check.

New information is often the best aphrodisiac.

As I stood there imagining Annabelle seated beside me in Sally's dining room, the words of all those people talking between us began to sound like falling raindrops. When Annabelle looked over at me and smiled, I saw a woman who was anything but ordinary.

That's when Laura Married to Silent Howard stepped in front of me, basting my perspective with her butter-yellow hair. The blood rushed out of me as fast as it rushed in. Laura's words came across loud and clear. "Hello, Henry. Do you have a second?"

She pulled me into a nearby bathroom and closed the door.

"You took advantage of me," she said, full of indignation.

"I don't know what you're talking about."

"You know exactly what I'm talking about. And if you say anything to Sally about our conversation at my house, I'll tell her you made a pass at me."

That probably wasn't the best time to look up at the skylight above us, distracted by the sound of rain, real rain, falling down on that roof in Malibu. I swallowed hard, which Laura obviously misconstrued as a response to her threat.

"I'll tell her you're no different from Derrick Paulson."

Probably not the best time to flee the bathroom either. But there I was stepping around her, racing actually, as Laura just sort of stared at me, in awe of her own effectiveness.

The party was aflutter with guests and caterers scrambling to get everything inside, away from what was quickly becoming a steady downpour. I spotted Bill first, out on a balcony off the south side of the house, smoking a cigarette with Bridget Campanelli, who appeared to find him just as charming and funny as Sally had earlier. Both were enamored with the rain; it had been more than three months since we'd received a single drop, and they were out there to get wet. "Dude," said Bill when he saw me approach, "you were right. It wasn't your deodorant, it's actually raining."

"I have to go."

"You're leaving?" asked Bridget. "I haven't even had a chance to talk to you."

"I'll be back. Keep an eye on him for me."

"Go where, dude? We just got here."

I caught up with Sally as she reentered the living room from the deck outside, carrying one half of a cocktail table with Jonathan on the other end. "There you are," she said happily, rain rolling down her face. "Isn't this great?"

"I have to run over to Rebecca's. I'll be back as soon as I can."

"Rebecca's?"

"I opened up a section of her roof to fix a leak. I need to throw a tarp over it."

Sally heard the anxiety in my voice. "Okay."

"I won't be long," I said, taking her face in my hands, giving her a kiss. When our lips parted, I ran my left thumb over her right cheekbone, brushing away a bead of water. Then I bolted for the front door, passing Laura, who had witnessed the good-bye. The expression that formed on Laura's face when I fled the bathroom after she'd threatened me had metamorphosed into absolute bewilderment. She just stood there staring at me, like a young witch who had discovered her supernatural powers.

Poor Howard, he was in for one hell of a night.

.   .   .

The alarm system was already going off when I pulled into the driveway, validating my fear that enough rain was entering the house to trip the floor sensors. I ran inside and punched in the code, shutting down the alarm as the landline started to ring. I reached the phone and picked it up just as Rebecca's outgoing message began to play. A dispatcher from the security company was on the line, needing the password and my identity to rule out a break-in. If I had gotten there a couple of minutes later, and that call had gone unanswered, I would have been up to my ass in part-time patrol officers willing to empty their guns for eleven dollars an hour. Rebecca and Derrick would have been notified on their cell phones before I had a chance to deal with the damage. And Clyde the cat might have returned to his fort of shoes to die alone, as the alarm system deprived him of any sense of peace in his final moments on earth.

But he was still on the floor in the living room, begging me to make it stop.

Leaks follow the path of least resistance. In a pitched roof with asphalt shingles, like the one on the Paulson house, water can enter through one compromised area and run its course down through the rafters, along cripple studs and top plates, through insulation, past ceiling joists, and enter another room through a light in the ceiling. And it can get sidetracked along the way, branching off into an entirely new path aided by gravity, inflicting its wrath on an area that has been recently plastered and painted; a finished floor that hasn't completely cured.

I grabbed a blue tarp out of the garage and rushed up a ladder to secure it over a valley in the roof where the U-shaped house made a ninety-degree turn away from the street. I won't get into the particulars, but when I'd located the leak days earlier, and saw that the valley flashing was corroded, I hauled it out and cut away the section of plywood sheathing that had started to rot beneath it. I then left the area open to breathe in the dry summer air, planning to seal it back up after the holiday.

The water damage would have to be dealt with later. Clyde was on his last legs, literally, down to only two—the front ones he used to crawl across his own path of least resistance. He had abandoned his temporary bedroom and dragged himself through the door that separated phase one from phase two, all the way out to the water pooling on the living room floor. He'd used the last of his strength just to get there, only he was too weak to drink once he'd arrived. The bowl of water in his closet had lost its appeal; the rain was something he could smell, something he knew he needed. And he wanted someone to know that.

Rebecca answered her cell phone on the second ring. "Hey, I was just thinking about you," she said in a hushed voice.

"Clyde's sick. Really sick. I need to take him to a vet."

A waiting room in an emergency veterinary clinic open at night and on holidays is similar to the waiting room of an oncologist, in that if you're there, it's the last place you really want to be. There is an unmistakable aura about it. No one is browsing through old magazines or engaging in small talk with the person next to them. No one will remember the fading prints in the cheap frames on the walls. They're hunkered down with their own thoughts, struggling to stay positive. If hope is a matter of mood, in these places, it swings back and forth with the opening of every door.

Clyde was in my arms, wrapped in a cotton pillowcase I took off Rebecca's pillow, hoping her scent would put him at ease, which it seemed to do until I entered the clinic and he responded by pissing on me, relieving himself of what little he had in his bladder. The smell he had developed in the days leading up to this was there in his urine, only stronger, more pungent, closer to death. I had called Sally in transit and told her what was happening. She remembered Clyde from years back, and asked me if there was anything she could do to help. I said I'd call her after I spoke to the vet. Rebecca was also standing by. Derrick and the girls had already gone to bed. She was all alone, waiting for an update.

This wasn't the first time I spent a holiday helping out a client. Christmas Eve, 2005, was a long night as well. A woman I had worked for was killed in a car accident in the fall of that year, and her husband, Mike, was left with three kids under the age of eight. He'd called me in a panic from his garage around eleven p.m., desperate to show those kids they would have the Christmas their mother wanted them to have. But the toy manufacturers had other plans for Mike that night. The swing set he'd bought his boys was packaged without directions on how to assemble it. The prefabricated toy kitchen for his daughter came in twenty-seven different pieces, five of which were missing, and those directions were originally written in Chinese, translated into English, legible only to a dyslexic who spoke both languages fluently. We put the swing set together out in the yard, holding small flashlights in our teeth. Then we went to work in the garage on the missing pieces for the toy kitchen. I cut some scrap wood down to size, sanded it, and painted it to match the pieces the manufacturer was kind enough to include. Mike sped up the drying process with his wife's old hair dryer. Once we'd assembled the little kitchen, we brought it into the house and placed it next to the Christmas tree. The sun was rising when I got home that morning, but Mike's kids never knew we spent all night working on their gifts. They still had a dad, and a pretty damn good one at that.

When the vet was done performing emergency surgery on a dog that had been hit by a car, Clyde and I were called into the examination room. Clyde started shaking, nudging his little head between two buttons on the front of my shirt. The veterinarian knew what was wrong just by looking at him: Clyde's kidneys were failing.

I told her the whole story anyway.

You do that because providing the history of someone's decline is your last real chance to feel in control, like you can make a difference, like you will include one small detail that will be the key to nursing that being back to health. I watched for something to flicker in the veterinarian's eyes, hoping she would suddenly stop me and say something like, *"Back up. His fort in the closet . . . were any of those shoes made of Microsuede?"*

"I'm not really sure."

"You're not sure?! Think, goddamn it! Think!"

The vet just sort of nodded and continued to feel Clyde's organs. She checked his mouth and his eyes, then called for one of her assistants to take Clyde into the back to draw blood and run some tests to confirm her diagnosis. She said they would hook him up to an IV to get him fully hydrated to correct his electrolyte balance, which would make him feel better while they determined what percentage of his kidneys were still functioning. She answered all my questions and assured me no one was at fault. She said bringing him in earlier wouldn't have made much of a difference. Nearly thirty percent of all cats over fifteen suffer from renal failure, an irreversible condition that is commonly overlooked until it reaches this stage because cats are stoic creatures when it comes to their health. I still felt horrible for thinking Clyde was just reacting to the renovation.

I called Rebecca back and told her everything the vet told me. If the test results indicated that a certain percentage of Clyde's kidneys was still working, there was a way to extend his life. Rebecca could give him Ringer's lactate a few times a week through a needle inserted into an area of his hide located on his upper back near his neck. That would keep him hydrated and flush his system until his kidneys stopped working altogether. Rebecca sounded like she was outside her hotel, closing in on an empty pack of Parliaments. "How long?" she asked.

"Depends. Some cats have been known to live a couple of years, some even longer, most go within a year."

"Are they happy? Do they like being alive like that?"

"Depends on the cat. I can put you on the phone with the vet if you want."

"No. I just . . . I just want to talk to you." Her voice cracked, a hairline fracture snapping from another blow, a tattletale crack above a door or window that indicates the header needs more support. "Fuck," she said, letting it all go. The frustration, the loneliness, the sorrow, all came pouring out of her with enough moisture to extinguish the cigarette she was smoking. Nothing was said until she began to dry.

"I asked the vet what she would do if it was her cat."

"What'd she say?"

"She said she'd put him down."

Rebecca must have sensed that was a forgone conclusion because she just continued to inhale and exhale, each breath searching for a foothold that wouldn't collapse the moment she started talking again.

"It's not your fault, Rebecca. The vet said he's just old."

"She was taught to say that. What's she going to say? You've been neglecting your cat ever since your daughters were born, and if you weren't so fucking self-absorbed in your own stupid problems you would have recognized that?"

"We can try and stabilize him until you get back."

"No . . . that's selfish . . . I've put him through enough as it is."

"Then I should . . . go ahead with it?"

Her voice cracked again, worse than the first time. "I don't want him to suffer."

"He won't. I promise."

"Henry?" she asked as I was making the transition to hang up.

"Yeah?"

She couldn't get it out and it was tough listening to her struggle through it. "Will you . . . will you hold him for me and tell him . . . tell him . . ."

"I'll tell him."

The vet found it odd that I wanted to stay with Clyde, seeing as how I was just cat sitting for the owner. She said we didn't have to wait, we could put him down right away; the blood results weren't needed to put an animal in his condition to sleep.

I asked her to hold off a little longer.

After I had spoken with Rebecca, I called Sally and told her I wouldn't be able to make it back to the party. She said she understood, although not very convincingly. She'd been looking forward to that party. My decision to spend a few helpless hours with Rebecca's fifteen-year-old cat instead of returning to share in the celebration of her forty-second birthday was enough to taint her voice. She was, as I discovered the day we met, a believer in signs from the universe. I didn't inquire about Annabelle, or bring up my feelings on the subject. That was something Sally Stein didn't need to hear before blowing out her birthday candles, flush with whiskey and champagne.

Once Clyde finished his IV, he began to feel better, and when he began to feel better, he became more afraid of his surroundings, and when he became more afraid of his surroundings, that really screwed with my head. I found myself struggling with the fact that I was about to put him down in the one place he spent his entire life fearing the most. It felt like I was all but saying to him, *You were right to think this place would kill you.*

So I gathered Clyde into my arms, and took him back out to the truck.

FOURTEEN

Things you put off until later are like extension cords or head-phones placed in a drawer. If you put them away without taking the time to wrap them up, both become an intertwined mess all on their own, as if in your absence they learn how to move in the dark. Your Earbuds appear to be fine when you drop them in on top of those two-dollar headphones you got the last time you flew and forgot your iPod, but when you pull them out a week later you discover the two have mated and become inseparable. That's why we wrap up all the extension cords on the job site at the end of every day. They don't need a week. They'll wiggle their way into a time delay as soon as we leave.

This was the logic I took into my second session of couples therapy with Gia, a monumental step I made during our first session. I went into therapy thinking it was asinine to pay someone to listen to us jabber on and on for fifty minutes, while that person gently tried to steer us toward an awakening without interfering with the process. That had to be a little frustrating for a therapist. Dorothy from *The Wizard of Oz* could spend months talking about the color of the road, and the problem with straw, and how it all feels strangely familiar, and yet it would still be frowned upon by the psychological community if her therapist said, *"This is absurd. Just click your heels."*

No, I didn't think it was necessary to pay anyone to help us figure out what was wrong with our relationship. That was for all those other couples who didn't know how to communicate. The ones who were still together. But the fallout from the Fourth of July inspired me to reconsider my position as I sat there evaluating my actions in our therapist's gray, monochromatic office in the Miracle Mile District. I had made enough mistakes for one summer. It was time to commit myself to saving my breakup with Gia.

Our therapist was a woman named Celeste. She was in her late forties with a zaftig figure and an expressionless face. Her hair was silver and worn close to her head. Her mastery of stillness made me wonder about all the people she'd had to sit through to become that still.

Gia and I spent the first fifty minutes together telling Celeste about all the things you already know: Why we came to see her. How long we lived together. How and why we broke up. Gia had a slightly different account than the one I shared with you. According to her, I drove her into the arms of another man because I wasn't emotionally available. I was more invested in my work than I was in our life together. If I hadn't been, I would have been more receptive to her ideas, particularly the ones that involved our future. Gia did most of the talking, which was okay, because she was still harboring a lot of anger toward me, anger that was preventing her from going to the next level of intimacy with that buyer from Trader Joe's who had since proposed to her. And I was exhausted from all the overtime I had been putting in to repair the damage of that freak rainstorm.

The rain had brought the whole crew back together again.

We fired up the Gale Force air movers to dry out the plaster, replacing and patching the areas that needed it. We fixed the roof and installed new flashing and new shingles over the section that was leaking. We primed and repainted the new plaster inside the house. Then we stripped the living room floor and refinished it a second time, all before the Paulsons returned from their vacation on July 8.

As Gia educated Celeste on her version of the past, I thought about my questionable decision to let Rebecca's roof breathe for a couple of days instead of fixing it immediately. Hector and Miguel had warned me about spreading myself too thin back in April, and they reminded me of that with their silence in July. They barely said a word to me as we worked to get the Paulson house back on track, so we could resume work on Sally's guesthouse, which basically just sat there for a week, framed and sheathed, nothing more than a wooden shell of itself. Because the deconstruction of phase two at Rebecca's wouldn't be completed on schedule, I would have to push the electricians and the plumbers and wait for their next opening. I couldn't start them up at the guesthouse; we weren't ready for them there either, and Sally wasn't quite ready for me.

It was one thing to go to her birthday party just long enough to let everyone know we were dating, before bolting out the door never to return—a departure that must have provided all sorts of fodder for her more talkative friends. But that was just the beginning of Sally's frustration with me. The hours it took to get Rebecca's house back in order added up to all the hours that had passed before I was able to get together with Sally and discuss her birthday party. When I was finally ready to confront my fear of what she might tell me, Sally said she had other plans.

At the end of that first couples therapy session, Celeste let the room come to a rest before addressing us both. "I see," she said without a trace of emotion in her voice. "Well, you obviously still care about each other or you wouldn't be here. Gia, what are you hoping to get out of this?"

"I don't want to be angry at him anymore. I need to find a way to move on."

"And you feel that resolving your issues with Henry will allow you to do that?"

"I can't get married like this. . . . We'll never make it."

"What about you, Henry? What are you hoping to achieve?"

Suddenly, I couldn't think of a single thing to say. I felt as if I were drowning in front of a licensed lifeguard, trying to pass myself off as that uncoordinated guy at the community pool who just swims that way. "I don't really know. Clarity I guess."

"Clarity on what?"

"Everything."

"All right, well, that's a start. Why don't you give that some more thought before our next session. The more specific you are, the more helpful I can be."

*   *   *

What a difference a week makes.

Now fully committed to tying up all those loose ends that were preventing me from becoming a better, more balanced, less tangled person, I kicked off that second round of couples therapy ready to talk about Clyde. The time was five p.m. The date was July 12. A Thursday. The same Thursday I nearly popped Derrick Paulson in the face.

"Who's Clyde?" asked Celeste.

"My client's cat. You said I needed to be more specific."

"How is the cat relative to your relationship with Gia?"

"I'm not sure. I thought that was your job."

An acrimonious little laugh from Gia. "See what I mean? It all comes back to his clients. And you wonder why I never trusted you."

"You're the one who cheated on me. I never strayed."

"Just because you say that doesn't mean it's true."

Celeste narrowed her eyes without doing so. "Is that what this is about for you, Gia? Trust?" Gia just shook her head and stared at the floor. Celeste tried to pull her back in. "Is that why you started a new relationship while you were still living together? To avoid getting hurt by Henry?"

Gia didn't respond. In fact, she ignored the question completely.

After a long, nurturing silence, Celeste changed gears, "All right, we'll come back to that when you're ready. Go ahead, Henry."

A moment was needed to clear my throat of the indecision that had settled there during the delay. I then took Celeste through a brief history of my interactions with Clyde. I told her about the development of his symptoms, and how I'd discovered him on the floor in the living room, and how I'd rushed him to the vet where I was faced with that predicament that really messed with my head.

"You killed the cat yourself?" asked Gia, interrupting me, looking horrified.

"What?"

"Please tell me you didn't do something awful that will stick with me for the rest of my life."

"What kind of person do you think I am?"

"Oh, I don't know. I'm sitting here in therapy, aren't I?"

An expression had formed on Celeste's face as well. It looked uncomfortable there, restrained by muscles that were out of shape. "What did you do with the cat, Henry?"

When I left the veterinary clinic with Clyde, I had no real agenda other than to get him out of the place he feared the most. We didn't flee the building, and no one chased us. We signed out. The veterinarian said she would call me with the test results as soon as she had them. Out in the truck, Clyde climbed out of Rebecca's pillowcase and laid down in the girlfriend seat with the left side of his body firmly positioned against my right hip. The fluids had restored the movement in his back legs. The sickness in his eyes was still detectable, but relief was a powerful steroid and it was pumping through his veins as I scrolled through the contact list on my phone. It was too late to call a former client of mine who had used a mobile vet to put her dog down, so Clyde and I headed east.

Clyde started a location scout of my apartment, grew weak, and settled for a cool spot on the tile floor in the bathroom. If he was surprised that I, the ringleader of scary noises who had turned his house into a construction site, didn't live in an equally loud setting, he didn't show it. The trip to the vet had lowered his standards.

I fixed him a bowl of tuna fish and a saucer of Gatorade, having purchased both at the 7-Eleven where I did most of my major grocery shopping. Clyde wasn't interested in the fish, or in boosting his electrolytes, prompting me to place the call to my former client earlier than I wanted to. The positive side of calling someone at four-thirty in the morning is they're usually home.

"Who?" asked the voice on the other end.

"Henry Sullivan, I renovated your house a couple of years ago."

Of course there were other ways to find the number of a mobile vet who traveled around the city putting pets to sleep, but I wasn't exactly functioning on all cylinders.

Dr. Walt Knoechel's outgoing message instructed the caller to page him in case of an emergency, which I did repeatedly until he called me back. He explained that his emergency rate wasn't cheap, and I told him I didn't expect it to be. He penciled us in for nine-fifteen, then told me to call him Walt—Dr. Knoechel was his father.

I asked Walt if there was anything I could do for Clyde in the meantime.

"Create a peaceful mood," he said. "Light some candles, play some music."

"What kind of music?"

"Something soft and soothing."

The only other time a living being has an appointment with death (subsequent to Jack Kevorkian) is if they've been sentenced to it by a judge and jury. And let me tell you something, it just gets weirder and weirder the closer you get to that appointment, especially when you're sitting on your bathroom floor, surrounded by candles, listening to Sade. I thought about Rebecca Paulson lying on her back, staring at the ceiling of a hotel that offered seaweed wraps for nearly every ailment except the one she was suffering from. I thought about Sally Stein, who for all I knew was about to wake up in the arms of another woman, a woman I would never be able to compete with. I chose to leave out these details when telling Celeste and Gia about the experience. That would have complicated an already complicated issue.

It was just an example of good timing if you don't believe in the fe-line intuition that brought Clyde into my lap when Sally and Annabelle got the best of my imagination. Whatever motivated him, the effort it took on his part just to complete the short journey made me feel a little less alone, and I'll be damned if I didn't get all choked up for the first time since my old man was taken down by that gripper.

Walt was late for Clyde's appointment. He arrived at my place at nine twenty-two, seven of the strangest minutes of my life. Overtime. Borrowed time. Take it if you can get it. Walt had big hands and a firm shake, with an honest face and eyes that were pushing sixty. A guy you'd expect to see getting off a John Deere on a farm in the Midwest, not outside your front door in the City of Houses. When I led Walt over to the bathroom, Clyde took one look at him and scurried into the shower to hide at a speed I didn't think he had in him. Clyde sensed this wasn't a social visit.

"He's not ready yet," Walt said matter-of-factly.

"Should I change the music?"

"It's not the music. He's not ready to leave."

Walt examined Clyde and gave him some Ringer's lactate, instructing me on how to do it with the supplies he would leave behind. He told me how the animals spoke to him, and how Clyde had basically said, *"Get your ass out of here."* Walt didn't put animals to sleep unless the animal told him to. The owner's wishes didn't interest him.

"When you get the test results back," he said with a midwestern drawl, "I'll wager a day's work that one of those kidneys is still working at over fifty percent."

There it was again. That magic number that separates the winners from the losers.

Clyde jumped down victoriously from the kitchen table where Walt had juiced him up, and went back into the bathroom to live another day. "Page me if he gets any worse. I'll come by in a week or so to see how he's doing."

"The owner doesn't want him to suffer."

"He's not suffering. He's making a comeback. Wait for the test results."

Celeste and Gia continued to stare at me as I provided this last exchange. They both waited for a follow-up to the story, only I was done talking. For a hundred dollars an hour, I was ready for some feedback.

"That's it?" asked Gia. "What happened to Clyde? Is he still alive?"

"Yeah. He sleeps with me at night."

Gia pulled her chin inward and made a face. "When I said we should get an animal, you said you didn't have time for one."

"I didn't think I did. I was wrong. About a lot of things. I'm sorry I didn't know how to say that before."

Gia softened, finding this as unexpected as I did. I'm not sure what came over me while I was recalling Clyde's story for them, but it felt good to get it off my chest. That area of my body was approaching full capacity.

"I never thought I'd hear you say that," she said.

"Yeah, well, anger has a way of blinding people."

Celeste never interrupted me or made any effort to steer me back to my relationship with Gia when it appeared Clyde was leading us all astray. She remained perfectly still, a pose she continued to hold as she waited to see how Gia would respond.

Gia bit down on her lips, holding them between her teeth for a long time before freeing them to speak. "I'm sorry I cheated on you."

We just sat there, looking at each other, both a little wounded. I didn't really have a response for that so I gave her a nod and looked over at Celeste, who unfolded her hands and asked: "What did the woman say when you told her the cat was still alive?"

I chose my words carefully. "I haven't told her yet."

Gia didn't even acknowledge this. Her accelerated sense of time had pulled her focus to the grave of an old idea. "You know what you should do? You should make Clyde a little house for his litter box. I bet he'd really like that."

.   .   .

We should back up for a moment. Something else happened during sessions one and two of couples therapy that prompted me to tell Celeste about Clyde on July 12. The confession actually came about as a result of my little get-together with Sally Stein on the morning of July 10.

Sally and I didn't really get together, because she was avoiding me just as I had avoided her. It was more spontaneous than that. I went to the job site an hour early and let myself in the door off her kitchen. I was still on Hector's shit list, but he had returned to work on Sally's guesthouse with me and two freelance carpenters I had brought in to assist us. After nearly a week of peace and quiet, the resumption of work inundated Bertram with a number of extremely important conference calls, which I had to ignore at the risk of falling even further behind. Bertram didn't like being ignored.

One episode I should mention before taking you into Sally's kitchen involved back-to-back Bertram cameos in his bathrobe, the second of which did not go well. He had a Dictaphone in his hand that he had used to record the noise, and he kept thrusting it at me as if it was a can of lighter fluid he was using to douse charcoal. I think I said something like *"Get that out of my fucking face"* before swatting it out of his hand, sending it skipping across the pavement, an impulsive reaction I would soon regret.

Sally was much more surprised to see me standing there in her kitchen than I expected her to be. I did, after all, have my own set of keys. The coffee she was making was just your standard Starbucks variety. The straight-from-the-ass-of-a-feral-beast java was long gone. The tie on her robe was cinched tightly, along with her demeanor. Sally didn't offer me a cup of coffee. I knew I had some explaining to do, and that became ever more apparent the moment I attempted to do so.

"About your birthday—"

"Forget about it," she said, cutting me off. "It's for the best. The party made me realize that we rushed into this."

"What are you saying?"

"I'm saying I think we should see other people."

"Why? Because of Rebecca?"

"Jesus, Henry."

"I meant her house. The reason I've been so busy."

"No. I get that you had to deal with the rain, and the house, and I think it's sweet what you did for Clyde. It's that you couldn't take an hour, an *hour* to sit down and talk about this before it ballooned into something else."

"I didn't have time."

"Bullshit. If the other person is important to you, you make the time, Henry. I thought I was important to you."

"You're right. I'm sorry." Sally made no effort to pull me out of the self-destructive hole I had spent the last six days digging for myself. "You're very important to me. I just didn't know how to say what I wanted to say. I still don't."

"Then maybe there's nothing left to say."

"If I knew a week apart was going to make that big a difference, if I could do it all over again . . ."

"You'd what?"

I was just about to launch into a better, albeit fictitious version of myself when Annabelle walked into the kitchen wearing the robe I used to wear in the morning when I spent the night. Sally shot her a look letting her know she wasn't pleased with the timing. Annabelle was looking at me when it left the gun.

"Oh . . . hello, Henry," she said awkwardly, trying not to sound awkward.

"Annabelle."

Sally shifted in her seat toward her friend. "Could you give us a moment? Henry and I are just finishing up."

"Sure," said Annabelle, before attempting to explain her presence. "You said you were getting coffee. You never came back."

The pit in my stomach suddenly felt big enough to swallow me whole. There were two coffee cups on the counter for three people in the room, horrible for everyone involved. Sally's eyes stayed fixed on the table as Annabelle returned to the master suite. There was remorse and a hint of shame in her voice when she finally spoke.

"I'm sorry. I never meant for you to see that."

"You were just gonna sneak her out when I went on a supply run?"

"You're early. I thought she'd be gone before you got here."

"How do you know this isn't just a phase?"

"I don't . . . I just know I like the way it feels right now."

I lingered, nodded; turned for the door. "I should get to work."

"If you could do it all over again, you'd what?" asked Sally a second time, stopping me with her voice. I thought about it long and hard, trying to separate the truth from all of the crap that comes up when a fear comes true.

"I still wouldn't have come back to the party. I never wanted to share you. I wanted you all to myself."

FIFTEEN

I couldn't tell Rebecca Paulson that she couldn't come over to my apartment and see Clyde when she got back from Napa, so I didn't tell her about Clyde when she got back from Napa. Not right away at least. Not until after my couples therapist gently steered me toward realizing I could wait no longer. Call it cruel, call it questionable, despicable, unscrupulous; call it whatever you want and you won't get an argument from me. I was completely out of my mind at the time.

I had managed to convince myself that waiting was the right thing to do based on the purpose of that trip to Napa Valley. The trip was devised to distance myself from Rebecca, not bring her closer. I didn't trust myself four feet away from the woman. If Clyde's reprieve brought her into my arms, I was afraid I wouldn't let go. Delaying the truth was a form of abstinence, I told myself, the lesser of two evils.

Derrick Paulson didn't pull out of the vacation early; he made it all the way to the end, backing up his earlier claim that he was sincere about wanting to reconcile with his wife of six years. Only I didn't trust it for a second. Something didn't add up. The man was more patient than I anticipated. It had to be the money.

My responsibilities up at Sally's guesthouse provided a legitimate excuse to be absent when the Paulsons got home. On July 12, however, the same day that would end with me telling my couples therapist about Clyde, Derrick Paulson caught up with me when I stopped by the house to check on Miguel, who was busy working on phase two with the younger guys on our crew. I went at an hour when I knew Rebecca would be at work, a strategy I employed when returning her phone calls. The cell reception in her office was lousy, giving me the opportunity to digitally acknowledge her desire to see me without actually seeing her, a scheduling glitch I blamed on the tourniquet wrapped around my daily planner. And Derrick had checked in on us only one other time, so I didn't even take him into consideration.

"Sully," he said, entering the guest bedroom that had functioned as their temporary kitchen. "You ought to think about doing this professionally."

"Hey, welcome back."

"This place is really starting to come together."

"We're getting there."

"I'll say. Think you'll be done by the end of August?"

"That's the goal. This side of the house looks good. No termite damage in the walls; no real problems other than a leak I found in the roof, which we already fixed."

"You are the man," he said looking around the room, taking it all in. "Where did all the time go? I'll tell you where it went. Right here in the house." He made a little drumroll face to accentuate the joke, obviously nervous about the cards he was holding. Answering his own question was Derrick Paulson's tell.

"Yeah."

"Hey, you weren't kidding about that spa. Exactly what the doctor ordered."

"Good. Glad to hear it."

"You have to let me return the favor."

"That's not necessary."

"Come on, Sully. That's what friends do."

"It didn't cost me a dime."

"All right," he said, holding up his hands. "Then at least let Rebecca return the favor. She enjoyed it even more than I did. At least until the cat died. Thank God that's over with."

"We're even. I needed you guys to leave."

"Doesn't matter, you're going to like this. The hospital where she works is having this gala on Tuesday to raise money for sick kids, or retarded kids—one of the two. Anyway, as much as I want to be there, I can't. I have a speaking engagement in Vegas. Problem is, I don't want her to have to go to the party alone."

I felt the fingers on my right hand come together in a fist.

"Then it hit me. All the big hitters in town are going to be there. This could be a great chance for you to get into business with some of those guys."

I picked up a drill and redirected my energy into driving screws into the subfloor. "I already know most of the big hitters in town."

"Even better. You can use them to introduce you to the ones you don't know."

"Appreciate the offer, but I have plans that night."

"Come on, Sully. You'll have fun."

"Sorry, I'm booked."

The rejection didn't sit well with Derrick. He forced a smile. "All right, it's your career. Why don't you take the weekend to think about it."

"And if I change my mind, who do I RSVP to? You or her?"

"Her. She would have asked you herself, but I already said you'd go in my place. Guess I was wrong about you." He gave me a pointed look, then turned to leave, stopping briefly to address Alonzo who had been working on the room during this conversation. "You missed a belt loop, amigo."

• • •

As hard as it was to avoid Rebecca the week after she came home, the separation was effective. There was real anger in her voice during the last message she left me. The chemistry between us had been properly diluted. That little smile had fallen off her face. So I called her at home on Sunday to give her the news.

"Sorry it's taken us this long to connect. It gets kind of crazy at this point in a job."

Her response was rightfully chilly. "You don't have to lie, Henry. If you think less of me for the way I handled things with Clyde, just tell me. Don't wait until I'm at the office to return my calls. You know my cell phone doesn't work there."

"Clyde's alive."

Dead silence.

I explained to her how I got a second opinion from Walt, and how the test results came back verifying his diagnosis, and how I was waiting to tell her until I knew Clyde was going to survive, which seemed like a fairly reasonable excuse that wasn't altogether untrue. Rebecca was shocked, relieved, somewhat speechless. I waited for her to lay into me for withholding this information, but she was so excited she dove straight into the predicament I was trying to avoid.

"When can I come over and get him?"

The excuses I devised to try and hold her off longer failed just as I'd expected, and Rebecca came over anyway. Unannounced. The night she went to the hospital gala. Alone.

My door buzzer rang around ten-thirty. I wasn't expecting anyone, so naturally I ignored it until the noise became an issue for Clyde, who was hanging out with me on the couch, listening to his favorite R&B

artist. When I went to the front window to see who was there, Clyde repositioned himself on the warm spot where I had been sitting.

There she was gazing up at me, bathed in shades of streetlight one floor below, wearing a sand-colored dress, holding a pair of shoes that looked brand-new, presumably with blisters on both feet. That look was back in her eyes, fueled by vodka and hours of standing alone in shoes she just had to own. I quickly surveyed the street to see if she was followed, a cautious reaction based on Derrick's uncanny timing the week before. Ever since he managed to intercept me at the house in that small window of opportunity, I couldn't shake the feeling that someone was watching me. I didn't see a private dick with a camera, but if he was any good, I wouldn't have.

The moment I buzzed her in, my heart began to gallop. I quickly closed all the curtains and looked around frantically. I grabbed a couple of pizza boxes off a table and started to usher them into the kitchen. Once I reached my destination, I realized I had it backward. If my objective was abstinence, I should have been using that time to mess up the apartment, not make it more presentable. I returned to the living room and tossed the pizza boxes back on the table, then opened the front door just as Rebecca knocked on it.

"Hey," she said.

"Hey."

Time passed as we both just stood there, her engine detailed and idling right in front of me. I pointed to her shoes and tried to defuse the tension. "I think those are supposed to go on your feet."

"I should have worn something more practical. Can I come in?"

She entered my apartment.

When she saw Clyde curled up on the couch, the sight of him caught her square on the chin. Her lips came inward, against her teeth. Her brow furrowed and bottomed out. As she moved closer, she started to cry and laugh at the same time. "Look at you," she said kneeling down beside him. "You look *sooo* much better." Clyde flicked his tail happily and that pretty much unraveled the last of her mascara. I tore off a sheet of paper towel from a roll on my coffee table and offered it to her. She wiped her eyes, looking around Clyde's temporary living room. "Did you buy all these cat toys just for him?"

"No. They're actually mine. I've been playing with them for years."

More laughter, less crying. "How much money did you spend?"

"Thirty, forty grand."

I was a regular riot. I couldn't shut up.

"Look at them all. They're everywhere."

"None of them interest him. He prefers balls of paper."

Rebecca blew her nose one nostril at a time. This went on for at least a minute. She wasn't self-conscious about the amount of noise she made, nor did she have any qualms about needing two more sheets just to finish the job. And yet I was completely enthralled by her as she did all of this ridiculous nose blowing, and that scared the shit out of me. When she was finally finished she took a deep breath and exhaled. "So this is what you do in your spare time? Listen to Sade and play with cat toys?"

"Why do you think I'm in such a hurry to get home every night?"

She smiled. "I haven't heard this album since I was single."

"Clyde finds it soothing."

"It's very romantic. Are you going to offer me a drink?"

No. I wasn't. But I started for the fridge anyway. "Beer okay? It's all I got."

"Beer sounds good."

I popped open a couple of longnecks and started back.

"This isn't how I imagined you."

"We can shut it off. I'm actually getting pretty tired of this album."

"No, I like it. . . . I meant your life. I always saw you as this guy with a great house, filled with all of these beautiful things you made. I never saw you in an apartment."

"My lease is up at the end of September. I have to find another place."

"Where are you going to move?"

"Don't know."

"You're not thinking about leaving L.A.?"

"No."

She nodded and took a pull off the beer I handed her. She was still on the floor, seated on the backs of her calves, her knees parted just enough to catch my eye.

"What are you doing here, Rebecca?"

We held this look for a moment. "I want you to tell me about those other two women you were with. The ones who were married."

"I gave up on that truck a long time ago."

"Tell me anyway," she said without hesitation.

I saw myself go to her and take her right then and there. Whatever happened after that wasn't my problem. I'd spent my entire life waiting to feel this way. Why should I allow it to die one of those slow deaths enslaved by reason? When I realized I was still standing there, on the verge of doing what I'd just imagined, staring into eyes that seemed to be wondering why I hadn't, I willed myself over to the far end of the couch, away from Rebecca and Clyde, and took a seat while I still could. "I've already ruled out one of the husbands. They reconciled and moved out of the state."

"Tell me about the woman who still lives here."

There were other things I could have said to get her back in that maroon minivan, moving away from me in seat setting number two.

But as I sat there looking at her all dressed up for a special occasion that was special only to her, I realized that there was just one story I needed to tell, that Rebecca Paulson needed to hear.

"Valerie and Rob lived in Santa Monica with their three kids. . . . Valerie didn't work anymore. She came from money, and her husband made a fairly decent living. I got the feeling they were having marital problems when I went to look at the house, but I took the job anyway against my better judgment."

"How'd you know?" she asked, scooting closer.

"The house told me. They didn't have a lot of pictures of themselves as a couple. And the few they did have out were strange. Most people at least try to appear happy once a camera is pointed at them, and they couldn't even do that. I liked the wife immediately. There was something about her I couldn't explain. The husband, on the other hand . . . he and I didn't exactly click. I don't think his life turned out the way he envisioned it. And that made him aggressive, tough to be around when we were working on the house."

"The type of person who would steal your truck?"

"I'm getting to that. He wasn't abusive to his wife, at least physically. He just stopped giving her what she needed in the marriage. She thought renovating the house would make her happier . . . make it easier to continue on for the sake of the kids."

"Did it?"

"No."

Rebecca thought about that. "Why'd she marry him?"

"I don't know. She didn't say. Her friends didn't seem to understand it either, the few I met anyway. They were uncomfortable around him, which I think kept her from cultivating those friendships. She was old-fashioned that way. She'd bet on a man when the odds probably weren't in her favor, and she was determined to be right about him even at the expense of her own happiness."

Rebecca's eyes had fallen into a lifeless stare.

Clyde got up, walked the length of the couch, and sat down beside me.

"But it became harder and harder for her to maintain the façade. She held out for years, hoping another child might repair the walls around her. Once she realized that wasn't going to happen, she began to think about her escape, afraid that the environment she'd found herself in was affecting the children she already had. I'd seen clients in that position before, preparing for the long good-bye. They feel like they need to have everything in order before they make a run for it. They need to get their computer fixed, their car looked at. Right now, there's a couple out there shopping for a new bedroom set even though one of them knows they'll be gone before it's time to flip the mattress."

"Was the husband having an affair?"

"She thought he was, but she couldn't prove it."

"What did you think?"

I hesitated. She waited. Neither of us looked away.

"I thought he was, too. His behavior was all over the place, which only made it harder for me to resist the feelings I had developed for his wife. I fell in love with her. I knew it was wrong and nothing but trouble, so . . . I started avoiding her. I did whatever it took to keep from being at the house whenever she was home, which put Miguel and Hector in a tough situation. They began to resent me for not being around when they needed me."

Rebecca dropped her eyes to the ground just as I had done the night of the Dodgers game. "How did the wife feel about you?" she asked in a voice as thin as her nightgown.

"It was mutual, or so it seemed. She wasn't thinking clearly . . . only I couldn't see that until after I fucked everything up."

"What happened?"

"We got involved. We got caught. And her husband used it against her in court. He took her for a load of money and got shared physical custody of the kids. And he didn't even want the kids. He just wanted to be right."

Again, Rebecca grew quiet.

When we are lost, it's easy to see ourselves in every story that involves the plight of another. But as Rebecca Paulson sat there staring at me, I got the feeling that she knew I had made it all up, that I had concocted every single detail.

Sure, I could have just told her about my encounter with Derrick years earlier in Kirsten Janikowski's Spanish Colonial out in the Valley, except that wasn't my style. And I think my couples therapist would have supported that decision if she had been there on the couch serving as our mediator. People need to come to their own conclusions. They don't need someone who's just as messed up as they are telling them what to do.

"Do you still think about her?" Rebecca asked after a long silence.

I let the silence return before giving her my response. "Every single day."

A sad smile brought some light back into her face. She got up and made her way over to me and Clyde, who was purring beside me. She bent down and ran her hand over the top of Clyde's head. While she was petting him, a tear rolled down her face and fell onto my left knee. I stood up to give her more room.

"He's much happier here with you," she said, standing to face me.

"I'm gonna miss him."

"I want you to keep him. I told the girls he's in Heaven. He should stay there."

She then reached out and pulled me into her lips. It wasn't a kiss that was moving to the bedroom, or down to the floor. It was a kiss that began somewhere near the end. I held the small of her back until I felt my hands grabbing at the fabric of her dress, at which point I pulled away from her lips and lowered my head toward her shoulder. Our faces remained that way, side by side, still touching on behalf of all the places we could not touch.

At some point, she turned and walked out the door.

At some point, I went over and closed that door.

*   *   *

The moment you fall in love with the sound of progress is the moment you stop hearing everything else. If you find yourself operating heavy machinery under the influence of this sound, a hurricane could blow into town and you won't realize it until that hurricane has already hit.

Things began to fall into place on both jobs during the last two weeks in July.

I took another pay cut to keep us on budget and to throw the crew a little something extra to keep their spirits up. Freelancers and subcontractors were moving in and out of both locations at a pace that only escalated my feud with Bertram, except I was too busy to appreciate just how bad it had gotten.

Throwing myself into my work was the only way I could envision making it to September. In addition to completing both houses, there were a number of things still standing in my way. The mood at Sally's was bleak, weighted down by the length of summer. Sally and I had split up, but during business hours, we were forced to continue to cohabitate. I could sense when she was home, and feel her when she wasn't. I never saw Annabelle again, and still that wasn't enough to keep me from placing her there anyway. To maintain what was left of my pride, I kept myself moving at all times. I ate with a tool in my hand. I stopped taking breaks to banter with Hector, which wasn't much of a sacrifice because he still had very little to say to me despite my apologies. He would just have to come around on his own, I told myself.

Fortunately, the designs I'd labored over back in April worked in our favor. Phase two of the Paulson house wasn't nearly as ambitious as phase one. Three bedrooms, two baths, Rebecca's office, and the main hallway. I needed only a few more weeks to finish the first half of the job, so barring another time delay, another kiss, another move by Derrick Paulson, hitting our deadline was still a possibility.

The guesthouse above Sally's garage was conceived with a loft in mind: one large room capped by a twelve-foot ceiling. A space that also could be used as an art studio or a home office, a duality that would make the listing more attractive if and when Sally decided to sell. The bathroom would be sectioned off by frosted tempered glass. The rest of the space would remain wide open, motivated by light from three large rectangular windows in steel frames. Against the fourth wall, we would inset two concealed closets with a media center and a wet bar between them, using reclaimed tobacco barn beech. The floor would be paved in honed Icestone made from a combination of recycled glass and concrete. A metal spiral staircase in the northwest corner of the room would lead up to a rooftop garden. The exterior would be covered in basalt stone cladding to match the main house.

Gia wasn't real happy that I had to cancel the couples therapy sessions that had been scheduled during this time period. She said she had something important she needed to talk to me about. Pregnant didn't work out mathematically, and I wasn't in the most talkative mood heading out of that kiss with Rebecca Paulson. I eventually broke down and committed to another session in early August.

I couldn't get the kiss out of my head.

As conflicted as I was for allowing it to happen, I wouldn't have traded a single second of it in a memory of twenty for a pill that would remove the feeling it left me with. Camouflaging myself in all that progress we were making up at Sally's kept Bertram from slowing me down. But I knew I couldn't stay away from the Paulson house forever. Not if I was going to get it finished in time for Rebecca's family reunion. So I decided to switch places with Miguel at the end of July and start the cabinetry work in Rebecca's living room. The younger guys didn't care what I did as long as they were making a good wage, and Miguel and Hector always worked best as a team. Maybe reuniting them would bring Hector around.

It was hard to concentrate that first day back. I parked just down the street beneath a sycamore tree and watched from afar as Rebecca loaded the twins into her minivan to drop them at day camp before continuing on to work. I hadn't seen her or spoken to her since the night she showed up at my apartment, and I wanted to see how she was doing. Watching her interact with her girls put things into perspective. She was a good mother, and she looked as if she had committed herself to that with the same amount of determination that had me trying to submerge myself in my own work.

Derrick walked out the front door and gave the girls a kiss, letting them know he was still one heck of a dad. When he went to kiss Rebecca, she turned her cheek at the last available second. Derrick remained in the driveway, waving until they were out of sight, then he jumped into his hunter green Jaguar and drove away, destination unknown.

Miguel had the younger guys, who were all capable workers once they had been given direction, working in pairs in the guest bedrooms plastering new blue board. When I went to check in on them, Juan asked for my take on the time. I was off by thirty-five minutes. My worst time-check on record, even worse than the day Hector brought in a couple of joints of this stuff he called baboon weed. Seven guys stumbling around, looking for tools as if we'd all suffered a pot stroke. Baboon weed was banned from the job site the following day, or maybe it was that same day. For some reason, I don't really remember.

As I stood in the living room studying the area where I was going to build the fireplace mantel, the built-in shelves, and the bar, I began to question myself. I had been looking forward to tackling this project for months. It was going to be my signature piece inside the house. Except my original vision suddenly felt common to me. Manufactured. Ordinary. Out in the garage, where we had set up a wood shop, I placed my drawings on top of the table saw and tried to reexamine them in a neutral place. Before I came up with a solution, my phone rang. It was Sally Stein calling from her landline. I considered letting it go to voice mail, then answered it anyway.

"They got Hector and Miguel," she said in a panicked voice.

"What are you talking about?"

"ICE. They're taking them away right now."

"I'm on my way. Don't let them leave before I get there."

A number of traffic violations were committed as I raced across town, desperately trying to turn back the clock using the wheel of my truck. If it was fate that got me there without being pulled over, it was fate that Hector and Miguel were gone when I arrived. Technology had surpassed us. The fake green cards Bill secured years earlier had failed to pass inspection.

Sally briefed me on what had happened. How field agents from the Immigration and Customs Enforcement agency just showed up as if they had been tipped off, as if someone had given them the address. ICE was looking for large groups of illegal immigrants. Two Mexicans working on a guesthouse up in the Hollywood Hills were hardly worth their time. Unless someone called in a favor, beating me at my own game.

I looked across the street and caught a fraction of Bertram watching us through a break in his blinds. When he saw that I had seen him, he ducked out of sight as I marched over to Sally's garage. The bastard had waited me out, waited for me to vacate the job site before making the call, and he landed both of the Bautista brothers by doing so.

He was probably feeling pretty proud of himself until he saw me walking toward his front door with a cordless drill in one hand and a cordless Sawzall in the other. I could hear Sally yelling as I drilled a starter hole, pleading with me to handle it another way. After I fired up the saw and began tearing through the door, all I could hear was the reciprocating teeth of revenge. Sally entered right behind me, afraid I was going to use the tools on her neighbor.

That was precisely what Bertram thought when I found him cowering in his office, clutching a phone and his Daytime Emmy, claiming he would hit me with the statue if I got too close. I got good and close anyway. Close enough to smell the bitter in his breath. Close enough to hear the reverb in the poorly chosen words that came tumbling out of my mouth.

"Fucking with me is one thing. But if you ever fuck with my crew again, I swear to God, I'll renovate every goddamn house on this street."

SIXTEEN

The cops who take you down the hill in the back of a squad car don't treat you any different for going peacefully after you've committed a breaking-and-entering crime. Once they get that call from 911 telling them there's a contractor holding a neighbor at saw-point, threatening to renovate the entire neighborhood, the cops don't mess around. I used the time it took us to get to the station the same way I would use the time it took the cops to book me, fingerprint me, and document me with an After photograph of their own. I tried to come up with a way to get Hector and Miguel out of the shit-storm I didn't hear coming.

The Bautista brothers had a plan if it ever came to this. They wouldn't call their wives to notify them. They didn't want to involve their families and possibly jeopardize the duplex in East L.A. They would contact Inez and Reina through me once they had been deported. There was no contingency on what they would do if I'd been thrown in jail for threatening someone with a Sawzall, which left me with a dif-ficult decision: I could use my allotted phone call to contact Inez and Reina and give them the bad news, something I was hoping to do in person, or I could call Bill and have him come get me once bail was posted.

Sally Stein rescued me from having to make that decision.

Sally wouldn't tell me what she said to Bertram to get him to drop the charges, and she was equally vague about the call she placed to someone she knew in the D.A.'s office. Since I had already been booked, there was a fair amount of red tape to cut through to get me out of there before the sun began to set.

We said nothing to each other as we were leaving the station; nothing until we were headed back up to her place to get my truck. I had about an hour and a half left before Inez and Reina would be expecting their husbands to walk through the door.

"I'm sorry for dragging you into this, Sally."

"You don't have to apologize."

"Yes I do. I lost my cool."

"You stood up for your friends. That's what friends are supposed to do."

"I only made it worse."

"You did what you thought was right." I couldn't even look at her. I didn't want her to see me like that. Maybe that's why Sally decided to let me know I wasn't the only one who had mishandled a friendship. She kept her eyes fixed on the road as she drifted back through the silence between us. Although she didn't say anything until she was ready, I sensed she was speaking long before she spoke. "That's all I tried to do for Rebecca."

She paused, looking for the right words.

"Have you ever seen something in someone you're close with, something they can't see in themselves? A potential, an inner beauty, that thing that makes them unique? And you don't understand why they don't recognize it, but you keep trying . . . you keep thinking there has to be a way to help them see that thing you've always seen."

"Yeah."

"I never found that way."

"Maybe there isn't one."

Sally fell back into the rhythm of the road.

"I never messed around with Derrick Paulson as some of my friends would like you to believe. I'm not sure how that rumor got started. Probably because I wouldn't talk about it." She shook her head at the notion, knowing I had gone to look at Laura's house, knowing what Laura would tell me if the subject came up. "She was my best friend . . . that friend you only get once."

"I don't think you're the only one who has regrets."

Sally turned to me. "What did she say?"

"Nothing."

"She didn't tell you anything?"

"Just that you used to be friends. I got the feeling that she'd given up on her version of the story."

Sally filed this among the facts she had been carrying around for years. It loosened her vocal cords. "I shouldn't have been so righteous. I should have handled it differently."

"How'd you handle it?"

"I sort of . . . I sort of threatened Derrick with a fork."

"The way I sort of threatened Bertram with a saw?"

"It was just a salad fork. But I did tell him that if he ever hurt her, I'd destroy him."

"That couldn't have gone well."

"No, it didn't. I knew he was involved with another woman when they were engaged. I saw him in a restaurant with her. But Rebecca didn't believe me."

"Tan, fake tits, nice legs?"

"Yeah. How'd you—"

"Lucky guess."

It took Sally the better part of a red light to resume her train of thought. "It wasn't just that he couldn't keep his dick in his pants. . . . It was the way he looked at her. She deserved more, yet she was willing to sacrifice that just to start a family. Without kids, she didn't think her life would have any meaning." Sally stopped and considered the statement, giving me a glimpse of her own struggle with that decision. "I didn't go to the wedding . . . and that was pretty much the end of it."

"Do you ever think about calling her?"

"What am I going to say? She's still with him." As this lingered, Sally weakened. "And maybe that's okay . . . maybe that's what she needs."

I offered nothing to the contrary. The subject faded back into a memory as we climbed up Laurel Canyon, out of the urban jungle below. When we reached Sally's house, I thanked her for everything she had done for me and got into my truck.

Sally approached my window as I was backing up.

"Do whatever you have to do to help Hector and Miguel. There's no hurry on the guesthouse."

* * *

On my way to East L.A. I called Bill and told him to meet me at my place at nine.

He asked why. I told him. Bill said he'd be there at eight-thirty.

The entire Bautista family ate dinner together every night, alternating back and forth between the two sides of the duplex. That night belonged to Hector and Inez. The children of both marriages were already gathered around the table when I arrived. Inez and Reina knew something was wrong the moment they saw me standing on the doorstep. Reina barked instructions at the kids before both women stepped outside to talk to me in private. Inez closed the door behind them.

"ICE came to the job site."

Reina was more volatile than her older sister, and she reacted by searching for a place to put her reaction, the way someone looks for a place to spit something out of their mouth. She started for the street, turned back after a few steps and walked toward me, then veered off again and kicked the screen door. Inez just stared at me, her eyes blackened by the news. I sensed that I had been a popular topic during those dinners they shared together, those dinners that, for the past two months, Hector and Miguel had been late for.

"Have you heard from them?" Inez asked in a cold, quivering voice.

"Not yet. But you'll know the moment I do."

Reina began to weep, an agonizing sight that became more troubling when Gabino appeared in the window to see what all that kicking was about, looking how I probably looked when I was his age, when I didn't know I was saying good-bye to my mother.

"Don't worry," I said to Reina before thinking it through. "I'm gonna fix this."

"How? How are *you* going to fix this?"

Gabino ran back to the dinner table.

.   .   .

Bill thrived in a crisis. All of that methodical preparation for the apocalypse had served him well. He paced around the room for a while, then stopped suddenly in front of the stereo. "Dude, you gotta shut this shit off. I can't concentrate. We're up to our asses in alligators, not bridal showers."

"Then stop pacing. You're making Clyde nervous."

"Clyde doesn't understand a single word Sade is saying. He's a cat. Cats are killing machines. If you were ten inches tall he would tear off your head and eat it. Your head would be in the litter box covered in sand."

"I'm not ten inches tall."

"Then stop acting like it. Who's in control of the remote around here? You or Mr. Genie Pants?"

I shut off the music to shut off Bill. Bill resumed pacing. It was after nine and still no word from Hector and Miguel. At some point, Bill started thinking out loud. "Even if they make it back into the country, top-of-the-line green cards will take a few weeks."

"That's not soon enough."

"That's how it works. You think those things just materialize out of thin air? They have to be state of the art. CIA shit. Nothing less."

"Set it in motion. In the meantime, we need to get them home."

"That's not gonna be easy. It's a hell of a lot harder than it used to be."

"I know . . . that's why we have to go all-in."

Bill liked the sound of a big bet. "What have you got in mind?"

"How long would it take you to line up a boat?"

"You serious?"

I hesitated to ask myself that same question, making sure I was fully cognizant of what I was getting us into. "The border's too risky."

Hector called the next morning after he and Miguel had been deported to Tijuana. His mood was somber, anger at the mercy of fatigue. He was concerned only about his family. He didn't sound too happy about having to depend on me for anything at that point, and probably debated calling Inez directly before Miguel talked him out of it.

The Bautista brothers were from Zacatecas, a city located thirteen hundred miles from the pay phone he called me from. Their cell phones had been confiscated. They had no friends or family anywhere near Tijuana. And they were low on scratch, about sixty bucks between them. I gave Hector the address of a Western Union I had picked out the night before when Bill and I started drawing up the blueprint of our plan.

"I'll wire you the funds you'll need on your end. Head south to Ensenada and grab a few of days of R and R. I want you guys good and rested when Bill and I pick you up."

"You're coming to get us?" asked Hector, somewhat confused.

"I never took that fishing trip I was gonna take. Now's as good a time as any."

*   *   *

Bill called his guy who knew a guy who knew the right guy for the job.

It took him less than thirty-six hours. While he was doing that, I went over the plan, looking for holes and things that could go wrong—the same way I would approach a house, only more carefully. The two I still had to complete had taught me that.

I told the younger guys to take some time off and wait to hear from me. We were on a bad streak, and until we got a win, I didn't want to leave myself open to an unsupervised disaster at the Paulson house.

I left Rebecca a message while she was at work and told her about Hector and Miguel, and how we wouldn't be around for a few days. But not to worry, I'd make arrangements for Clyde, and figure out a way to get her house finished even if I had to do it while I was in custody. Rebecca returned my call within the hour and left me a message wishing us good luck.

Then I balanced my checkbook.

Some people save money for retirement, college funds, a second home. It seemed I had spent the last seventeen years saving for the summer of 2007. Just in case there was any doubt about how poorly I had handled everything, it was right there in front of me in that little blue book. It was a virtual roadmap of destruction, each toll clearly marked by the carbon copy that remained. Camera money, bribes, a new old truck, a real estate seminar, a birthday painting, vet bills, couples therapy bills. It was a good thing I was sitting on a sizable nest egg, because it was about to take an even bigger hit.

The captain, as he liked to be called, had as many rules as I did. To charter his boat for three days and employ his services and those of his first mate, it would cost me fifteen grand, plus fuel, permits, and fishing licenses. Due to the risk involved, his price was nonnegotiable. He wasn't a coyote, he was a legitimate, third-generation fisherman of Croatian descent, who every once in a while helped out families in our position. But before he would commit to the job, he had to hear our story.

He wouldn't make a run for just anybody. He didn't care about that operation your crippled cousin needed, or that your grandmother was working as a prostitute in the parking lot of a slaughterhouse governed by drug lords. He would only smuggle an immigrant *back* into the country, no first-timers. And only if the immigrant who got deported had lived here responsibly, contributing to the system. They couldn't have a criminal record of any kind. No DUI. No citation for littering. Not even an unpaid parking ticket. And because he also knew a guy who knew a guy, he had ways of knowing these things. The captain's code was built on one simple principle. He believed that once an upstanding individual had lived in the country he loved, the country he had fought for in Vietnam, it was inhumane to send that person back.

"You need to try and make him cry," said Bill on our way down to San Pedro to meet the captain at a dive bar frequented by longshoremen.

"Cry?"

"My guy said the captain likes a good cry now and then. He'll do just about anything if you move him to tears."

"Why didn't you tell me that before? You said it was pretty much a done deal. Hector and Miguel cleared the background check."

"They did. I'm just saying it wouldn't hurt to milk it a bit."

Good thing I spent a little extra time going over that blueprint.

I took the captain through the whole ordeal. Not only was he not moved to tears, he didn't even appear to be listening. He spent most of the story studying my hands. He was fifty-eight according to our own background check, but the sea and the sun and the wind had done a number on him. His eyes looked like two olives sitting on top of a beet salad. Below that, a bird's nest of a beard covered his jaw and most of his neck. His hair was long and gray and styled by the sea.

When I finished trying to make the captain cry, he looked over at Bill and said: "You got the hands of a lady. But you . . ." he said, turning back to me. "You look like you could hold your own on a boat. You know how to fish?"

"I do."

He nodded and got to his feet. "I'll think it over and get back to you."

"How long is that gonna take?"

"Don't know. I'll be in touch."

I followed him out of the bar. "I need an answer now."

"It doesn't work that way. This ain't your game."

"That's them over there," I said, pointing to Inez's car where she and Reina and the kids were packed inside, exactly where I asked them to be. "That's who they left behind."

The captain gave me a look. Then he studied their faces one at a time, releasing a sigh that reminded me of my own. "Those kids need fathers," he said more to himself.

"I know."

The captain looked up at the sky and filled his lungs with air as if the air would tell him what to do. "We leave the day after tomorrow. I got your number. I'll call you with the details."

* * *

The caretaking instructions I left my neighbor were fairly routine. I didn't want to come across like one of those people who place all of their anxieties onto their animals.

In the morning, scoop the litter box right away. Clyde won't do his big business unless the box is completely clean.

Give him an ounce of tuna fish. Make sure it's good and wet.

Check his dry food bowl and make sure he has crunchies.

Give him fresh water.

Throw him balls of paper for fifteen minutes and don't take it personally if he looks at you like you'll never make it in the majors.

Turn on the TV before leaving for the day. The station will be tuned to the Animal Planet. Check programming to make sure it's suitable.

In the evening, repeat the instructions above, then shut off the TV and turn on the stereo. He can listen to his favorite CD once, but that's it—no ifs, ands, or buts.

Check to see if he's dehydrated by pulling up on the back of his neck. If the flesh doesn't snap back into place immediately, page Dr. Walt and he'll come over and give him some fluids. If you can't get ahold of Walt, call Rebecca, Clyde's emergency contact. Both numbers are below.

With Clyde all squared away, and the crew on hold until I got back, there was only one thing left to do on my list before leaving town. Bill inquired about it when I told him we had to make a quick stop on our way down to San Pedro.

"Where? The Grove? You gotta swing by and pick up a fanny pack?"

"I need to make an appearance at couples therapy."

"Right. I'm gonna pretend like you didn't just say that."

Celeste and Gia were waiting on me in Celeste's office in the Miracle Mile District. Celeste was in her chair, legs crossed, perfectly still. Gia was fidgeting in one of the two chairs across from her, wearing a simple, somewhat conservative dress without all the accessories, the bells and whistles. I apologized for being late.

"Gia has something she wants to tell you, Henry."

"I have something I need to say first. I think we're pretty much done here, Gia. You don't have to explain yourself, and I don't want you to feel guilty about anything. You were lonely and I was too busy to see it, and for that I'm sorry. I'm sorry I let you down, and I'm sorry I wasn't more supportive of your ideas. Go, live your life. You have my blessing."

"I stole your truck."

My reaction clearly took longer than expected because she repeated herself as I tried to backtrack through the fallout just to get to the crime. "*You?*"

"Please don't hate me."

Celeste waited for me to do something, say something, express what I was feeling. But I didn't really feel anything other than confusion. "Is that why you wanted to go into counseling? Just so you could tell me that?"

"No. It was all the other stuff, too. That was just . . . the bigger reason."

I turned to Celeste, who offered her input. "I just found out myself."

Back to Gia who looked ashamed. "Why?" I asked.

"That's what my fiancé wants to know."

"He's the one who suggested therapy?"

"I told him I was holding on to the truck for a friend who was out of the country. But then I realized that wasn't the right way to start a marriage, so I told him the truth."

"Why?"

"Because I couldn't live with myself."

"I mean why did you steal my truck in the first place?"

Gia looked away. I looked at Celeste. Celeste looked at Gia. All of that looking only left me looking more befuddled. Celeste brought out the gentle stick. "Gia?"

"All right, all right," she said, coming around. "I thought I did it because your dad's truck was holding you back. That it held us back. That it was a symbol of your inability to let go of the past and make a commitment to the future." She stopped for a moment and shook her head. "But now I think I might have stolen it because I'm a little crazy."

A strong possibility. So what was preventing me from agreeing with her?

"Why the trumpet?" I asked.

Gia shrugged. "Because I always thought someone like you should know how to play music."

Suddenly I began to feel an overwhelming sense of clarity. A couples therapy clarity that had nothing to do with the trumpet Gia had bought me with my stolen credit card. I wasn't inspired to go out and sign up for music lessons in Larchmont Village just so I could play "Amazing Grace" at someone's funeral. I was, and still am, rhythm-impaired. The clarity came from somewhere else.

Everyone who exits your life leaves you with at least one gift. A shirt, a Sade CD, a cat, a lesson learned, a mistake you will never make again—something. Even if you haven't found it yet. When I was compiling my list of suspects who might have stolen my truck, I never even considered Gia or anyone else in my personal life. I just assumed the thief was work-related because my work felt like the only thing in my life at the time. But it wasn't. I had just pushed everything else into the background, out of sight, to the point where I didn't even recognize it anymore.

"You think I'm crazy, don't you?" asked Gia, needing some kind of response.

"Maybe a little. But not any crazier than I am."

This provided that mind of hers with a clear path to the exit. "It's down in the parking garage, all washed and waxed and ready to go. My fiancé made me buy you a new set of tires."

The history of that truck pulled at me with the power of all those horses under the hood of nostalgia. Those horses that'll drink you dry if you don't rein them in as soon as they begin to run.

"Why don't you keep it," I said once the feeling had passed. "Consider it an early wedding present."

"You don't want it?"

"I got a truck. I like this one better."

SEVENTEEN

If your contractor or your project manager and his crew don't show up one morning, you wonder why. If they don't show up the morning after that, you get a little worried. But it's that three-to-five-day absence that really gets under your skin, especially if you're in the final stage, feeling like you've been holding your breath for months just below a plane of water that has left everything out of focus.

If you're a history buff, you might even equate the feeling to what runners must have felt prior to the 1908 Olympic games in London, when the marathon was officially extended from 24.85 miles to 26.2 miles just so the runners would finish in front of the Royal Family viewing box. What's another 1.35 miles to a bunch of exhausted athletes who are already crapping themselves on the world's biggest stage? What else could we do to make it harder on the athletes and more entertaining for the Royal Family? I know—we'll put the viewing box on wheels and when the runners approach we'll begin moving the box away from them. Splendid. Brilliant. God save the King.

Your contractor doesn't think that way. He and his crew want to finish your house as badly as you want them out of there, if not more. For some of you, you may have sensed this during your interactions with them. The pleasantries you've been exchanging for months aren't quite as pleasant as they used to be, unless of course you're sleeping with the contractor, and if that's the case and you're still reading this, your house is the least of your troubles.

That punch list you have going—that list of tweaks and polishes that just keeps growing the longer you stare at things—isn't helping matters. It's good that you have it. Essential, in fact. It's your right as a homeowner to get exactly what you paid for. Just keep in mind that these lists should be handled with care if you want to get everything completed in a timely fashion. This is the stage when you will start to see less and less of your contractor and his crew. They have other punch lists to deal with and other jobs to start. To make sure you stay in the mix, don't let that list turn you into an expert, a common mistake at this juncture. Avoid saying things like, *"They built the Empire State Building in just over a year. How long does it take to putty a nail hole in my baseboard? It's four inches off the ground."* That's not going to persuade anyone to putty a hole in your baseboard. That's only going to make you sound like the king or queen who keeps moving the finish line.

The worst thing about the three-to-five-day absence is the amount of time you spend wondering where in the hell they went. You're supposed to be using that chunk of mental real estate to daydream about your new life inside your home. How you're going to arrange your furniture when the house is finally completed. That first dinner party you're going to have for all your friends. The five to seven pounds you're going to lose before throwing that dinner party.

But instead, you can't get past the fact that your dreams aren't moving forward. Other jobs, other punch lists, you understand that, you're a sophisticated person. But don't the workers need their tools for that? Don't they need all of those things they left sitting in the bathroom, on the floor of the kitchen, in the garage, on the stairs? It's as if the last thing they did before vanishing into thin air was make a concerted effort to spread all of the tools around, like that would somehow put you

at ease. Do they do that on every job when they know they're not coming back for three to five days? And if so, are some people really stupid
enough to think the crew is still coming to work every day just because
they left their stuff everywhere?

No. This spreading of the tools is not a premeditated act to make
you think any of those things. You haven't stumbled across a secret
code. It just means something more important came up, like smug-
gling two gifted carpenters back into the country. Not that your house
isn't important.

We always cleaned up after ourselves at the end of each day, so any
random tools that were left lying around Rebecca's would have to remain there due to the predicament we were in. It didn't matter what
house we were working on, I never gave out the code to the alarm system to anyone other than Hector and Miguel. It wasn't that I didn't
trust the younger guys; they wouldn't have been on my crew if I didn't.
It was out of respect to the client. If Derrick Paulson chose to revert
back to his old cantankerous ways just because I didn't send Alonzo
over to clear his eye line of a tool bag or a ladder, then I would welcome
that grievance as an admission that his own plan had failed. And I
would do it with a smile on my face. For Derrick Paulson would be dealt
with soon enough.

*　*　*

The captain's boat was called the *Juana Maria*.

She was a fifty-foot Delta with twin Caterpillars that tallied seven
hundred horsepower. She had four bunks to sleep in and a bathroom
for Bill to get sick in. Germ exposure does nothing for nausea once
your inner ear gets all cattywampus. The galley was cozy. It had a stove,
a refrigerator, an oven, and a prep area tailored to the wishes of the
captain, who liked to cook whenever the horizon gave him a hunger.

The *Juana Maria* was worn around the edges, yet she was equipped with the latest in nautical technology. Radar, scanning sonar, a VHF radio, depth finders, and a satellite phone if everything went horribly wrong.

As the captain took us out of the Cabrillo Marina in San Pedro, past Terminal Island, past the tankers and the cargo ships, into the vast freedom of open water lit by a setting sun, I wondered about *Juana Maria*. Only a fool would change the name of a boat, and the captain didn't strike me as a fool. If he'd bought the boat used, she was just a name in another man's memory, only I didn't get that feeling. I sensed a hallowed hull deep within him, an empty hold still haunted by the one who got away. The one who made him a man of a few words, a captain who would risk his boat and his charter business for two immigrants he'd never met. Was *Juana Maria* just the name of a boat, or was she the reason he was on that boat, making exceptions, occasional runs to the south?

Some mysteries were better left unsolved, I reminded myself.

It was roughly one hundred and ten miles from San Pedro to the banks we were traveling to off the coast of northern Baja. Once we got up to a cruising speed of twelve knots it would be about a nine-hour trip, putting us there just before sunrise if the weather cooperated and we didn't have to change course. The *Juana Maria* did nineteen knots at full throttle, but there was no need to tax the engines. We weren't in a hurry. The art of deception works best without a clock.

The captain's right-hand man was a guy named Tillman, a sun-drenched angler who whistled and hummed songs no one else knew. On day trips with larger groups of people, the captain brought in an additional deckhand to help bait and untangle lines, which seemed kind of excessive since Tillman did the work of three men in half the time. If Rebecca Paulson was born to drive, Tillman was born to roam the deck of a boat. He was a monkey without a tail, a forty-six-year-old trapeze artist in a younger man's clothes, who swung from port to starboard, stern to bow, moving in a manner that only made Bill more seasick.

Part of Tillman's job was to take care of clients like Bill so the captain didn't have to. The captain wasn't one to coddle anyone. It didn't matter how much you were paying him. The *Juana Maria* was docked in San Pedro, not Marina del Rey. She wasn't a vessel for cloth napkins or extended warranties or gardenia-scented candles. Encouragement was viewed similarly.

"Get a line on him" was all the captain said when Bill emerged from the head to get some fresh air and throw up over the side of the boat.

Seasickness affects people differently, and no single treatment has been proven to work consistently on everyone. It's a malady that has produced a number of crazy remedies over the years, many of them conveyed to Bill as Tillman strapped him into a harness. Tillman talked about a captain he once crewed for who believed the best cure was to go swimming. Then there was his buddy on a boat out of Anchorage who swore the only way to kick it was to sit in the center of the boat and sip beer and eat gingersnaps.

The captain didn't believe in theories. He believed in time. The nausea would eventually pass, and until it did, the softy who was suffering should just wait it out and try not to make a spectacle of himself. It didn't help that Bill had become self-conscious about his hands after the captain's comment that they looked feminine. Bill asked me for my honest opinion after the captain agreed to take the job, and I told him his hands were fine. They were just on the thin side, that was all. Bill showed up for the voyage wearing his Moped gloves. The captain laughed for nearly a minute.

The scopolamine patch that Tillman slapped on Bill's arm at the onset of his symptoms began to work after a few hours, and by then Bill looked downright shattered. You had to love him for fighting through it though. If he was the guy I was neck and neck with in the race to keep it together, maybe I had done a few things right after all. Bill was the reason we were able to make that run, the friend who provided me with a chance to repair my other friendships.

*   *   *

Just after one a.m., I went into the cabin to try and grab a little shut-eye. Tillman and the captain would continue to navigate in shifts, although I didn't get the impression either of them needed much sleep. Bill remained on deck, drinking beer and eating gingersnaps. He wasn't ready to go inside and risk getting seasick again.

The plan from that point forward was closely guarded by the captain, yet I wanted to review what I imagined it to be. I couldn't stop thinking about it. I wanted to be fully prepared. All I really knew was that the transfer would take place at sea. The captain had arranged for a boat in Ensenada to take Hector and Miguel out to meet us. That boat wouldn't have to travel outside Mexican waters, meaning I had little reason to think there would be a problem on their end. Beyond that, I had no idea what to expect. Something covert. I was sure of that. A dinghy ride through the dead of night perhaps. Something that wouldn't show up on the radar screens of a Coast Guard cutter or an ICE boat patrolling the area. But what if it didn't work? What if one of those agencies spotted us anyway and stopped us for an inspection? Then what? What was the captain's contingency if it all came down to that?

My experience in the field of fantasy arguments helped me conduct a fantasy inspection of such a boarding as the bow of the *Juana Maria* loped through the salty Pacific. House inspections were rarely troublesome. Every once in a while I'd come across an inspector who needed to leave his mark, but I knew all the building codes so any adjustments we were required to make were usually small and didn't take a lot of time. A failed inspection at sea, however, would be catastrophic. Those inspectors would not instruct us to do it over again. They wouldn't tell us to take our undocumented passengers back to Mexico and return for a second inspection once we had dropped them off.

I imagined the scrambling that would take place once the Coast Guard contacted us on channel sixteen, the hailing channel on a VHF radio, informing us that we should prepare to be boarded. I could see the looks on the faces of Hector and Miguel when the captain told them to climb into the hold and hide beneath the fish. I heard myself offer to hide with them as a sign of solidarity. Then I heard the captain try to explain to the Coast Guard that Bill, and Bill alone, had chartered the boat to eat gingersnaps and fish in gloves he wore on his Moped. This was the weird left turn that let me know I was falling asleep. The dream blinker that signaled I was merging out of one world and entering another.

At sunrise, I was awakened by Tillman. We had arrived at one of the banks south of the border. The boat was hardly moving. When the captain saw me topside, he instructed me to wake up Beatrice, the moniker he had given Bill, who was asleep in one of the fishing chairs. He then briefed us on what was about to happen.

Most experienced fishermen agree that tuna are pound for pound the toughest fish in the sea. They're strong, fast, and they strike hard. If it's a fight you want, tuna fight back and then some; they do not tire easily. To find these fish, you need to find what they're looking for. Albacore are a migratory species that only move in water within two degrees of sixty-five degrees Fahrenheit. The best place to find that water is the offshore banks. The banks off southern California and northern Baja are basically undersea mountains that impede the flow of deep-water currents, creating upwellings of cooler water rich in nutrients that rise to the surface, attracting sardines and anchovies that feed off the floating kelp patties that tend to coagulate against the rims of these upwellings. And where there are bait fish, there are predators such as albacore looking for an easy meal.

I had assumed the captain chose to leave on August 5 because it would give us a three-day window to travel down to Mexico and back under a dark moon, one of many clever elements to a plan so mysterious he wouldn't discuss it. But the moonless sky wasn't chosen for safe passage; it was chosen because of the effect it had on the fish. Without the light of the moon, albacore have trouble finding sardines and anchovies at night, giving the bait fish a chance to rest and school up. By dawn, the albacore are ravenous and looking to hunt. This was the only component to the captain's mysterious plan to get Hector and Miguel back home to their families. He had nothing else worked out after that. No tricks up his sleeve. No contingency. Nothing. We were simply going to catch fish to avoid getting caught. There was no time to get another captain.

The captain had spotted a floating kelp patty about forty yards upwind of us, just west of Hidden Bank. Tillman quickly baited three troll lines with feather jigs and threw them off the back of the boat. The captain returned to the helm on the upper bridge, talking as he climbed. "If we catch a yellowtail, we move on. If we hook a tombo, get ready to show us what you're made of."

"What's a tombo?" asked Bill.

"It's Hawaiian for albacore. Like Beatrice for Bill."

Minutes later, we had our first strike.

"Hook up!" yelled Tillman, manning the pole.

The captain throttled back on the twins.

It didn't take Tillman long to get a feel for his opponent. "She ain't no yellowtail," he announced, pulling against the drag of the fish with just enough resistance to let the fish know he was there. "Ain't no tombo either. Feels like a bigeye."

Bluefin and bigeye (ahi) tuna grow to be much bigger than albacore. They prefer slightly warmer water, but if they're in the neighborhood they'll dine with their smaller cousins. "Give her to Sullivan," the captain ordered. "Get some live bait in the water."

I jumped into one of the chairs and strapped myself in.

"Hope you're ready," said Tillman. "She's a real handful."

"Aren't they all."

Tillman brought in the other troll lines and quickly switched them out. He inserted hooks crossways through the noses of live sardines and tossed them into the water, letting them swim toward the kelp patty. He then handed one of the rods to Bill. "The bait speeds up right before it's hit. Let her run for a few seconds, then clutch the reel into gear."

Both of the live-bait lines were hit almost simultaneously.

Men have no problem heaping ridiculous amounts of meaning on small things. Football games, office pools, parking spots, getting a fish into a boat. If the outcome is the one we are looking for, our little worlds expand temporarily, making us feel like everything else in life will work out in the end.

All I had to do was get that fish in the boat, and Hector and Miguel would get home to their families safe and sound. We wouldn't get caught or lost along the way. I wouldn't turn into my great-grandfather during our migration to the United States and have to spend the next three years working in a cannery. I wouldn't have to hide beneath the fish alongside my brothers in arms and say a little prayer that the Coast Guard wouldn't look there. I would return to Rebecca Paulson's house and get it ready in time for her family reunion, and I would deal with Derrick Paulson while doing so. After that, I would complete Sally Stein's guesthouse and find a new place to live, an even better place to live, and all would be right once again.

The fish did not receive this memo.

It forced me to take my time, an approach that was always good to me, one I had drifted away from as of late. The fish darted back and forth trying to shake the resistance that was slowing it down, convincing me I had snagged the back of a small submarine. I waited for it to grow tired and run toward me, shortening the line each time it did.

While I was waging my existential war, Bill and Tillman each landed two more rounds of albacore, all more than thirty pounds, which I think secretly impressed the captain. Bill's hands weren't a problem. They did just fine. The captain got on the radio and let the other captains in the area know the fish were biting off Hidden Bank. Boats on the horizon were soon headed our way.

It was indeed a bigeye, nearly two hundred pounds of meaning.

It took me an hour just to get the fish close enough so Tillman and the captain could gaffe it on opposite ends. They made sure they had a good hold on my future. Then they hoisted it up and over and into the boat.

"Holy fuck," said Bill. "Look at the size of that thing."

The captain cocked his head. "Not bad for a Mick."

I was obviously feeling pretty good about the outcome because I didn't even see or hear the boat approaching from the southeast until it was nearly upon us. It all happened so quickly. Tillman tossed a couple buoy bumpers over the starboard side as the captain threw the twins into reverse and maneuvered the *Juana Maria* around, effectively placing us between the boat that was about to join us, and two other boats making their approach a few miles away. The captain called over to his Mexican peer. "We're running low on bait. We'll swap you our spot for a bucket or two."

The Mexican captain put two fingers in his mouth and whistled.

A moment later Hector and Miguel emerged from the cabin, each carrying a bucket of sardines just as their boat began to roll by us. They stepped up and over the small wavering gap and jumped down onto the deck of the *Juana Maria*, as if they were stepping over a puddle, not the Pacific. "Thanks," said the captain to his accomplice. "You're gonna like it here."

And with that, he spun the helm and accelerated toward a new horizon.

Hector and Miguel never stopped moving, not even when they set the bait buckets down. They just kept walking right past me and disappeared into the cabin, looking the way I imagined they would look if the captain told them to hide beneath the fish prior to being captured. They were just as shocked as I was that the transfer took place in the vulnerability of broad daylight, and in that moment, I think they held me responsible.

Bill and I didn't move. I couldn't speak for Bill, but I was multitasking. Half of me was silently questioning the sanity of the captain, while the other half was contemplating the abracadabra powers of a bigeye. Tillman put us to work loading the fish into the slush-hold before I had the chance to make a wish and rub its belly. Probably for the best. "Business as usual," he said, giving us direction. "Mop up when you're done."

The captain brought the *Juana Maria* up to cruising speed.

Hector and Miguel remained inside the cabin.

I waited for one of the other boats approaching the bank to alter its course and follow us, only none of them did. The crew on the boat that brought Hector and Miguel out to sea wasted no time getting their lines into the water, maintaining the appearance that this was the only reason they went there.

Time passed slowly, uneventfully, and with each passing minute I began to recognize the beauty of the captain's plan. It was so overt, it was covert. Any sensible smuggler would wait for the cover of night before making such a transfer. The morning belonged to fishermen, and even if one of them was using fish as a front, he sure as hell wouldn't get on the radio and bring attention to himself by sharing his location with all the other captains on a chatting channel. Only a real fisherman on the move to another bank would do something like that.

Once I realized it was that simple, that we were not about to be chased, boarded, or apprehended, that we were in the hands of a true craftsman, I grabbed a six-pack out of the cooler and went into the cabin. Hector and Miguel were each peeking out of a window on opposite sides of the boat, coming to the same conclusion that brought me in there.

Goddamn it, it was good to see them again.

"Who's ready for a cold one?" I asked.

Miguel smiled. Hector tried to fight it, held his own for a beat or two, then blew me shit for the first time in over a month. *"Pinche culero,"* he said in a tone I had missed. "Where'd you find these fucking guys?"

"I didn't. The credit goes to Bill. He made it all happen."

Bill gave us a moment to sort things out before coming inside with his gingersnaps. But Hector and Miguel didn't seem to need another moment. The effort on our part was all that needed to be said.

The captain steered us over to Mushroom Bank, another spot he liked to frequent, and we spent the rest of the day battling albacore. Hector and Miguel were cautious to leave the cabin at first, but soon they, too, got caught up in the rush, the freedom of the moment. When we had reached the legal limit of ten fish per person, the captain went to work in the kitchen, cutting up one of the albacore, preparing a lavish platter of sushi and sashimi. He then broke out a bottle of cold sake he'd been saving for a special occasion, and he and Tillman joined us as we floated aimlessly, eating and drinking and swapping lies as only old friends can.

Hector and Miguel grew quiet as the sun began to set. It didn't matter how sublime the setting was, or how good we were feeling, the journey wasn't over. They were anxious to get moving again. The captain said nothing to assure us that all would go smoothly when he sensed we were ready to leave. He just got up and returned to the upper bridge deck and put us on a course for San Pedro, one of two directions available to us.

And it did feel different, heading home from beyond. And it wasn't just the stars that came out in a moonless sky, or the sake, or the gratification of digesting a meal you caught with your hands. It was the realization that home doesn't just represent a part of us. Home is who we are, wherever we are.

As I listened to Tillman chatting up our day on the radio, I found myself revisiting the simplicity of the captain's plan, and how it pertained to my own unfinished business. I didn't have to take Derrick Paulson down; he was already there. I didn't have to threaten him or remind him we had met before in the house of a previous mistress. I just needed to highlight him, make him stand out a little bit more. Then it would be up to Rebecca to see that thing she couldn't see in broad daylight. And to do that, I didn't have to change the design of the piece I still had to build in her living room. The design wasn't the reason I questioned myself, the reason it felt common to me. It was the materials I had selected.

We arrived in San Pedro just before sunrise.

The captain guided the *Juana Maria* into her slip at the Cabrillo Marina and Tillman secured ropes around the cleats. There were no touch-and-go moments along the way. The compass I packed for the migration remained in my pocket. With the exception of Bill's bout with seasickness, the voyage could not have gone more smoothly.

Alonzo answered the call I had placed, and he, Juan, Eddie, and Marco were there waiting for us, ready to implement my contribution to the plan. They boarded the boat and began unloading our catch, transporting it to the bed of my truck, which they'd already filled with ice. When they had established a steady flow of traffic, Hector and Miguel joined them, blending in seamlessly, which the captain seemed to appreciate.

Bill and I shook hands with Tillman and the captain and we all agreed to get together again sometime soon. The captain held his grip on Bill and gave him a nod. "The next charter's on me. You don't need them gloves."

Out in the parking lot, Hector and Miguel slipped into Inez's car as if they'd been gone only an hour. The two couples tried to maintain that ruse, except they couldn't keep their hands off each other. It brought to mind that intangible expression in the bones of every great structure. The motivation that drove mankind to reach for the sky, to erect the great pyramids, skyscrapers, churches, synagogues, and mosques around the world. Each is a testament to what we are capable of feeling, not building. And yet for all of their grandeur, those institutions of gratitude can still be knocked down without a moment's notice. But that didn't stop people from building them anyway.

Bill and I drove north to Little Tokyo to hook up with a buyer on the black market.

Selling sport fish was considered a crime in the state of California, only Bill didn't think it was any more of a crime than letting eleven hundred pounds of fresh tuna go to waste. I suggested we donate the fish to a shelter. Bill didn't take kindly to the idea.

"Yeah, that'll make a difference. Maybe we should just drive around skid row and hand them out individually. Homeless people love fish. They spend all their free time lying around their little cardboard huts dreaming about all the wonderful things they would do if only someone would stop and hand them a big fucking fish."

The buyer bought our catch for five bucks a pound. I kept two albacore for Clyde and me, and gave Bill his cut of the money. I then dropped Bill off at his apartment in Eagle Rock, and went back downtown to the L.A. Mission to give them the rest of the cash. The executive director looked at me kind of funny, like he smelled something kind of funny. He accepted the donation just the same.

EIGHTEEN

On the deck of the *Juana Maria*, I told the Bautista brothers to spend some time with Inez and Reina before returning to work. I updated them on Bertram and Sally, and how Sally had given us an extension. Bill was still working on securing the fake green cards, so until then, they should remain with their families. I would resume work on Rebecca's house with the younger guys.

The morning after we returned from our trip, I drove over to my storage unit and loaded up the back of my truck with a good portion of the old man's wood. I then drove over to Rebecca's, making sure I got there before she left. Hector and Miguel were waiting in their truck when I arrived. I pulled up next to them and rolled down the passenger window, assuming the worst. "What are you doing? You're suppose to be laying low."

"You're never gonna finish this place on time without us," replied Hector.

"That's my problem. It's not worth the risk."

"ICE doesn't know shit about this house. East L.A. isn't any safer."

"Doesn't matter. We're still better off waiting for Bill."

"We've been looking over our shoulders for the past seventeen years. Good documentation isn't gonna change that."

"Do Reina and Inez know you're here?"

Miguel leaned forward and looked over at me. "We may be fools, but we're not stupid."

"And they're cool with that?" I asked skeptically.

Hector got out and closed his door. "You're family. You know we take care of our own."

Derrick had already left to drop the girls at day camp, a first for him. He must have been feeling the pressure, the turned cheek of his wife. A cheek he would have to turn back until he found another way to get a piece of the equity he needed to make a fresh start. I had to imagine he was working on something pretty special for Rebecca's family reunion. I could just see him pulling out diamond earrings in front of the whole clan. At a moment when everyone was watching.

Rebecca gave Hector and Miguel a big hug when they walked in the door ahead of me. It was genuine and sweet and perfectly Rebecca. Hector and Miguel's response was completely unexpected. They thanked her for her concern in perfect English, and told her not to worry, we'd have her house finished before her family got there. Rebecca may have asked about their sudden understanding of the language if I hadn't been standing behind them. Instead, she just thanked them and stepped aside to let them begin their day. Then she looked at me. "I'm glad you're okay. I'm glad it all worked out."

That was still debatable. I nodded anyway. "I'd like to make an adjustment in the living room."

"You want to move the windows again?" she asked with a smile.

"I want to use different wood for the cabinetry. Cherry's not right."

"What's wrong with it?"

"Nothing. It's a beautiful wood. But I think the space deserves something more unique, a mixed species of African Blackwood and Waterfall Bubinga."

"How much is that going to cost?"

"There's no charge. I've been saving it for the right project."

"You don't have to do that, Henry. I'm sure cherry is fine."

"You'll like this better."

Rebecca contemplated making the change. "Okay."

We weren't building a cathedral, as Hector used to say whenever I obsessed about a certain project. And that was true, it was just a fireplace mantel, a bar, and some built-in shelves for books or knick-knacks or accomplishments on display. But it was also a chance to say good-bye. A chance to do it right this time. My dad's desire to use that wood to build something that would last forever kept him from using it to build anything at all. That was a Sullivan tradition I didn't need to uphold.

Over the course of the next three weeks, we worked exclusively on the Paulson house. Sally Stein's guesthouse became that five- to twenty-eight-day absence that makes your neighbors wonder if you ran out of money before completing your renovation. Hector, Miguel, and I worked together like we did in the old days. We gave the younger guys on the crew more responsibility and forced them to develop on their own. While they worked to finish phase two of the house, we concentrated on the woodwork—the reason we got into the business. We checked the time and were never more than ten minutes off. Miguel was still the king, but Hector and I had our own runs on the boom box. We ate lunch together out in the driveway. We bantered between bites.

My landscape designer started on the grounds around the house on our second day back. She and her crew used a Bobcat to accent areas of the yard with large boulders that would supplement my color palette for the exterior of the house. She installed a small pond with a fountain in the center of a flagstone patio outside the master bath, and bordered the area with a garden of succulents, lilies, papyrus, Mexican sage, and night-blooming jasmine, all visible from the bathtub inside. Against the back fence that defined the property line, she planted passion-flower and black-eyed Susan vines.

I wanted to get the rocks in place so I could draw from them to mix the paint before the painters arrived. Color swatches were rarely accurate over the years, forcing me to constantly doctor batches of paint just to get them to my liking. I eventually grew tired of this and began mixing the paint from scratch using my own pigments. My painters had no problem with that. They were a team of six Chinese guys all in their forties and fifties who never got rattled by anything. Hector called them *huffers* due to his belief that it was the paint fumes that had left them so even-tempered. They drove two white vans saddled with ladders. They all wore matching white jumpsuits. And they judged their abilities on how pristine they kept those jumpsuits. You didn't have to speak Chinese to understand how much they enjoyed ridiculing one another whenever one of them got paint on himself, lighting up the cotton scoreboard.

The most time-consuming task the painters faced was stripping the window frames of layers of old paint and restoring the wood beneath, a look that would connect the house to a yard featuring two fifty-year-old oak trees. They would then paint the wooden lap siding of the house a granite-based color found in the rocks that represented the earth on which the house was built.

I prepared three different batches in small amounts, carefully documenting the measurements to duplicate the process once I had the colors just right—anything other than the exact shade I was seeking would look like a sandy bland mess once it was applied, instead of that soft, organic color found at the bottom of a shallow riverbed. The second coat of paint would be lighter than the first, and the third would be lighter than the second, giving the exterior of the house more depth, a subtle transparency aroused by light. The painters would then apply all three coats by hand, using four-inch, horsehair brushes.

Whether you are putting a budget together for a full renovation, or just getting bids to have the outside of your house painted, do not let anyone talk you into painting wood siding with a sprayer. Do not buy into that commercial where the guy paints his entire house on a Saturday afternoon and has enough time left over to fix himself a sandwich and catch the late game. He didn't save time, he just borrowed it. Sprayers apply a much thinner coat of paint than a brush or a roller, which is why the paint goes on so quickly. After a few harsh winters and a couple of hot summers, that same guy will be wondering why it began to peel and fade nearly as fast as it went on. Sprayers are fine for stucco exteriors and landlords and people looking to flip a house. Pay the extra money and do your wood right. There is no substitute for sweat equity.

Other than the painters and the landscapers, I chose not to bring in any more subcontractors to lighten the load. We became a team again, without free-agents coming and going for a price. It allowed us to move faster and more efficiently throughout the day. The cohesion made us better at what we did best.

Before electricity and central heating, the fireplace was the heart of every house, the center of existence that made the house habitable. It provided warmth and a place to cook. It was the television you stared at long after the kids went to bed. Only the images it produced, night in and night out, came from the imagination of whoever was watching it. The scenarios and the plots were your own. The dénouement was up to you. That was the basis of my design for Rebecca's living room.

The fireplace was located in the center of a wall twenty-two feet wide, sixteen feet high, capped by a vaulted ceiling. The chimney ran up the back of that wall on the outside of the house, and that left the fireplace looking detached, undersized. The raised hearth that lead into the fireplace was made of brick that had been painted the *color* of brick with a faux-finish I couldn't even begin to describe.

Hector and Miguel began by paneling the entire wall with plywood veneered in Waterfall Bubinga, a caramel-colored wood dripping with lines and rolling waves, a pattern that made it appear like it was actually flowing, ergo the name. While they did that, I built the fireplace mantel out of four solid pieces of the same wood in the garage.

They say a surgeon should never operate on a family member. The bond makes it difficult to separate the person from the task. Without a certain detachment, you run the risk of compromising your judgment. My job was downright trivial compared to even the simplest procedure involving anesthesia, yet I could relate to the reasoning behind that medical point of view. I felt the old man looking over my shoulder as I made that first cut. It was like I was ten again and he was forcing me to confront my fear of the saw, as if it was a bike I had fallen off of while learning to ride. I wanted him to be proud of what I was building. I wanted him to understand why I was using his wood. But it got easier, and strangely cathartic with each subsequent cut. Each piece that went into the project became one less piece I had to carry around.

We brought the mantel into the house and anchored it into place, hiding the gaps where it met the wall with molding we milled out of African Blackwood, a dark wood with hints of red and caramel running through the grain. We liked the contrast of the Blackwood so much we used it for all of the molding on the face of the mantel, which gave the piece a Cubist quality. We used it like frames to capture patterns in the grain, to draw the eye to specific places the way a photograph would. When you stood back and looked at the space in the light of the new windows, it appeared as if the entire wall was cascading toward you, a

feeling that would only intensify once it had been properly shel-
lacked.

Still, something was missing.

The wood brought the wall to life, but the distance between the
top of the mantel and the vaulted ceiling still made the fireplace look
like it had been left behind. I wanted to feel the chimney that ran
up the exterior of that wall, the length of it, the journey from flame
to smoke. So we took salvaged, split-face Fieldstone—the same material I had chosen to cover the old hearth—and used it to create the presence of that chimney. Within two unmarked vertical lines forty-two
inches apart, we mounted stones randomly against the panels of
Waterfall Bubinga all the way to the ceiling, using special bolts, not
mortar. We positioned them in a way that made it look as if the back
of the chimney was protruding through the wooden waterfall, as if
the water had washed away all the mortar, and the stones you could
not see.

Derrick Paulson didn't like anything about this wall.

Neither he nor Rebecca were around much those last three weeks.
The saws were loud and the clock was ticking for us and Rebecca. She
had her own mountain to climb before her family arrived. Hector
caught her staring at the wall one day while he was working on the bar,
stage right of the fireplace near the sliding glass doors that led to the
backyard. Miguel and I had stepped away to help the younger guys keep
pace in the rooms they were working on. Time was always a good editor
for me. I needed to clear my head and test my perspective before we
made the final push.

Hector didn't have to give me a client update. It was, in fact, a violation of a policy he attempted to implement that would put a halt to crew
members passing along information to me on the job site. Yet he told
me anyway. He said Rebecca just stood there for a good fifteen minutes

gazing at the wall, at the tumbling Fieldstone suspended in the center of it, with a far away look in her eye.

Derrick expressed his opinion more overtly.

He stopped by the house one afternoon in the middle of our second to last week and said he needed to talk to me. Before I could respond, he turned and went outside into the backyard where the painters were working. He looked around briefly for a more private place, then he raised his hands to his hips and got straight to the point.

"What's with all the weird wood?"

"We altered the design."

"No shit, Sherlock. I can see that."

"You don't like it?"

"No, quite frankly, I don't."

I couldn't resist repeating what he said to me after he tackled Bill at the end of the street. "You should have said something."

"I was trying to give you the benefit of the doubt."

"What don't you like about it?"

"Everything. It looks out of place. It looks . . . it looks like it doesn't belong in this house."

"Not everything has to match. That's what I like about it."

"I don't give a crap what you like about it. I'm the one paying for it."

He clenched his jaw muscles and waited for a response he didn't get. This was the Derrick Paulson I knew. The man lurking behind the man he was pretending to be.

"Finish it," he demanded. "Then take down the rocks and paint over it."

"I can't do that."

"It's not a request. It's an order."

"Rebecca likes it. If you want it painted, it'll have to come through her."

Derrick shook his head and leaked a laugh that wobbled like the end of tug-toy in a dog's mouth. "All right. If you want to make it difficult on yourself, fine. I'll get her to tell you." He started back inside, then stopped to face me. "My offer to help you expand your business is off the table. Don't even think about using me as a reference."

That was the last exchange I had with Derrick Paulson.

I went back inside, grabbed the shim I had written a measurement on, and walked through the house out to the garage where Hector was ripping a piece of molding on the table saw. Hector shut off the saw and stepped in beside me as I watched Derrick accelerate down the driveway in reverse without bothering to look behind him. He spun the wheel of his hunter green Jaguar and sped off. His preoccupation with me and Hector prevented him from seeing the brown Buick parked on the street beneath a sycamore tree. The driver of that Buick waited for a moment before starting the engine and driving off in the same direction as Derrick. Probably just a coincidence, I thought to myself.

Rebecca never told me to paint over the wall or the mantel. The subject was never even raised. Whatever Derrick said to her, he said it unsuccessfully. We finished the top of the bar using the best pieces of African Blackwood in my pop's arsenal. We used a smattering of Macassar ebony to give the built-in shelves—stage left of the mantel—a hint of separation from the rest of the wall. We then coated all the wood with three coats of natural shellac, and covered the old hearth in split Fieldstone set in mortar, sealing the area when it was completed.

Rebecca didn't have a punch list, but mine was long enough on its own. I didn't want to have to come back once I finally walked out that door. While we addressed each remaining task, room by room, the painters finished the exterior of the house, demonstrating some of their finest work. In the evenings, Tess helped Rebecca stage furniture in the rooms we had already backed out of. On Thursday, August 30, the day before Rebecca Paulson's family arrived, we completed renovating her house.

My second favorite moment on every job is actually the conclusion of my first—the one that follows deconstruction, when I get to stand inside an empty room and imagine how it will all look when it is finished. As I stood in Rebecca's living room, gazing at the wall one last time before leaving, it felt strange to have deviated so far from my original vision. I never imagined seeing my dad's wood in a house I would never return to, nor did I anticipate the feeling that brought the wood into the picture. I guess it was fitting that Rebecca entered the end of this moment the same way she entered the beginning of it: from the archway of the foyer. She didn't have lunch in her hand, and she wasn't carrying a purse designed by Sally Stein. Her hair was pulled back in a blue bandanna. She was wearing her ratty old sweatpants designated for cleaning, and a pair of tennis shoes she kept outside at night. The woman never looked better.

"It's so beautiful I don't even know what to say, Henry."

"It's a little much. But I'm glad you like it."

"Like isn't the right word."

I turned back to the wall as she moved further into the room, closer to me.

"The whole house," she said. "It's perfect."

Nothing, I'm afraid, is ever perfect. Not in my line of work. There are always little flaws whenever something is built by hand, and you should keep that in mind when you discover one after your contractor has left. Building is all about fractions and trying to keep things square. It only takes one miscalculation to derail a project. Go into any five-star hotel and look at the grout lines on the floor in the bathroom of your suite. They're a long way from perfect. If the work in your home was done by someone reputable, you won't notice these imperfections unless you are actively trying to find them, which is why your contractor didn't point them out to you.

On that day, I wasn't that contractor. "There's a spot on the bar I'm not real crazy about, but other than that I think this room turned out pretty good."

"Where on the bar?"

I showed her a spot in the back corner along the wall where two pieces of molding came together at a forty-five-degree angle. "It was the last piece of molding we had, and I was in a hurry. I cut it short by a sixteenth. I don't like the look of wood putty, so I just left it alone."

"It's fine," she said. "No one will ever know."

"You will."

Rebecca looked at me for a moment, as if there was some greater meaning behind my response, and I took that as my cue to get the hell out of there, claiming I had to help the guys load up the trucks. She started to thank me for all the work we did, then she just stopped and gave me a hug. We held each other longer than we should have. As long as she was against my chest, it wasn't good-bye until our eyes met.

There were no After pictures taken of the Paulson house.

. . .

I took a couple of days off to find another place to live before returning to work at Sally's with the younger guys on the crew. Even though Bill had secured fake green cards for Hector and Miguel, and Sally had assured me Bertram wouldn't be a problem, I was still nervous about bringing them back to the location where they were apprehended. The Bautista brothers agreed to a forced vacation. There was no need to tempt fate.

Sally Stein's guesthouse was completed the last week of September.

Sally and I kept threatening to get together in the months that followed. But she was busy with her various charities, and I had gotten caught up in working on my own house, a three-bedroom Craftsman I bought in the foothills of Silver Lake.

I received a card in the mail from Rebecca Paulson in December of that same year, only I didn't recognize the return address on the outside of the envelope. When I opened it up, I discovered one of those Christmas photographs people send out to their families and friends. The one that says *Happy Holidays from the Paulsons!*

In the picture, Rebecca and her two daughters were standing on the Santa Monica Pier eating cotton candy. Derrick Paulson was nowhere in sight. The photograph was taken from the exact same perspective as the first photograph, except in the updated version Rebecca looked happy.

The renovation network soon revealed that Derrick Paulson didn't get anything when Rebecca filed for divorce. Whatever he had been up to, she had acquired the proof she needed to start over, to sell the house and move on with her life. Maybe it came from the driver of the brown Buick parked beneath the sycamore tree. Maybe Rebecca had done it on her own. Either way, I'd like to believe my old man had a hand in it, that his field trips to all those lumberyards around the state of Illinois were not in vain. And even if the new owners of that house in Brentwood painted over the wall, or hauled it out altogether, that hadn't kept us from building it.

There is something about the light in southern California that is nearly impossible to describe to anyone who hasn't experienced it. When most people think of the region their minds reproduce images they saw on the news: earthquakes, wildfires, mudslides, young celebrities jacked up on fame, slamming into each other on their way to rehab. Images that make you ask yourself *Why in God's name would any-one live there?*

Because of the light. And by light, I don't mean the weather.

That might sound like an answer you'd expect from one of the de-mented who call this place home, but it has captured the eyes of poets and painters, architects and scientists ever since the city was founded, and probably long before that. It is a light that can only be generated by a desert positioned between mountains and the sea. A light that reflects off tiny particles in the air creating a dreamlike feeling, at times defined by crisp shadows, at times diffused to where there are no shadows at all. A light so magnificent it's easy to get seduced into a timeless trance, and not realize it until years have passed. A light that can make a bad break look like a blessing, an empty promise seem like it will keep.

The light coming into my house the day I received that photograph of Rebecca and her daughters was a particular blend of gold and green with hues of blue sapphire. The windows didn't need to be moved. Clyde liked them just the way they were. As I entered the kitchen to tape Rebecca's photograph to the face of my refrigerator, I realized that the envelope the card came in had my new address written on it. It hadn't been forwarded from my old apartment. But I never told Re-becca Paulson where I was moving to. And I wasn't listed. The only way she could have gotten the address was to pick up the phone and call her old friend Sally Stein.

Acknowledgments

Thank you to all the people who employed me when I was renovating properties, as well as all the people I worked with, especially Mark Schultz, Steve Gregory, Donnie Stroud, and Antonio Martinez.

I would like to thank my family and friends for all their years of support, and those who offered their input while I was writing this book: Steve Gregory, Adam Levine, Jeff Spira, Fred Beese, Marie Colabelli, and most of all, my wife, Cheryl. For everything.

I'd like to thank Jeff Okin and Lydia Wills for making the book happen, and my editor, Peternelle van Arsdale, for making the book better. I'd also like to thank Ivan Held, Marilyn Ducksworth, Stephanie Sorensen, Chris Nelson, Lisa Amoroso, Catharine Lynch, Andrea Ho, Rachel Holtzman, and everyone else at Putnam. Also, Leslie Gelbman at Berkley.

Thank you to the great Elizabeth Jennings for encouraging me to write when I was young. Thank you to my father who handed me that first hammer.